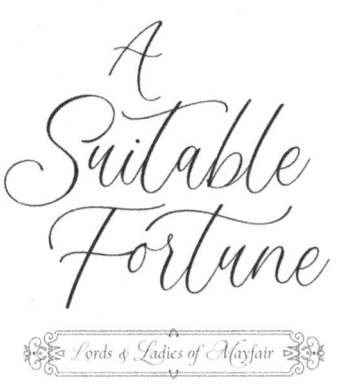

Laura Beers

Text copyright © 2024 by Laura Beers
Cover art copyright © 2024 by Laura Beers
Cover art by Blue Water Books

All rights reserved. No part of this publication may be reproduced, stored, copied, or transmitted without the prior written permission of the copyright owner. This is a work of fiction. Names, characters, places and incidents either are the product of the author's imagination or are used fictitiously. Any resemblance to actual persons, living or dead, business establishments, events, or locales is entirely coincidental.

Chapter One

England, 1813

Miss Emilia Hembry was utterly unremarkable. She had to work harder than anyone else just to survive. It had been this way since her mother died three years ago, leaving her entirely on her own.

Through sheer determination, she had managed to secure employment at Mrs. Allston's Seminary for Young Women. She was an accomplished needlewoman, just as her mother was, and she used these skills to teach her students.

Emilia held up the embroidered and beaded reticule that she had just completed for her class's inspection. "Are there any questions?"

A blonde-haired girl in the front of the room raised her hand.

"Yes, Susan," Emilia acknowledged.

Susan gripped her reticule tightly and a slight pout came to her lips. "Mine doesn't look like yours," she said.

Emilia rose from her chair and came to inspect the poorly

stitched reticule. "That is because you just need more practice. I will be happy to help you with that."

"Practice won't help her," Anne admonished from the back. "For me, it won't matter. I am going to marry a wealthy lord and have a lady's maid that will tend to my every whim, including making me reticules."

Emilia worked to keep the displeasure off her face. Anne was far too opinionated for her young age and she was cruel to the other students. No doubt her parents had spoiled her to no end, making her entirely unbearable.

"Any genteel young lady is proficient in all types of needlework," Emilia started, "and it is important for you to possess this skill."

Anne didn't look convinced. "I just think it is beneath us to learn such a thing. I would rather be riding my horse than sitting in the drawing room."

Some of the other students cast disapproving looks Anne's way, but no one spoke up. Not that Emilia expected any of them to. No one wanted to cross Anne. It never ended well.

Emilia approached Anne's desk and asked, "Did you at least attempt the assignment?"

"I did," Anne replied as she retrieved the reticule from her lap. "I never said I couldn't make one. I just think it is stupid."

"Everyone has a right to their own opinion," Emilia said as she studied the reticule. To her surprise, it was far better than what she had expected. The embroidery could use some more work, but it was a functional reticule.

Anne offered her a smug smile. "I daresay that mine is better than yours."

Emilia had just about enough of Anne's pretentious attitude, yet she refrained from voicing her thoughts. She knew she had to hold her tongue and remember her role. It was her job to instruct Anne in needlework, not etiquette. The headmistress had explicitly warned that she wouldn't tolerate criticism of her students. Her overprivileged, opinionated students.

"Your embroidery is sloppy, but you did complete the assignment," Emilia said, placing the reticule down onto the table.

A knock sounded at the door.

Emilia turned her head and saw her one true friend standing in the doorway. She could always count on Lily to lift her spirits. They had both arrived the same day to start work, and they had quickly formed a close connection due to their shared hardships.

"Mrs. Allston wishes to see you," Lily informed her.

"Now?" Emilia asked with dread in her voice. Mrs. Allston had never asked to see her during one of her lessons before. Why would she do so now?

Lily nodded. "She said it was most urgent and for me to take over your class."

Emilia glanced at the wall clock. "We were about to start work on their slippers."

Stepping further into the room, Lily said, "I will teach them until you return, but you don't want to keep Mrs. Allston waiting."

Lily gave Emilia a meaningful look, a silent communication that conveyed their mutual understanding. It was the kind of look that hinted at Mrs. Allston's impatience, as if she didn't have time to wait for anyone.

"Very well," Emilia agreed. "I shall return as quickly as I am able to."

As Emilia walked past Lily, her friend whispered, "I wish you luck."

"Do you think I need luck?"

Lily shrugged. "Everyone needs at least a little luck when speaking to Mrs. Allston. But do try to remember that she does have a kind heart. She just works hard to hide it."

Emilia hoped she looked more confident than she felt. "I

am sure it will be fine," she said before departing from her classroom on the second level.

While she descended the stairs, Emilia started racking her brain about why Mrs. Allston could have called for this meeting. Had she done something wrong? But she already knew that answer. No. She had always done everything that was expected of her, and she did so without complaint, knowing she couldn't risk losing her only source of income.

Emilia had worked hard, and she had managed to put aside some money, nearly three pounds. It was an inconsequential sum to some, but to her, it meant everything.

It wasn't long before she arrived at Mrs. Allston's office and the door was slightly ajar, revealing she was not alone. A short, white-haired man with a protruding belly was sitting in a chair that faced the desk. His cheeks were red, and he had a big nose, but he looked as if he had a pleasant enough demeanor.

It was best that she got this over with, she thought.

Emilia knocked on the door and waited for Mrs. Allston to acknowledge her. She wasn't bold enough to enter the room without being invited to do so.

"Enter," Mrs. Allston ordered.

Pushing open the door, she saw Mrs. Allston sitting behind her desk, the familiar look of impatience on her face. Her black hair was pulled back severely into a chignon at the base of her neck, and Emilia wondered if that was what always caused her unpleasantness.

"Good, you have finally arrived," Mrs. Allston said with a terseness in her words. "You have a visitor."

The man had risen when Emilia had walked into the room. He performed a bow when she turned to acknowledge him.

"Miss Hembry, I presume," he said in a kind voice. It had been a long time since a gentleman had spoken to her with such consideration.

Remembering her manners, Emilia dropped into a curtsy. "Yes, sir."

"Allow me to introduce myself," the man started. "My name is Mr. Allen Rymer and I am the late Sir Charles Sutherland's solicitor." He paused. "Does that name mean anything to you?"

Emilia shook her head. "I'm afraid not."

"That is to be expected," Mr. Rymer said. "I am here on his behalf."

With a glance at Mrs. Allston, Emilia responded, "I do not understand. Why would this Sir Charles have anything to do with me?"

Mr. Rymer gestured towards a chair. "If you will have a seat, I shall explain my purpose in being here."

Emilia sat down on the proffered chair. She was curious as to why he was here, but she feared that he had made a terrible mistake. She had no affiliation with this man.

After Mr. Rymer returned to his seat, he continued. "Sir Charles died a few days ago, and he has requested that you be at the reading of his will, alongside his family."

Her eyes grew wide at this unexpected news. "Why would Sir Charles request such a thing?" she asked. "I do not know this man."

"That may be true, but it was his dying request," Mr. Rymer shared.

"But, why?"

Mr. Rymer offered her an understanding look. "I cannot explain anything more than I already have, but I will expect you in London in two days' time. The reading of the will shall be done at Sir Charles' townhouse in Mayfair."

Mrs. Allston spoke up. "That is quite impossible. Miss Hembry is employed as a teacher here and can't just up and leave us shorthanded."

"I do understand the terrible position that I am putting

you in, but it is in Miss Hembry's best interests if she comes to London," Mr. Rymer responded.

As intrigued as Emilia was, Mrs. Allston was right. She couldn't leave and risk losing her position at the school. Besides, even if she wanted to, she didn't have the funds to travel to London.

Mr. Rymer must have sensed her concerns because he pressed on. "I took the liberty of securing a coach for your travels and I was instructed to give you fifty pounds for your journey."

"Fifty pounds?" Emilia repeated back in disbelief. That was more money than she would earn for ten years of teaching. Why would he bestow upon her such an enormous sum?

"If you leave now, you will be in London tomorrow afternoon, where I secured lodging in anticipation of your arrival," Mr. Rymer said. "It is a quaint boarding house near Mayfair and it will only be a short walk to Sir Charles' townhouse."

Emilia sat back in her seat as she considered the solicitor's words. Not only was she to receive fifty pounds but everything else was taken care of. It would cost her nothing to travel to London to listen to Sir Charles' will being read. Was she foolish to even consider doing such a thing?

Mrs. Allston rose from her seat. "Will you kindly wait for us in the entry hall, Mr. Rymer?" she asked. "Miss Hembry and I have much to discuss."

"It would be my pleasure," Mr. Rymer replied, rising. "I shall wait for Miss Hembry's decision."

After the solicitor departed, Mrs. Allston came around her desk and closed the door. "Well, that was exciting, but you must know that you cannot go to London. You are needed here."

"If I did go, I would only be gone for a few days," Emilia attempted.

"That is far too long." Mrs. Allston clasped her hands in front of her and pursed her lips. "If you do decide to go to

London, I will have no choice but to let you go from your position."

Emilia had a choice to make. She could do what was expected of her, just as she always did, or she could do something for herself. But was she willing to face the consequences of her actions?

She didn't know why Sir Charles wanted her there, but it must be important if he had sent his solicitor to collect her, especially since it had come at a great expense to him. Could she take the risk of going, even if it meant she would lose the position at the school?

In her heart, she knew she needed to go.

"I think it would be best if I went," Emilia said softly, knowing she was about to stoke Mrs. Allston's ire.

Mrs. Allston inhaled swiftly. "For what purpose?" she asked. "You must know that nothing will come from this. You are just a poor country bumpkin. You no more belong in London than a pig belongs in a home."

Emilia winced, knowing there was some truth to her words. Her gowns were simple and might draw some unwanted attention on the fashionable streets of London. But if she didn't go, she would always wonder what could have been. And she couldn't abide that thought.

"Please, Mrs. Allston," Emilia said. "I have never asked for a day off since I started working here nearly three years ago. I will come back as soon as I am able."

"I took a chance on you and gave you employment," Mrs. Allston stated, lifting her chin. "And this is how you repay me?"

Emilia rose from her chair and hoped to appeal to Mrs. Allston's sense of decency, assuming she had any. In a calm, collected voice, she said, "I am most grateful for everything that you have given me, but I must go to London. If there is even a chance that I could have a change of fortune, I must go."

Mrs. Allston's expression softened slightly. "I won't give you my blessing, but I do understand," she responded as she sat down behind her desk. "If you do come back, I will let you have your job back…"

"Thank you," Emilia gushed.

"… but I will dock your pay and lower your wages to ten shillings for three months," Mrs. Allston finished.

Emilia decided to take what she could get from the ornery headmistress. "That is fair, Ma'am," she said.

"As much as I dare to admit it, you are not completely incompetent at your job and the girls seem to be taken by you," Mrs. Allston remarked as she waved her hand in front of her. "Now, be off with you. You must pack quickly if you want to leave soon."

As Emilia left to inform Mr. Rymer of her decision, she felt happiness well up deep inside of her. It was something she hadn't allowed herself to feel in quite some time now. She found a strange comfort in sadness. It's what she was accustomed to and no one could ever take it from her because there was nothing to take.

But now, hope bloomed in her heart. She didn't know what lay ahead of her, but surely it was better than what she was leaving behind.

Fredrick Westlake, Earl of Chatsworth, felt like an imposter. He was sitting amongst his friends at White's but his mind was far away. He was thinking about his comrades on the Continent, knowing full well what they were enduring.

Misery.

Death.

War had turned out to be nothing like he had expected. He had started off fighting for a purpose, but as time passed, that line began to blur, leaving him to question what was truly right or wrong.

But that wasn't the worst part. It was the faces that he saw when he closed his eyes; the faces of the men that he had killed. They relentlessly tormented him, depriving him of any peace. He was trying to learn to coexist with them, but he was failing. Miserably.

Sitting around a table at White's, he couldn't help but wonder what he was even doing here. His comrades were out on the battlefield, risking their lives, and here he was, doing nothing to help them.

Lord Rushcliffe's voice interrupted his thoughts. "Are you with us, Chatsworth?"

Fredrick lifted his gaze, noting the concerned expressions of Greydon, Viscount of Rushcliffe, and Mr. Tristan Westcott. "I am fine," he said, forcing a smile to his lips. It was the same evasive response he had grown accustomed to offering.

"You don't look fine," Tristan stated. "Quite frankly, you look rather troubled."

Not wanting to continue down this line of questioning, Fredrick knew the one thing to ask to shift Tristan's focus away from him. "How is your lovely wife, Lizette?"

Tristan seemed to radiate happiness at the mere mention of his wife. "Lizette is well," he said. "She is increasing."

"How wonderful," Greydon expressed. "I have no doubt that Enid will be overjoyed at the news."

Fredrick would have found his friends' marital bliss to be rather vexing if he weren't so happy for them. It seemed like everyone was falling prey to the parson's mousetrap, but not him. He had no intention of taking a wife.

Turning towards Greydon, Tristan asked, "Is it me or was Fredrick trying to distract me by asking about Lizette?"

"He most definitely was trying to distract you," Greydon replied. "But the question is why."

Fredrick tightened his hold on his teacup. Perhaps he had

attempted that diversion far too often and his friends had finally caught on. "Surely there is something else we could discuss other than me?" he asked.

"Nothing else is as interesting," Tristan remarked. "You could always tell us about the war. You have been rather tight-lipped on the matter."

"That is because there is nothing to say about it," Fredrick asserted.

Greydon studied him for a moment before asking, "Dare I ask about your mother?"

"She is still alive, for now," Fredrick replied. His mother was withering away right before his eyes and he was struggling with the fact that she didn't remember him anymore. To her, he was just a stranger.

Tristan's eyes held compassion. "You have our deepest sympathies," he acknowledged.

Fredrick didn't want their sympathy or their pity, but that's what it felt like- pity more than anything else. He was just trying to keep one foot in front of the other. Life had gotten far too complicated for him, and he didn't see a way out of the hole he found himself in.

Tristan rose and pushed in his seat. "It is time I return home to my lovely wife."

"Tell Lizette we said hello," Fredrick remarked.

After Tristan walked off, Greydon glanced over his shoulder before lowering his voice. "I am concerned about you, as we all are. You have seemed rather despondent since you returned from the war, and we want to help you…"

Fredrick put his hand up, stilling his friend's words. "I am fine. Just fine. Now, can we end this line of questioning?" There was that elusive response again. It rather suited his emotions.

"I know what it is like to grieve the loss of someone close to you and—" Greydon began.

Fredrick cut him off. "No one can understand what I have

gone through. I appreciate what you are trying to do, but it won't help me. Nothing will."

He knew that he couldn't simply wish away his problems as if waving a magic wand. Life didn't work that way. There were some things that were irrevocably broken, and he felt like one of those things.

"I should go," Fredrick said, shoving back his chair.

Greydon looked at his nearly full teacup. "But you haven't finished your tea," he attempted. "Stay, just for a moment longer, and I promise I won't question you further."

Before Fredrick responded, his brother, Lord Roswell, approached the table with a smile on his lips, but it didn't quite meet his eyes. "We have a problem," he informed them as he sat down.

"Which is?" Greydon asked.

The smile left Roswell's lips, and he dropped all pretenses as he revealed, "Caleb appears to be missing."

"Missing?" Fredrick repeated. "How is that even possible? We just saw him at Octavia's wedding not too long ago."

"Anette's mother came to visit and informed us that Caleb hasn't been home in three days," Roswell responded.

Greydon grew solemn. "That is unlike Caleb."

"I know," Roswell responded. "Kendrick isn't worried, though. He thinks Caleb might have gone undercover in the assignment he was working on."

"Can you tell us what he was working on?" Fredrick asked.

Roswell's eyes held regret. "I'm afraid I can't, at least, not yet," he said. "Did Caleb say anything to you that would cause concern on your part?"

"While you were on your wedding tour, Caleb spoke of visiting the rookeries and I could tell he looked troubled. He even looked slightly disheveled if you could imagine," Fredrick revealed. "I should have followed him, or offered some assistance, but I was dealing with the attempts on Harred's life at the time."

A server arrived at the table and addressed Roswell. "May I get you something to drink, my lord?"

Roswell glanced at Fredrick's teacup before saying, "I will just have a cup of tea."

"Very good," the server said before he walked off to do his bidding.

As Greydon brought the glass up to his lips, he remarked, "You must be worried if you aren't drinking."

"I need a clear head," Roswell said. "I have no choice but to go into the rookeries tonight and search for Caleb."

"That is like searching for a needle in a haystack," Fredrick advised. "Surely Caleb gave some indication as to where he has gone."

Roswell knitted his brow. "He might have, but I have been so distracted by Anette as of late that I might have missed what was right in front of me."

"That is hardly your fault since you two are still newlyweds," Greydon said. "If it would help, I can ask around and see if anyone knows anything about Caleb."

"I would greatly appreciate that but do so discreetly," Roswell urged.

Greydon pushed the empty glass away from him. "That won't be an issue," he assured. "My informants are paid well for their silence."

"Kendrick did want me to remind you both that there is a place for you at the agency," Roswell said. "We are shorthanded and could always use the help."

Fredrick no more wanted to be a spy again than he wanted a thorn in his boot. It was a life that he had left behind when he had left the Continent. He had been one of Wellington's spies and that had taken a great toll on him. What he was forced to do… no, he couldn't do that again.

Wellington had sent him home to care for his ailing mother and that is what he intended to do. The spy life was behind him. It had to be, for his sanity's sake.

"Does your silence mean you are considering it?" Roswell asked.

Fredrick shook his head. "My answer is no."

Roswell looked disappointed. "I expected as much, but I was hopeful that you would reconsider." He shifted his gaze towards Greydon. "Dare I hope you want to be an agent?"

"Enid and I discussed it and we thought it was best if I focused on running the estate," Greydon said. "I already have far too many secrets."

The server came and placed a cup of tea in front of Roswell and asked, "Will there be anything else, my lord?"

"No, thank you," Roswell said as he reached for the cup of tea.

After the server walked away, Greydon pushed back his seat and rose. "It is best if I depart. I find that I miss Enid."

Fredrick watched as Greydon headed for the main door and asked, "Do all men turn into love-craved fools after they get married?"

"Only the lucky ones that are fortunate enough to marry their true loves," Roswell replied. "Speaking of which, where is your wife?"

Fredrick huffed. "I have no desire to take a wife."

"I said something similar until I managed to convince Anette to marry me."

"Yes, well, you had been in love with Anette since we were young," Fredrick said. "It was no surprise to me that you two ended up together."

Roswell took a sip of his tea before saying, "You must trust me when I say that a wife is a good thing."

"I know you are happy, but not everyone deserves to find happiness," Fredrick said. "I am content on my own."

"Are you?" Roswell questioned.

Fredrick pressed his lips together, knowing his brother was only trying to help. But he didn't need his help. Or anyone's help, for that matter. He was happy for his brother, he truly was, but that didn't mean he had to follow in his footsteps. They were on different paths.

"I apologize. I feel as if I am being a little too preachy," Roswell said.

"You aren't wrong," Fredrick muttered.

Roswell pushed the teacup away from him. "Octavia told me that she was worried about you."

"When did our sister tell you this?"

"The moment I returned home from my wedding tour," Roswell replied. "She says that you are just keeping up pretenses, but you are truly miserable. Is there any truth to that?"

Octavia had raised her concerns to Fredrick before, but he didn't think she would run to Roswell to try to help him.

Fredrick shoved back his chair and rose. "I tire of this conversation," he said. "I'm going home."

Rising, Roswell responded, "Don't think I failed to notice you not answering the question."

"You live your life, and I will live mine," Fredrick asserted. "I know Octavia means well, but she doesn't understand what I've been through."

Roswell put his hands up in surrender. "All right, you have made your point. But I am here if you ever want to talk."

"I would not count on that," Fredrick muttered before he started walking towards the main door.

"You will find that I am an excellent listener," Roswell said as he caught up to him and matched his stride. "Sometimes Anette accuses me of not listening to her, but I can repeat back every word that she said to me."

Fredrick grinned. "That is a quality of any good husband. It would drive Mother mad when Father would do that to her."

At the mention of their mother, Roswell grew solemn. "Mother isn't going to last much longer, is she?"

"I doubt it."

A Suitable Fortune

Fredrick stepped out onto the pavement and glanced up at the sky. He had so much to be grateful for, but he was miserable, just as Octavia had determined. He didn't know what his future would bring, but he hoped it was a chance at redemption.

Chapter Two

Emilia stood outside of Sir Charles' grand townhouse as she attempted to gather enough courage to enter. She had come this far, but the fear was unrelenting. Despite wearing her finest gown, she knew that everyone would see she didn't belong.

But she hadn't come this far to give up now. Taking a deep breath, she squared her shoulders and hoped she looked more confident than she felt, despite the nagging doubts. She wondered what she had to be nervous about. After all, Sir Charles had requested her presence at the reading of his will. He must have believed that she belonged here.

Emilia approached the main door and knocked.

The door was promptly opened, and a tall, white-haired butler greeted her. "May I help you, Miss?"

"I am here for the reading of the will," Emilia replied.

The butler's eyes crinkled around the edges, and that one simple gesture allowed her to relax her tense shoulders. "I must assume you are Miss Hembry," he said.

"I am."

He opened the door wide. "Mr. Rymer informed me that

you would be coming. Allow me to show you to the parlor where the family has assembled."

Emilia stepped inside the grand entry hall and forced herself not to gawk at the opulent decor. Deep blue paper adorned the walls, intricately carved woodwork graced the length of the room, and the freshly polished marble floor gleamed underfoot.

"If you will follow me, Miss Hembry," the butler said before he started down a corridor that was lined with portraits.

She trailed after the butler but her eyes strayed towards the portraits of the genteel women and gentlemen. She wondered what it must be like to sit for a portrait such as these. She could hardly imagine wearing such fine clothes and having elaborate jewels hanging around her neck. It was a life that would always be out of her reach.

The butler came to a stop outside of an open door and gestured for her to enter. His expression remained stoic, yet his eyes, just for a fleeting moment, seemed to betray a hint of concern. Which was ridiculous, was it not? Why would he even show the least bit of concern for her? She was nothing more than a stranger to him.

Emilia hesitantly stepped inside of the room and saw Mr. Rymer engaged in a conversation with a young blonde-haired woman, who was elegantly dressed in a black muslin gown, and a fashionably dressed gentleman, both appearing to be of a similar age to her. The solicitor's expression, however, bore traces of frustration, suggesting that their discussion wasn't proceeding as smoothly as he had hoped.

Mr. Rymer glanced over at her and his eyes flashed with something that looked very much like relief.

"Miss Hembry," Mr. Rymer greeted loudly.

The young woman followed the solicitor's gaze and her eyes narrowed on Emilia. "Who is *she?*"

"As I told you, your father invited Miss Hembry to the reading of his will," Mr. Rymer replied.

The gentleman leaned towards the young woman and said in a hushed voice, "I will never understand what Father was thinking, but if he left her a penny, I intend to contest the will."

"She probably is the daughter of his whore," the young woman remarked with a hand covering part of her mouth.

Emilia shifted nervously in her stance. They had spoken loudly enough that she had heard their every word, leading her to believe that had been their intention. If their aim was to make her as uncomfortable as possible, they had certainly succeeded. She began to wonder whether her decision to come had been a mistake.

Mr. Rymer approached her and bowed. "You are most welcome here." He paused. "Miss Hembry, I do believe introductions are in order. Allow me to introduce you to Miss Clarissa Sutherland and Mr. Calvin Sutherland."

Mr. Sutherland acknowledged her with a cursory nod while Miss Sutherland merely huffed, then returned her attention to her brother. It was evident that they held her in low regard and didn't consider her worthy of their time or notice.

"Now that everyone is here, shall we begin?" Mr. Rymer asked.

"It is about time," Miss Sutherland complained. "I don't know why my father thought this meeting was necessary."

Mr. Rymer gestured towards the available seating. "Would everyone care to take a seat?"

Miss Sutherland glided effortlessly to a camelback settee. Emilia chose a chair that was the farthest way from Miss Sutherland and tried her best to ignore the disdainful glances that were being directed her way by the brother and sister.

"I will stand," Mr. Sutherland said.

"Very good." Mr. Rymer walked over to the desk and picked up a stack of papers. "As you were informed, Sir

Charles amended his will just days before his death, in the presence of two witnesses. A Lord Billingsly and Mr. Crawshay. It has since been recorded in probate court and approved by the judge. Furthermore, Sir Charles appointed me to be the executor of his last will and testament."

"Father always made much ado about nothing," Mr. Sutherland said. "I don't understand why no one could read the will until now."

Mr. Rymer came to stand in front of them and said, "It was his request, and I had no choice but to honor it."

"How long is this going to take?" Miss Sutherland asked, glancing at the long clock in the corner. "I have a meeting with the dressmaker this afternoon and I won't be late for the fitting. I need a whole new wardrobe now that I am in mourning."

"It shouldn't take too long," Mr. Rymer assured her. "Are there any questions before I begin reading the will?"

Miss Sutherland shot Emilia a disgruntled look, daring her to speak up. Not that she had any intention of doing so. Being in this room was becoming increasingly unpleasant with each passing moment.

Mr. Rymer cleared his throat and began reading in a clear and precise voice. "I, Sir Charles Sutherland, of the parish of St. George's, do by this, my last will and testament, give and bequeath to my daughter, Emilia, everything of which I may die possessed, or which may be hereafter due to me, minus twenty thousand pounds which will be divided equally amongst my two illegitimate children, Clarissa and Calvin."

Emilia stared at the solicitor in disbelief as a deafening silence filled the room. Did she dare believe what had just been read to her? How was it possible that she was Sir Charles' daughter? None of this made any sense.

Miss Sutherland jumped up from her seat. "This is preposterous! Father wasn't in his right mind when he wrote this will.

We are not illegitimate; she is!" she shouted, pointing at Emilia.

Mr. Rymer lowered the papers to his side. "Unfortunately, you are misinformed," he said. "Sir Charles eloped to Gretna Green with his first wife, Rosie, and hadn't annulled the marriage when he married your mother, Lady Diana. Therefore, Emilia is Sir Charles' only legitimate child and is entitled to his vast fortune."

"I will need to see proof of this," Mr. Sutherland demanded.

"I shall send it over at once. But I should warn you that the marriage documents were submitted to the probate court and have been reviewed by the judge, confirming that Sir Charles did, in fact, commit bigamy," Mr. Rymer shared. "It is within your rights to contest the will, but it will come at a great expense to you."

Miss Sutherland turned her attention towards Emilia and spat out, "You may think you have won, but you will be returning to the sewer from whence you crawled out of soon enough."

Emilia was taken aback by the harshness of Miss Sutherland's words, not knowing how to respond to such an insulting remark.

"That was uncalled for," Mr. Rymer chided. "I should note that you are now residing in Miss Hembry's residence and she has every right to have you removed."

"Removed?" Miss Sutherland exclaimed, her voice becoming shrill. "This is my home!"

"It *was* your home, but I have seen to your trunks being packed," Mr. Rymer said. "Sir Charles did graciously purchase you a townhouse in Cheapside that you may reside in."

Miss Sutherland's face went slack. "You wish us to move from Mayfair to Cheapside?" she asked in disbelief. "No, there must be some kind of mistake. Father wouldn't treat us this way. He loved us!"

"Allow me to continue to read what your father wrote," Mr. Rymer said, bringing the papers back up. "To Clarissa and Calvin, who never would follow my advice, and constantly treated me rudely in very many instances, I tire of your ungratefulness. It is time for you to carve your own paths and learn to make do with what you have. If you—"

Mr. Sutherland went and grabbed the papers out of Mr. Rymer's hand. "Let me read it," he commanded.

As everything was going on around her, Emilia just sat in stunned silence. She was trying to make sense of what had been told to her. Was this truly happening? Did she just become an heiress? It just seemed too good to be true.

"As you can see, everything is in order," Mr. Rymer said.

"This can't be happening," Mr. Sutherland muttered under his breath. "This is just a joke, isn't it? Father is just having some fun at our expense."

Mr. Rymer shook his head. "I'm afraid not."

"What will people think of us?" Miss Sutherland asked, dropping down onto the settee. "We are ruined."

"I will give you some time to come to terms with what just happened while I speak to Miss Sutherland privately," Mr. Rymer said, turning his attention towards Emilia. "Shall we?"

"That is my title of address," Miss Clarissa snapped.

"Not any longer," Mr. Rymer corrected. "Miss Sutherland is the oldest daughter, and the only legitimate one. It is her right to be addressed as such. You will now be known as Miss Clarissa Livingston, after your mother."

Emilia slowly rose from her seat and tried to act as calm as possible, despite her heart pounding in her chest. Not only did she just discover she was the daughter of Sir Charles, but she was to take a new name, as well. She followed Mr. Rymer from the parlor, and he led her towards a room that was situated in the rear of the townhouse.

After he had closed the door, Mr. Rymer put his hands up and said, "I suppose you have some questions for me."

Yes.

Where did she even begin?

Mr. Rymer must have understood her hesitancy and smiled. "Perhaps I shall start. You have inherited this townhouse, a country estate in Sussex and a hunting lodge in Scotland. Furthermore, Sir Charles died with a fortune totaling nearly two hundred thousand pounds."

Emilia's mouth dropped. "Two hundred thousand pounds?" she repeated back.

"Yes, and it is all yours," Mr. Rymer replied.

"I don't understand," Emilia said. "I was told that my father was a soldier and that he died in the war when I was young. Why would my mother lie to me?"

Mr. Rymer's eyes held compassion. "Sir Charles eloped with your mother to Gretna Green but his parents disapproved. They kept their marriage a secret, hoping time would soften his parents' stance. Unfortunately, it did not, and they threatened to cut your father off if he didn't marry his betrothed, Lady Diana."

"Why didn't my father get an annulment then?"

"Because he loved your mother, more than anything; at least that is what he told me," Mr. Rymer said. "Your mother understood the terrible position your father was in and decided it would be best if she removed herself from his presence, not knowing that she was increasing. By the time she learned of you, Sir Charles was already married to Lady Diana."

Mr. Rymer continued. "If she came forward, then Sir Charles would have been disgraced and lose everything that he had worked so hard for."

"When did Sir Charles learn about me?"

"It wasn't until you were older," Mr. Rymer shared. "Your mother sent a letter and asked for funds to send you to a boarding school. She hoped to educate you to give you a better future than what she had provided for you."

Emilia brought a hand to her forehead. "Why didn't my mother say anything?"

"I do believe she thought she was doing right by you," Mr. Rymer responded. "As far as everyone knew, you were the legitimate daughter of Captain Hembry."

"Did my mother lie about being married to Captain Hembry?"

"Your mother did go through the pretense of marrying Captain Hembry before you were born, but it was not a valid marriage," Mr. Rymer said. "I know this is a lot to take in, but there is no mistake in it. You are Sir Charles' true heir and he wanted you to have what was rightfully yours."

Emilia couldn't quite believe her change of fortune. But where did she go from here? It just seemed too overwhelming, and she was afraid to make a misstep.

"Would you care to meet your staff?" Mr. Rymer asked.

She blinked. Her staff? No, she wasn't ready to meet them. They would know that she didn't belong here the moment they looked at her. What she needed was a moment alone to process this information.

"I would like to take a walk if you don't mind," Emilia said. She found great solace in a good walk. She always felt better after one.

If Mr. Rymer seemed surprised by her request, he didn't show it. "Of course. Would you like to take along a maid or perhaps two footmen?"

"No, I would prefer to go alone."

Mr. Rymer looked unsure. "It would be best if a maid accompanied you for propriety's sake," he said. "I'm afraid the freedom that you have been accustomed to in the countryside is no longer an option afforded to you in London, given your circumstances."

Emilia decided it was best to concede, knowing he spoke true. "Very well. Do I just ask a maid to accompany me?"

"I shall speak to Dalby, your butler, and he will see to collecting a maid for your walk," Mr. Rymer said. "If you will wait here, I shall return shortly."

After the solicitor left, Emilia's eyes wandered over the room. A stately desk sat in the center and tall bookshelves lined one wall. She couldn't quite believe it. Those books all now belonged to her. All of them. She had never owned a book of her own before now.

The realization hit her as she recognized that she didn't just own everything in this room. But the entire townhouse. The portraits. The furniture. It was all hers.

Emilia was conflicted about how she should feel. On one hand, she was happy about her change of fortune, yet on the other, she felt overwhelmed. What did she know about managing a household, let alone an entire estate? When she had arrived here, she had never expected this outcome. Not in her wildest dreams.

But then distant shouts of disgruntlement reached her ears and she came to an abrupt stop. Her fortune came at a great expense to others and she was well aware of the bitterness and resentment that her newfound wealth might stir. It would be best if she contained her emotions until she was far away from the townhouse.

Fredrick sat on a bench in Hyde Park that overlooked the Serpentine River. He always came here with the same purpose- to find the solace that he once had. And he always left disappointed. He had done too many things he had come to regret during the war to ever think he would be free from these wretched memories.

There was one image that haunted him above the rest. It was the face of Timmy. His eyes were opened, staring up at him, telling him that he was to blame for his death. No matter how many times he tried to banish Timmy from his mind, he was always there. Lingering. A painful reminder that he could never go back to his old life.

"May I sit here?"

Fredrick looked up and saw a dark-haired young woman standing near the bench. Her face had delicate features, a pert nose, and rosy cheeks. Her eyes were perhaps her most striking feature, large and expressive, and a rich shade of green. Long, dark lashes added depth to her gaze and her lips held a subtle, graceful smile.

As irritatingly beautiful as she was, Fredrick had no desire for her scheming. No doubt she was here to cast coy smiles and bat her eyelashes at an eligible lord.

But he didn't dare be rude.

Fredrick gestured towards the end of the bench. "You may," he said as he went to angle away from her.

The young woman turned back and shouted, "I am going to sit here. You can remain where you are."

He quickly glanced over his shoulder and saw a maid standing watch a short distance away. Why was she announcing her intentions to the maid?

She sat down and stared out over the Serpentine River. She made no attempt to speak to him or even glance his way. How odd. Perhaps she had no idea who he was. Which would be a first. Every unattached young lady seemed to know of him and his family.

After a long moment, she asked, "Do you believe one should be happy when the cause of one's happiness makes others so miserable?"

Fredrick had no desire to engage in a philosophical debate with a stranger. He just wanted to sit in silence and be miserable. But he couldn't just ignore her question. He decided to be honest with the young woman and, hopefully, she would leave him be after that.

"I do believe happiness is a fleeting emotion and attempting to hold onto it is pointless," he said, knowing how depressing he must sound.

She seemed to consider his response before saying, "Normally, I would agree. However, I just had the most wonderful change of fortune, though it was at a great cost to others. I do not know how I should feel about that."

"I'm afraid I can't answer how you should feel."

"No, you are right," she said with a wave of her hand. "I do apologize for my brazenness."

If Fredrick was a smart man, he would just let the conversation end there, but he heard the sincerity in her voice. She was greatly troubled by something, and he couldn't just ignore that. Could he? No. A gentleman always helps a woman in distress. His mother had engraved that into his very soul.

He shifted towards her on the bench. "Perhaps I could help with your dilemma, assuming you tell me more of the predicament that you find yourself in."

"I do not wish to trouble you, sir."

Sir? This young woman truly didn't know who he was. Which came as a great relief to him. Would she have spoken so freely if she knew he was an earl? He doubted it. Women were far more interested in flirting with him than speaking to him. It was obnoxious, considering he had no desire for a wife.

"I have the time," he encouraged. "In fact, I have nowhere pressing that I need to be at the moment."

Indecision flickered on the young woman's face, leaving him uncertain about what she would decide. Since they weren't introduced, this conversation was entirely inappropriate, but he didn't think the young woman's intention was to trap him.

She turned to face him and asked, "What would you do if you were just given two hundred thousand pounds?"

He lifted his brow. "That is a large sum of money."

"It is," she replied.

"Dare I ask if this happened to you?"

She pursed her lips before saying, "I would rather not say."

Fredrick had always prided himself on knowing when someone was lying, and this young woman was not good at hiding her emotions. She was an heiress. An heiress that was far too naive that she would confess such a thing to a stranger.

This young woman didn't know who she was talking to. What if his intentions hadn't been honorable? He could have easily absconded with her and taken her to Gretna Green, forcing her into an unwanted marriage. He felt it was his duty to tell her that she was unwise in being too forthright.

As he opened his mouth to chide her, she spoke first. "I don't know what to do," she murmured, her eyes holding him transfixed. "Will you help me?"

For some inexplicable reason, an intense sense of protectiveness surged within him concerning this young woman. Her innocence and self-doubt stirred his determination. He couldn't let her fend for herself in high Society. She would be a target for every rake and fortune hunter, if she wasn't already.

"Before we start this conversation, it might be best if I introduce myself to you," Fredrick said. "My name is Fredrick Westlake." He intentionally left out his title to ensure she was more at ease with him.

She bit her lower lip. "I do not think it is wise if I reveal my name, at least, not yet."

"You would prefer anonymity then?"

"I would," she replied. "Is that all right?"

Fredrick smiled. "I have no objections." He was fairly confident he would be able to deduce her name by the end of this conversation. There weren't too many families that had such a vast fortune in London.

She fidgeted with the reticule in her lap. "Before today, I was a teacher at a boarding school and now I don't know who I am."

"You are an heiress."

Her eyes grew wide, as if it were inconceivable that he saw through her. "I didn't say that," she said.

"You didn't have to," he responded. "Please proceed. I find myself intrigued, and that rarely happens."

With a brief glance at her maid, the young woman said, "I don't know why I am telling you all of this. You are a stranger to me."

"I know you have no reason to trust me, but I can assure you that I will not betray your confidences."

A line on her brow appeared as she studied him. "I believe you," she said after a long moment.

Fredrick didn't know why her words affected him so deeply, but they did. She trusted him, despite only just meeting him.

"Everything I thought I knew about my life was a lie," she shared. "I am someone else entirely."

"Is that a good thing?"

"It is just different," she replied. "And now, I am a part of this world that I know nothing about, and I fear that everyone will know how vastly incapable I am."

Fredrick leaned back in his seat. "I must assume you are speaking of the *ton*."

"Yes, are you familiar with it?"

"A little," he lied. He knew all too well about the trappings of the *ton*. He had no doubt that this young woman would be treated horrendously by members of high Society. She was far too innocent to be treated in any other fashion.

"Will you teach me?"

He lifted his brow. "About the *ton*?"

She nodded. "Yes, about the *ton* and about everything."

"That could take some time."

Perking up in her seat, she said, "I have time. Lots of time. In fact, I have more time than I know what to do with now."

A thought occurred to Fredrick. He had an idea on how he could help her, and he hoped she would be willing to try it. "I am not opposed to helping you, but my sister-in-law, Anette, would be a far better teacher than me."

"I don't know," she said. "Do you think she would be willing to help me?"

"I do, but I should warn you that she tends to speak her mind freely," he replied.

The young woman appeared thoughtful. "I would appreciate her help, and yours, if you are still willing."

"I am. But in order for me to assist you, I must know who to call upon," Fredrick said.

"I suppose you are right." She hesitated, a subtle hint of vulnerability in her eyes. "My name is Miss Hembry... no... Miss Sutherland."

"Which one is it?" he questioned.

She squared her shoulders and replied, "Miss Sutherland."

Realization dawned on him as he asked, "Are you related to Sir Charles Sutherland?"

"I am," she replied.

"I hadn't realized he had any other children."

She offered him a timid smile. "It was rather a recent development."

Fredrick knew there was more to the story but he didn't want to press her. Not yet. He suspected she had revealed far more than she had intended to. He didn't want to make her uncomfortable.

"If you are not opposed, I shall call upon you tomorrow and I will bring Anette with me," he said.

Her smile grew, and he found himself smiling back at her. Which was odd since he hardly smiled anymore. "I would like that very much," she responded.

"May I escort you back to your townhouse?"

"Do not trouble yourself," she said. "I brought a maid with me."

Fredrick shifted his gaze towards the petite maid and he found himself worried on her behalf. Miss Sutherland may not know what kind of danger she was in, but he did. That maid could hardly fend off a persistent suitor.

"I would be remiss if I did not recommend you start bringing footmen along with you for your walks in Hyde Park," he started. "It is far safer for a woman of your standing."

Miss Sutherland rose. "I'm afraid I am used to walking everywhere by myself. I shall have to resign myself to the fact that I can no longer do things that I had once taken for granted."

Rising, Fredrick tipped his hat. "It was a pleasure to meet you, Miss Sutherland."

She dropped into a curtsy. "Thank you, kind sir," she said before she turned to leave.

As he watched Miss Sutherland continue down the path, he had the strangest urge to follow her and ensure she returned home safely. But that would be far too presumptuous of him. It would be best if he let her find her own way home, without him.

Why had he not heard of this Miss Sutherland? He was acquainted with Sir Charles' other children, as was everyone, and he found them to be rather arrogant, which didn't sit well with him.

Fredrick did have an issue. A very pressing issue. He owed Sir Charles a great debt and he thought it had died with him. But he now realized that he could ease his conscience if he helped Miss Sutherland.

But where did he start? How could he teach Miss Sutherland everything she needed to know before she ventured into the treacherous waters of high Society?

The further Miss Sutherland progressed along the path,

the stronger his conviction became that he must follow her to ensure her safe arrival home. He couldn't just leave it be. He would never forgive himself if any harm befell her.

With a sigh, Fredrick hurried after her, being mindful not to draw Miss Sutherland's attention. Not that it mattered. She kept her gaze straight ahead as she navigated the bustling streets of London, seemingly oblivious to the numerous perils that surrounded her.

Chapter Three

Emilia stared up at the townhouse and still couldn't quite come to terms that this now belonged to her. All of it. What was she going to do with a grand townhouse? She had been raised in a cottage that had fit their needs and all her belongings fit into a trunk. Not even a large trunk.

Feelings of inadequacy coursed through her, leaving her uncertain about how to proceed. For once, she found herself without a plan.

"Is there a problem, Miss?" the maid asked, standing behind her.

Emilia shook her head. "No," she replied. "I was just thinking."

"It would be best if you did your thinking inside the townhouse," the maid advised. "You wouldn't wish to cause unwanted attention by standing on the pavement."

"You are right," Emilia said. "Thank you."

Taking a deep breath, Emilia headed towards the main door of the townhouse. It was promptly opened and the butler greeted her.

"Welcome home, Miss Sutherland," he said, opening the door wide.

She stepped into the entry hall and saw a silver-haired, portly woman that was dressed in a drab brown gown.

The woman smiled kindly at her. "My name is Mrs. Harvey and I am your housekeeper. Whatever you require, all you need to do is ask."

Emilia winced, aware that she didn't even know what to ask for.

Mrs. Harvey must have read her mind because she continued. "I know this might be a bit overwhelming for you so I have taken the liberty of arranging a few things for you," she said. "The dressmaker will arrive tomorrow to fit you for a new wardrobe."

"That is most kind of you," Emilia said, glancing down at her simple gown.

The butler cleared his throat. "It is my turn to introduce myself. My name is Mr. Dalby and I have been in Sir Charles' employ since I served him as an under-butler."

"It is a pleasure to meet you, both of you," Emilia acknowledged. "I'm afraid everything feels like a whirlwind right now."

"That is to be expected," Mrs. Harvey assured her. "But we shall help you."

The sound of heels clicking on the marble floor resonated just before Mr. Rymer appeared.

"Good, you are back," Mr. Rymer said. "How was your walk?"

"It went well. I met the most interesting gentleman," Emilia revealed. "His name is Mr. Fredrick Westlake. Are you familiar with him?"

Mr. Rymer nodded. "Yes, but you should know that Mr. Westlake is more commonly known as Lord Chatsworth. He is the eldest son of the Marquess of Cuttyngham."

Emilia blinked. "Are you quite sure?"

"Yes, Lord Chatsworth is considered one of the most eligible gentlemen of the Season," Mr. Rymer shared.

She had never spoken to a lord before, and she found herself curious as to why he hadn't revealed who he truly was. But she was glad that he hadn't. If he had, she wouldn't have been so open and honest with him.

Mr. Rymer clasped his hands together. "We still have much to discuss. Shall we adjourn to the study?"

Mrs. Harvey spoke up. "I am sure that Miss Sutherland would like to rest before the seriousness of your conversation."

They both turned their expectant looks to Emilia and she wasn't sure what she should say. She didn't dare disappoint either one of them.

Knowing that they were waiting for a response, Emilia said, "Perhaps I could be shown to my bedchamber before I speak to Mr. Rymer."

She waited for Mr. Rymer to argue with her, but instead he just bobbed his head. "Yes, of course, I shall wait for you in the study."

Mrs. Harvey gestured towards the stairs. "I would be happy to show you to your bedchamber. It is on the second level and it was recently remodeled."

As she walked towards the stairs, Mrs. Harvey matched her stride and said in a low voice, "You are doing well, given the circumstances."

"Am I?" Emilia asked. "I have no idea what I am doing."

"That is to be expected, but your household staff is loyal to you," Mrs. Harvey revealed. "Just be patient with yourself and know that you will make a few missteps."

Emilia placed her hand on the iron railing as she started up the stairs. "I have never been in such a grand home before. I feel out of place."

"It is one of the finest townhouses in all of London," Mrs. Harvey remarked with pride. "But just give yourself some time and it will get easier."

She wanted to believe Mrs. Harvey's words, but she was

fearful. She didn't know the first thing about running a household. She just felt inadequate.

Mrs. Harvey started down a corridor and it wasn't long before they arrived at a wooden door. She opened the door and stepped inside.

Emilia followed her into the room and came to an abrupt stop on the lush carpet. The rich, green-papered walls were adorned with an intricate, patterned design. Heavy drapes framed the tall windows allowing just a soft, filtered light to enter.

In the center of the room was a large, four-poster bed, draped with sumptuous silk fabric. A vanity table with a gilded mirror sat in the corner and it was covered in porcelain jars.

Mrs. Harvey turned back towards her. "I hope this room is to your liking."

"It is beautiful," Emilia said.

"This room belonged to Sir Charles' wife... er... second wife... I mean, his not wife." Mrs. Harvey stopped. "I do apologize."

"There is nothing to apologize for. This is an adjustment, for all of us."

Mrs. Harvey offered her a grateful look before saying, "I have asked one of the maids to see after you until we hire you a proper lady's maid."

"I have never had a lady's maid before," Emilia admitted. "I have always just learned to make do on my own."

"Well, you shall have one now," Mrs. Harvey responded. "In fact, you have an entire household staff to see after you."

Emilia walked over to the bed and ran her hands along the silk bedding. She had never slept in anything so fine before. She didn't even have a feather mattress at her boarding school. Mrs. Allston had provided only a straw mattress for each of her teachers, and they slept in the cold, damp attic.

"Would you care for me to turn down the sheets so you may rest?" Mrs. Harvey asked.

"No, I think it would be best if I spoke to Mr. Rymer now," Emilia replied. "I have so many questions for him."

Mrs. Harvey nodded her understanding. "I will show you the way, unless you are more comfortable going on your own."

"I'm afraid I would get terribly lost if you left me to my own devices," Emilia admitted.

"Very good, Miss," Mrs. Harvey responded. "It would be my pleasure."

Emilia pointed towards a door that was along the far wall and asked, "Where does that door lead to?"

"That was Sir Charles' bedchamber," Mrs. Harvey revealed. "It hasn't been touched since his passing."

Finding herself curious, she asked, "Was my father happy with Lady Diana?"

Mrs. Harvey pressed her lips together before saying, "I'm not quite sure how to answer that. They both seemed to tolerate each other, I suppose. Quite frankly, they spent more time apart than they did together."

"Did my father laugh often?"

"No, he was more a solemn man, but kind," Mrs. Harvey replied. "He would give every member of his staff a Christmas bonus, no matter how long they had been working for him."

Emilia's eyes strayed back towards the door, knowing she would need to go into his bedchamber and try to get a sense of who her father truly was.

As she followed Mrs. Harvey into the corridor, Emilia found herself wanting to know more about Lady Diana. "When did Lady Diana die?"

"About five years ago, Miss," Mrs. Harvey said over her shoulder. "One day she was here, and the next she was gone. The doctor said her heart just gave out."

"How terrible." Emilia found herself feeling sorry for Clarissa and Calvin. How awful would it be to not be able to say goodbye to your own mother?

Mrs. Harvey came to a stop at the top of the stairs and shared, "When your father was dying, he kept calling out for Rosie. I have come to realize that this was your mother."

"She was."

"It is not my place to say so, but when Sir Charles died, he seemed at peace, as if he had finally found his Rosie," Mrs. Harvey said.

Emilia wanted to believe that was true. Her mother worked hard to keep a roof over their heads and never complained, but there was a sadness in her eyes that was undeniable. She hoped that her mother was finally happy.

Knowing Mrs. Harvey was still waiting for a response, Emilia said, "Thank you for sharing that with me."

"You are welcome," Mrs. Harvey responded before she headed down the stairs.

Once they arrived at the study, Emilia saw that Mr. Rymer was sitting on the settee, and papers were set out in front of him.

Mr. Rymer rose and bowed. "Miss Sutherland," he greeted. "Welcome back. We have much to discuss."

Mrs. Harvey slipped out of the room as Emilia went to sit across from Mr. Rymer.

The solicitor returned to his seat and reached for a stack of papers. "I will send a coach to collect your belongings from Mrs. Allston's Seminary for Young Women."

A thought occurred to Emilia. "Would it be possible for you to collect Miss Lily from the boarding school, assuming she would be willing to travel to London?"

"That would be simple enough," Mr. Rymer acknowledged.

"May I hire Lily on as my lady's maid?"

Mr. Rymer smiled. "You do not need my permission. You can hire and dismiss whoever you would like."

"Then I shall draft a letter to Lily."

"I will ensure the driver delivers it to Miss Lily," Mr.

A Suitable Fortune

Rymer said. "Now, on to your various investments. I suggest you keep your father's man of business, Mr. Dryer. He is proficient at what he does and helped to grow Sir Charles' fortune."

Emilia bobbed her head. "I would concur."

"As to that matter of where Miss Clarissa Livingston and Mr. Calvin Livingston reside," Mr. Rymer said. "Sir Charles was in the process of transferring ownership to them but he died before that transaction went through. Since it still belongs to you, it is within your rights to retain the property for your own use."

"I have no intention of displacing them," Emilia responded. "We must honor my father's wishes and gift them the townhouse."

Approval shone in Mr. Rymer's eyes. "Very good, Miss." He placed the stack of papers down. "Let's discuss the particulars about your country estate in Sussex…"

Emilia glanced at the long clock in the corner and realized that she was tired. Emotionally and physically. Perhaps she should have taken a nap instead of meeting with Mr. Rymer. But she was here now and she needed to pay attention. After all, he was talking about her future. A future that still seemed quite unbelievable to her.

Fredrick stepped into the dining room and saw Roswell sitting at the table, reading the newssheets.

"Good morning," he greeted. "Where is Anette?"

Roswell glanced up from the newssheets and replied, "She should be down in a moment."

"I was hoping to ask a favor of her," Fredrick shared as he sat down.

Lowering the newssheets to the table, Roswell said, "You

have piqued my interest. What favor do you intend to ask Anette?"

"Aren't you being a bit nosy this morning?" Fredrick teased.

"I am terribly nosy, especially when it comes to my wife," Roswell said.

Fredrick leaned to the side as a footman placed a plate of food in front of him. "I met the most..." His voice trailed off. How would he describe Miss Sutherland? Intriguing? Perplexing? Ah, he settled on the perfect word. "I met the most *peculiar* young woman in the park yesterday."

"Do I know of this peculiar young woman?"

"I doubt it, because she didn't know who we were," Fredrick revealed.

Roswell's brow lifted. "I take it that she must not be in high Society, then."

"That is the odd part," Fredrick started. "She claims that she is the daughter of Sir Charles Sutherland."

"Wait a moment," Roswell said as he flipped the newssheets to the front page. "I just perused this article, not giving it much heed, but I do believe it pertains to this Miss Sutherland." He folded the pages back and read it.

After a long moment, Roswell shared, "According to this article, Sir Charles committed bigamy and was already married when he wed Lady Diana, thus making Clarissa and Calvin illegitimate. He had a daughter with his first wife, and she inherited the vast majority of his fortune."

Fredrick sat back in his seat. Parts of his conversation with Miss Sutherland came back to him and now it all made sense. No wonder why she was so conflicted. She had gained this vast fortune, but at the expense of others.

"Apparently, Clarissa and Calvin were seen entering a townhouse in Cheapside," Roswell said.

Anette's voice came from the doorway. "Are you speaking of Miss Clarissa Sutherland?" she asked.

"I am," Roswell replied. "Do you know her?"

"I do, but I try to avoid her at every opportunity," Anette replied as she sat down by her husband. "She is a terrible person and loves nothing more than to gossip about others' misfortunes."

Roswell extended her the newssheets and said, "Well, it would appear her fortune has just changed."

Anette accepted the paper and read the article. "I never thought I would feel sorry for Clarissa, but I can't believe this happened to her," she said. "She went from being highly sought after to losing everything."

"Well, if it helps, I met Sir Charles' legitimate daughter in Hyde Park yesterday," Fredrick revealed.

"What was she like?" Anette asked.

Roswell spoke up. "Fredrick said that she is peculiar."

"Peculiar?" Anette asked, appearing intrigued. "How so?"

Fredrick reached for his teacup and took a sip. When he lowered the teacup, he replied, "She is unlike any other woman I have met. She knows nothing about the trappings of the *ton* and I am worried that she will be ostracized by them."

"Surely she must know something about the *ton*, considering she is Sir Charles' daughter," Anette argued.

"Prior to discovering the truth about her parentage, she was a teacher at a boarding school," Fredrick shared.

"A teacher?" Anette asked. "What subject did she teach?"

"Does it matter?" Fredrick asked.

Anette shrugged her shoulders. "Not truly, but I find myself curious."

"Regardless, she is in need of our help," Fredrick said. "I can't in good conscience just leave her be and watch her fail."

Lowering the newssheets to the table, Anette studied him for a moment before asking, "Why is this so important to you, considering you only just met this young woman?"

Fredrick glanced at the open door before he lowered his voice. "After I received my commission in the Army, I made a terrible mistake. I gambled with money that I didn't have and I was in debt. I was too embarrassed to tell Father and admit my mistake. Instead, I went to Sir Charles for some advice."

"Why did you go to Sir Charles?" Anette questioned.

"Sir Charles is my godfather. He went to university with my father and they have been close ever since," Fredrick explained. "When Sir Charles heard my plight, he paid off my debt and strongly encouraged me to never gamble again. Which I have no intention of doing. It is a terrible vice, and I was fortunate to have learned from my mistake." He paused. "I feel as if I owe it to Sir Charles to help his daughter."

A footman placed a cup of chocolate in front of Anette as she asked, "Are you not worried about betraying Clarissa and Calvin by helping this Miss Sutherland?"

"I do not consider it a betrayal. Frankly, I was never particularly close with either of them, partly due to the differences in our ages, but mostly because of their pretentious attitudes," Fredrick said. "They took after their mother in that regard."

Anette glanced at Roswell and asked, "What do you think? Should I help Miss Sutherland?"

"It is entirely your choice," Roswell replied. "I have no say in the matter."

"You are of little help, Husband," Anette joked.

Roswell leaned closer and kissed her on the cheek. "I am a smart enough man to let you come to your own decisions, mostly because you always do the right thing."

"Now I have no choice but to help her." Anette brought her gaze back to Fredrick's. "Does she even want our help?"

Fredrick picked up his knife and fork. "She does," he confirmed. "But I should warn you that it might take a considerable amount of time. She has the poise of a lady, but she seems so unsure of herself."

"That is not surprising. My mother spent my entire life preparing me to enter high Society," Anette said. "I can't imagine being thrust into it at her age. No doubt she has no idea what to expect or how vicious the gossips can be."

Fredrick placed his fork and knife onto his plate. "Shall we call upon Miss Sutherland?" he asked as he pushed back his chair.

Anette grinned. "May I ask what the urgency is?"

"There is no urgency," he replied. "I just thought it would be best if we got it out of the way." Which was a lie. For some reason, unbeknownst to him, he was looking forward to seeing Miss Sutherland again.

There was a refreshing quality about her that piqued his interest, and he eagerly anticipated another chance to engage in conversation with her. Which never had happened before with a young woman. Most of the time, he grew tired of the overt flirtations, but Miss Sutherland had not once indulged in such behavior. Instead, she appeared to hold his opinion in high regard.

He wondered if she had discovered his true identity yet. If so, would she resort to the same desperate tactics that the other young women engaged him in to garner his attention? He hoped not.

Anette took a sip of her chocolate and lowered the cup back down to the table. "You must allow me to eat my breakfast first."

"Of course," Fredrick said.

Roswell glanced at the footmen before saying, "My trip into the rookeries was not very productive, I'm afraid. I made no progress on my case."

Knowing that his brother was being intentionally vague since they weren't alone, Fredrick said, "That is most unfortunate."

"I could always use your help," Roswell said. "Another set of eyes would be greatly appreciated."

Fredrick had already made his thoughts known on the

matter, but could he sit back and do nothing, knowing his friend was missing? That thought unsettled him.

But what if Caleb was just undercover and he didn't need- or want- their help? They could unintentionally reveal his identity.

After Anette swallowed her bite of food, she said, "Fredrick would love to help you."

"I would?" Fredrick asked.

Anette gave him a smile that held a hint of knowing satisfaction. "It is only fair that if I help you with Miss Sutherland that you help Roswell find my brother. Don't you think?"

Fredrick had to admit that Anette was rather clever. He suspected that she would help him with Miss Sutherland regardless, but she was using it to her advantage. And he didn't fault her for that. He probably would do the same thing.

"Anette is right. I am happy to help," Fredrick said.

Roswell clasped his hands together. "Wonderful," he responded. "I shall take you up on it soon enough."

Fredrick glanced up at the ceiling. "Have you visited Mother this morning?" he asked.

With a solemn look, Roswell replied, "I did, and she is not quite with us. She has reverted to when she was a debutante and was worried about her coming out ball."

"Has she asked about Octavia yet?" Fredrick asked.

"She did once, but that was only because she wanted another bag of dry sweetmeats," Roswell shared.

Fredrick sighed. "I can pick up a bag at Gunter's when I am out today."

"She would greatly appreciate that," Roswell said.

Anette wiped the sides of her mouth with her napkin and placed it down onto her plate. "I am ready to go visit Miss Sutherland. I do hope she isn't a bore."

"I can assure you that she is not a bore," Fredrick said.

Roswell rose and assisted his wife in rising. "I wish you luck, my dear. I will be home for supper."

"You better," Anette said in a serious tone but there was a lightheartedness to it.

"Will you miss me?" Roswell asked as he leaned closer to his wife.

"I most definitely will, my love biscuit," she gushed.

Fredrick worked hard not to roll his eyes at Anette's term of endearment for Roswell. He thought it would be best for them- and him- if he left them alone to say their goodbyes.

As he departed from the dining room, he found himself contemplating whether Miss Sutherland would be pleased to see him, although it held little significance either way. He simply harbored a hopeful wish that she did.

Chapter Four

Emilia sat in the drawing room as she worked on her needlework. It was soothing and familiar. Something she needed to be reminded of right now.

She pulled the needle through the fabric as she let out a sigh. Mrs. Harvey had recommended that she retire to the drawing room so she could welcome any callers that she might have. Not that she expected any. No one knew who she was. Well, that wasn't entirely true. Lord Chatsworth knew of her and had promised to call. But what if he had changed his mind, especially if he had read the newssheets this morning?

Emilia was in the most awkward of situations and she had no idea what she should be doing. Why was she even in the drawing room? It hardly mattered where she sat in this grand townhouse. No matter where she sat, it confirmed the one thing that she already knew- she didn't belong in this life.

What if she just retired to her country estate and lived out her days in peace? Would she disappoint her father's memory if she did just that? Surely he didn't think she could ever fit into high Society.

Just one look at her simple green gown would confirm that. It was made from a sturdy cotton material and did little to flatter her figure. Which was intentional. Why would a teacher at a boarding school need to attract the attention of a suitor?

Dalby stepped into the room and announced, "Lord Chatsworth and his sister-in-law, Lady Roswell, have come to call. Shall I show them in?"

"They are here?" she asked.

"Yes, Miss," Dalby confirmed.

Emilia lowered her needlework to her lap and tilted her chin. "Please show my guests in," she said, hoping she sounded more confident than she felt.

Dalby tipped his head as he went to do her bidding.

A moment later, a brown-haired young woman and Lord Chatsworth stepped into the room. He was just as handsome as she remembered, which had nothing to do with why she had initially struck up a conversation with him. His eyes carried a certain familiarity that eluded her explanation, yet she couldn't deny the powerful attraction she felt towards him, stronger than any she had experienced with anyone else she had met before.

Remembering her manners, Emilia rose and dropped into a curtsy. "Welcome to my home," she greeted.

Lord Chatsworth bowed. "Good morning," he said. "I do hope we didn't call too early."

"Not at all," Emilia replied. "I have been up for hours. I am used to waking up when the rooster crows to help fix breakfast for the girls..." She stopped and closed her eyes. Why had she just revealed that? He had only asked a simple question and she had blabbered on.

With a slight gesture at Lady Roswell, Lord Chatsworth said, "Miss Sutherland, allow me the privilege of introducing you to my sister-in-law, Lady Roswell."

"It is a pleasure to meet you, my lady," Emilia remarked.

Lady Roswell smiled. "Were you really a teacher before you came to London?"

"I was," Emilia replied.

"May I ask what you taught?" Lady Roswell asked.

"Needlework."

Lady Roswell made a face. "I am terrible at needlework. My mother says that I am hopeless but I find that I don't have the patience for it."

"Perhaps you never had a good teacher," Emilia suggested.

"I doubt that is it," Lady Roswell said. "I would much rather be practicing my shooting at the targets."

Emilia gave her an odd look. "You enjoy shooting?"

"I do," Lady Roswell said, holding up her reticule. "I carry a muff pistol with me wherever I go, and it even came in handy one time."

"Should I carry a pistol in my reticule?" Emilia asked.

Lord Chatsworth interjected, "Not unless you are proficient at it."

Emilia shook her head. "I have never held a pistol before," she admitted. "My mother didn't particularly care for them."

Lady Roswell retrieved the pistol from her reticule and held it up. "It is rather dainty and can do a great deal of damage to your attacker."

"Are the streets of London so terribly unsafe?" Emilia asked.

"In my experience, yes," Anette said. "And you are an heiress now. You should know how to protect yourself from rakes and fortune hunters."

Emilia felt her eyes grow wide. "Do you think they might hurt me?"

"It wouldn't be hard to toss you into a coach and abscond with you to Gretna Green—" Lady Roswell started.

Lord Chatsworth spoke over her. "Let's not frighten the poor girl, shall we?"

"My apologies," Lady Roswell said. "I'm afraid I tend to get carried away on certain topics, but I assure you that I do mean well."

A maid stepped into the room with a tea service and placed it onto the table. "Would you like me to pour, Miss?"

"I can pour, but thank you," Emilia replied as she returned to her seat. "Would anyone care for a cup of tea?"

While Lady Roswell returned the pistol to her reticule, she replied, "A cup of tea would be lovely, wouldn't it, Fredrick?"

"Yes, tea would be nice," Lord Chatsworth confirmed.

Emilia picked up the teapot and poured three cups of tea. It was silly that she felt so nervous, especially since she had done this hundreds of times.

After she handed them each a cup of tea, she picked up her own teacup and took a sip. She wasn't quite sure what she should say or do. What must they think of her? She was a terrible hostess since she had already run out of things to say.

Lady Roswell smiled. "I read about your incredible change of fortune in the newssheets this morning."

"Oh, you read that," Emilia murmured.

"How are you adjusting to your new life?" Lady Roswell asked.

Emilia bit her lower lip. Dare she admit what she was truly feeling? What if they betrayed her trust and she became a laughingstock amongst the *ton*?

Lord Chatsworth leaned forward and placed his teacup onto the table. "You may speak freely to Anette," he said. "She may say the most outlandish things, but she will not betray your confidences."

"It is true," Lady Roswell confirmed. "Whatever you say to me will stay between us, now and forever."

Emilia had no reason to trust them, but she found herself doing so anyways. Her voice remained remarkably steady, despite the whirlwind of emotions inside of her, as she admitted, "I have no idea what I am doing."

Lady Roswell laughed. "Truthfully, none of us do. We just pretend like we do."

"I doubt that to be true," Emilia said. "I grew up in a

cottage and I became a teacher. How can I possibly mingle with the *ton*?"

"You are overthinking this," Lady Roswell remarked. "You are an heiress now. The same rules do not apply to you."

Lord Chatsworth spoke up. "What my sister-in-law is trying to say, but failing miserably, is that you are in a unique position. You don't need to marry to provide for yourself."

Emilia glanced down at her gown and said, "But just look at me. It is evident that I do not belong, even with my fortune."

"Your gown is rather simple, but a new wardrobe would fix that problem," Lady Roswell said. "Until then, you can borrow some of my gowns. We are of similar size and I do not wear the pale colors now that I am married."

"You are being far too generous, but I couldn't borrow your gowns…"

Lady Roswell put her hand up, stilling her objections. "I shall have them sent over at once," she said. "You may wear them until you have your own gowns commissioned."

"The dressmaker is coming today to take my measurements," Emilia shared.

"Good," Lady Roswell said. "I cannot help but notice that you are not mourning your father by wearing all black."

"I didn't know my father so it seems silly to mourn him," Emilia admitted.

Lady Roswell grew quiet. "I think in your case it is appropriate for you not to mourn him, given the circumstances. Besides, it is more important for you to be seen in public, and often."

"That is a relief," Emilia said.

"Now that is resolved, we must speak about your hat situation. Do you have an abundance of hats?" Lady Roswell asked.

"I have two hats. One that I wear to church service and my other one that I take on walks," Emilia replied.

Lady Roswell's hand started moving at an animated pace. "We need to get you more hats, at once. It is imperative that you have a closet full of hats."

Lord Chatsworth chuckled. "I daresay that you are being a tad bit overdramatic. After all, you are making it sound as if it is life or death."

"It is," Lady Roswell insisted. "A proper lady is never seen in public without a hat. It just isn't done." Her eyes grew wide. "Good heavens, I sound just like my mother."

Emilia felt herself relax and she even let a laugh escape her lips. It felt good to laugh, even if it was just for a moment.

Lord Chatsworth met her gaze and said, "I knew that Anette would help you, albeit in her own way."

"Thank you," Emilia said, hoping her words properly expressed her gratitude. "I feel so lost, not knowing what to expect."

"You must expect to go into battle," Lady Roswell declared. "And I have the perfect idea."

"I'm afraid to ask what it is," Lord Chatsworth said.

Lady Roswell's eyes lit up. "I will help you plan a ball where you can show the *ton* that you do belong here."

"I know nothing about planning a ball," Emilia said. "In fact, I have never been to one before. I did attend a country dance once."

"A ball is just like a country dance but bigger and better in all aspects," Lady Roswell declared. "And fortunately for you, I have been preparing for this moment my entire life."

Emilia shifted her gaze to Lord Chatsworth. "What do you think?"

"I think it is a grand idea," he admitted. "People are going to be curious about you. Why not just get the gawking out of the way?"

"But who will come? No one knows me," Emilia said.

Lady Roswell grinned. "I will help you come up with a guest list. I promise that the *ton* will flock to your ball."

Emilia grappled with conflicting emotions. On one hand, she wanted to be brave and plan a ball, but on the other, she was terrified to do so. She hated that fear was ruling her life, yet the prospect of making a misstep was a paralyzing concern.

"What would a teacher know about planning a ball?" Emilia asked.

Lady Roswell moved to sit on the edge of her seat. "You are most fortunate that you weren't born into this life…"

"I doubt that," Emilia interjected.

"… it is true. I have spent my entire life wondering why I didn't fit in high Society. Do you want the answer that I finally came up with?"

Emilia nodded.

"I don't fit in, and that is all right," Lady Roswell shared. "I paint terribly. I am an awful dancer. I oftentimes speak of mating rituals of animals. But no one has the right to tell me that I don't belong. Only I do."

"Surely it is not that easy?" Emilia inquired.

"Do not get me wrong," Lady Roswell said. "You will have to work hard, possibly harder than you have ever worked before, but we will get you ready for that ball."

Emilia had never been one to shy away from hard work. In fact, she welcomed it. If a task required diligence and effort, she would readily embrace the challenge.

She squared her shoulders and summoned every ounce of confidence she could muster. "Let's plan a ball."

Lady Roswell clasped her hands together. "We shall have such fun," she declared. "If it is all right with you, I think we should ask my mother to help."

"The more help, the better," Emilia remarked.

"Since we are going to be working closely together, I insist that you call me Anette," she said. "I do not want to stand on formalities with you."

Emilia felt a sense of relief at her words. "I feel the same way, and you must call me Emilia."

As Anette started speaking in a rushed manner on details about the ball, Emilia stole a glance at Lord Chatsworth. His face bore an amused expression as he listened to his sister-in-law, but she couldn't help but wonder what he was thinking.

Dare she hope that he would ask her to dance at her ball? No, that was utterly ridiculous to even think such a thing. He was an earl and she was just a country bumpkin that happened to inherit a vast fortune.

Fredrick was pleased that Miss Sutherland had agreed to the ball. Anette had been right. It was the only way for her to enter high Society. He had no doubt that the gossips were already parading about, desperate to obtain any information on the mysterious Miss Sutherland. Why not control the narrative and give them what they wanted?

Miss Sutherland was beautiful, and she was an heiress. Two things that were in her favor. However, he couldn't help but concern himself with the air of innocence that surrounded her. She appeared untouched by the world's harsh realities, and he feared that she might lose some of her goodness as she took her place in Society.

As he listened to Anette's ceaseless chatter about all the preparations that needed to be made, he couldn't help but watch Miss Sutherland. Her lips were tightly pursed in deep concentration, but her eyes told him a different story- fear. He didn't hold it against her. A certain level of trepidation was entirely reasonable, especially since he would rather fight in the war than attend balls with scheming matchmaking mothers.

Anette took a breath and asked, "Do you have any questions?"

"I have many," Miss Sutherland admitted, "but I don't even know where to begin."

"Do not worry. We will sort everything out," Anette encouraged. "And I have the perfect ballgown for you to wear."

"Thank you for doing this, and for everything," Miss Sutherland said.

With an understanding smile on her lips, Anette responded, "Women in our positions must stick together. If we band together, we are stronger because of it."

"I'm afraid I haven't had much time to cultivate friendships," Miss Sutherland admitted. "My first priority has always been to survive."

"Well, that life is in your past and you now have the ability to thrive," Anette said.

A silver-haired woman stepped into the drawing room and announced, "The dressmaker has arrived, Miss. She is setting up in the parlor."

"Thank you," Miss Sutherland acknowledged. "Will you inform the dressmaker that I will be there shortly?"

After the woman departed to do Miss Sutherland's bidding, Anette rose and said, "We do not wish to keep you any longer, but I will return with reinforcements to help plan the ball."

Rising, Fredrick joked, "That sounds terrifying."

"It is a simple fact," Anette said. "We shall create a team unlike any other team that has ever been formed before."

Fredrick chuckled. He could see why Anette and his sister, Octavia, were such dear friends. They both said such outlandish things.

Miss Sutherland stood up, her hands clasped in front of her. "I can't help but thank both of you for what you are doing."

"You need to stop thanking us so profusely," Anette chided lightly.

"I'm afraid I am not used to people doing such kind things for me," Miss Sutherland admitted.

Anette's eyes held understanding. "Your life is very different now. Embrace the change," she encouraged.

Miss Sutherland bobbed her head. "I shall try."

"We should go," Fredrick said with a smile. "But it was a pleasure to further our acquaintance with one another, Miss Sutherland."

She eyed him curiously. "May I ask you a question?"

"You may," he responded.

In a hesitant voice, she asked, "Why did you not tell me who you truly were when we first spoke in Hyde Park?"

Fredrick should have known this question was coming, but he found he was no more prepared for it. He had many reasons why he hadn't revealed his true identity to her, but he didn't want to reveal too much.

"I suppose it was because I wanted to set your mind at ease and I thought you wouldn't speak so freely knowing that I was an earl," he said.

"You are right about that," Miss Sutherland shared. "Prior to speaking to you, I had never spoken to a titled gentleman before."

"Never?" Anette asked.

Miss Sutherland shook her head. "I did not mingle with lords and ladies when I lived in the countryside. The closest thing I got to that was when I spoke to someone that was landed gentry."

"Well, that will most definitely change and you must prepare yourself for that," Anette said.

With wide, vulnerable eyes, Miss Sutherland inquired, "How does one even converse with a lord?"

"You have been doing just fine," Fredrick assured her. "I do not want to be treated any different than anyone else."

Anette huffed. "Yes, but there are some lords that only wish to speak about their greatness and accomplishments."

"Yes, there are those, but I am not one of them," Fredrick said. "My title does not define who I am."

Miss Sutherland considered him for a moment before saying, "I shall treat you as I would anyone else."

"Except when you are in public," Anette interrupted. "If you two are too familiar with one another then people might assume you two have an understanding."

"I understand," Miss Sutherland said.

Fredrick bowed. "Good day, Miss Sutherland."

Miss Sutherland dropped into a curtsy. "My lord," she murmured.

Anette approached Miss Sutherland and reached for her hand. "We are going to become the best of friends. I know it."

"I hope so," Miss Sutherland responded. "It would be nice to have more than one friend."

Anette looked unsure as she asked, "You don't truly have only one friend, do you?"

"I'm afraid I meant what I said earlier about not having time to cultivate friendships," Miss Sutherland said.

"That is awful, and it is now my mission to ensure you have a plethora of friends," Anette declared with a wave of her hand.

"And with that, we should depart, Anette," Fredrick urged.

As Miss Sutherland walked them to the door, she said, "I do appreciate everything that you are doing for me; what you both are doing for me."

"We have only just gotten started," Anette assured her.

The butler opened the door and Fredrick headed towards the coach. After Anette stepped inside, he sat across from her.

The coach started rolling down the street when Anette let out a sigh. "I can't believe that Miss Sutherland only has one friend. That is awful."

"I daresay she has prioritized work over socializing," Fredrick said. "I find it to be quite exemplary."

"Do you think there is something wrong with her?"

Fredrick grinned. "I daresay that you are overthinking this."

"I'm going to have to become more acquainted with Miss Sutherland, just to be sure," Anette said. "If she is hiding anything, it is only a matter of time before I discover it. I just wish Octavia was here. I could use her spy senses."

"Octavia does not have 'spy senses.'"

"She told me that she did, and I have no reason to doubt her," Anette said. "Besides, if she didn't have 'spy senses' then how did she know that Ruth had tried to kill Lord Kendal?"

"Octavia used deductive reasoning to come to that conclusion," Fredrick remarked.

Anette shrugged. "We are going to have to agree to disagree on this one, especially since I side with Octavia."

The coach came to a stop in front of their townhouse and a footman opened the door. After they made their way into the entry hall, Carson lowered his voice and informed them, "Miss Clarissa Livingston and Mr. Livingston are in the drawing room."

Botheration. Those were the last two people he wanted to converse with.

Anette glanced at the drawing room and asked, "Would you like me to accompany you?"

"If you would like," Fredrick replied.

"I would rather go play fetch with Freddy than spend a moment in Miss Clarissa's presence," Anette said. "She is not a pleasant person."

Fredrick tipped his head. "I understand and I do not fault you for avoiding her."

"Will you be all right?" Anette asked.

"I have been shot, stabbed and tortured," Fredrick replied. "I can handle speaking to Clarissa and Calvin."

Anette patted his sleeve. "I still feel as if I should wish you luck."

Fredrick headed towards the drawing room and saw Clarissa and Calvin were pacing back and forth in the small room. He thought it was best if he made his presence known.

"Clarissa. Calvin," he greeted. "What an unexpected surprise."

Clarissa rushed towards him and stopped in front of him. "You must help us," she said. "Father wasn't in his right mind when he wrote that will, and he has ruined us."

"Why do you believe he wasn't in his right mind?" Fredrick inquired.

Tossing up her hands, she asked, "What other explanation is there?"

"We intend to contest the will, but we were hoping for your support when we do so," Calvin said. "If we can rally support for our plight, we might convince the judge to rule in our favor."

Fredrick ran a hand through his hair. He felt some compassion for their situation but it would be a grand waste of time and money. Furthermore, he had every intention of honoring Sir Charles' will.

"I'm sorry, but I do believe it is pointless to contest the will," Fredrick said.

"But we have to try," Clarissa cried out. "Father only left each of us ten thousand pounds. Can you imagine?"

"That is a fortune to some," Fredrick attempted.

"Not to me and certainly not to you," Clarissa said. "Can you believe that he left his entire fortune to a country bumpkin? You should have seen the way she was dressed at the reading of the will. She looked like a servant in her simple gown. It was pathetic, really. I would rather die than been seen in such a drab gown."

"Precisely, you have class, which is something that upstart does not have. I doubt she even knows what to do with

Father's fortune. She is probably too simple to understand the intricacies that go along with handling such a vast sum," Calvin stated.

"She will squander it on whatever poor people tend to waste their money on," Clarissa remarked.

Fredrick frowned. "I will not have you insult Miss Sutherland in my home. She is struggling with her change of fortune, just as you are."

Clarissa's mouth gaped open. "You have befriended the upstart?"

"We met briefly in the park yesterday and I called upon her today with Anette," he replied.

In a swift motion, Clarissa threw herself down onto the settee and let out a loud, drawn-out sigh. "How could you betray us like this?" she demanded.

"I do not see it as a betrayal..." Fredrick started.

Calvin put his hand up, stilling his words. "My father was your godfather. I just assumed you would be loyal to our family above all else."

Fredrick didn't dare point out that Miss Sutherland was now included in Sir Charles' family.

"Come along, Clarissa," Calvin ordered with a clenched jaw. "Fredrick has shown his true colors, and it is not a good look on him."

Clarissa rose from the sofa in the most dramatic way imaginable. "This isn't over," she said. "Once our fortune has been restored, we will remember how you treated us."

"I do apologize if I upset you—"Fredrick attempted.

Calvin cut him off. "You can stop pretending that you care a whit about us," he said. "You would stoop so low as to side with someone that isn't worthy to lick my bootstraps."

As Fredrick opened his mouth to argue that point, Calvin held his hand out to his sister. "Don't bother walking us out. We know the way."

Fredrick remained rooted in his spot as Calvin and

Clarissa departed from the drawing room. Surely they knew they were on the losing end of the fight. Sir Charles was nothing, if not meticulous. He had little doubt that the will would stand up in court.

Anette's voice came from the doorway. "They are gone," she informed him. "They huffed and puffed as they stormed out of the door."

"Are we wrong to help Miss Sutherland?" Fredrick asked.

"Now that I saw their treatment of Miss Sutherland, it makes me want to help her even more," Anette replied.

"Good, because I do believe we are doing the right thing."

Anette smiled. "I was hoping you would say that because we have a lot of work ahead of us."

Chapter Five

With the morning sun streaming through the windows, Emilia sat on her bed and stared at the door that led to her father's bedchamber. Did she dare go in? She wanted to, but she was afraid of what she would find.

But whatever she found couldn't be worse than not knowing.

She could do this. Rising, she retrieved her wrapper and headed towards the door. Her hand stilled on the handle and she took a deep breath for courage.

Emilia slowly turned the handle and pushed the door open. Her father's bedchamber was dark and had a musty smell to it. The burgundy-papered walls were much more masculine than her bedchamber.

She walked over to the windows and tossed open the drapes, allowing light to fill the room. A four-poster bed sat in the center of the room and a writing desk was placed adjacent to it. That is where she wanted to start.

Crossing the room, she sat down on the chair and opened the top drawer, removing a stack of papers that had string tied around them. She untied the string and perused the papers.

The documents were plans for a boarding school for underprivileged girls.

She wondered why her father would want to open a boarding school. As she examined one of the documents, she saw the proposed name of the school- *Mrs. Hembry's Seminary for Young Women*. Why would he name the school after her mother?

Emilia would need to speak to Mr. Rymer about this at once. Perhaps he could shed some light on the boarding school.

She placed the papers down on the desk and reached for the bottom drawer. As she slid it out, she couldn't quite believe what she was seeing. The top page of a very large pile of papers was a detailed sketch of her mother's face.

Tears came to her eyes as she perused the sketch. She had no images of her mother and she knew that she would cherish this sketch until the end of her days.

Why did Sir Charles have this sketch? Did he sketch it himself? If so, how did he create such a perfect rendering of her?

As she started rifling through the pages, she saw that they were filled with images of her mother. Some were of just her face, and others captured her whole person. But they all seemed to perfectly capture her essence, especially the eyes. They were a gateway into her soul, and they reflected the kindness that her mother always expressed.

She heard a door close and it was followed by a familiar voice, "Emilia."

"Lily," she greeted. "I'm in here."

A moment later, her friend appeared in the doorway. "Was I shown to the wrong bedchamber?" she asked.

"No, this was Sir Charles' bedchamber," Emilia shared. "But I found something that is most extraordinary."

Lily approached the desk and looked at the sketch in her hand. "That is beautiful. Who is that a sketch of?"

"My mother," she replied, "and there is a whole stack of them."

"Did Sir Charles draw them?"

"I think so," Emilia replied as she placed the papers onto the desk. "At least, I hope he did."

Lily retrieved a sketch and held it up. "The detail is exquisite." She placed the sketch down and continued. "I must admit that I am dying to know why you brought me here. Your note was rather vague, but you said it was of the utmost importance."

Emilia rose from her seat. "I have had the most remarkable change of fortune. It turns out that Sir Charles was my father and I inherited his estate. All two hundred thousand pounds of it."

Her friend's eyes grew wide. "You are rich."

"I am, but I need your help."

"What help could you possibly need from me?"

Emilia tightened the wrapper around her waist as she replied, "I was hoping you would consider becoming my lady's maid. I will pay you double what you were earning as a teacher."

"But I know nothing about being a lady's maid," Lily stated.

"Neither do I," Emilia said. "I just need a friend right now. Someone that I can trust to help guide me."

Lily grew silent. "I will do it, but only if I don't have to wear a maid's uniform."

"You can wear whatever you want. In fact, I would be happy to order you a whole new wardrobe, if you would like."

Her friend held out the sides of her skirt. "I could use another dress. This one is getting rather worn."

Emilia smiled. "I am so glad that you are here."

"As am I," Lily said. "I have never ridden in a coach before. I felt like a real-life princess."

"That is just one of my coaches, supposedly. I have yet to make it to the stables."

Lily giggled. "I just wish I could see Mrs. Allston's face when she learns that we both won't be returning as teachers. She might just march over here with her pinched, red face and demand that we return to our positions."

"I will inform the guards not to admit her entry through the gates," Emilia said.

A grumbling came from Lily's stomach and she brought a hand to cover it. "My apologies, but I didn't eat anything this morning."

"Then we must go down to breakfast."

Lily looked unsure. "I do believe I am supposed to eat in the kitchen."

"That is utter nonsense. You will eat with me in the dining room," Emilia said. "I insist."

Her friend looked as if she were going to argue with her. But fortunately, she relented. "Very well, but we must change you out of your wrapper."

Emilia headed back into her bedchamber and opened the wardrobe. "Lady Roswell sent over a few gowns for me to wear until my new gowns arrive."

Lily came to stand next to her. "A few gowns?" she asked. "There is a whole wardrobe here, and I have never seen such fine gowns before. They are quite lovely, are they not?"

"They are," Emilia agreed as she ran her hand down a pale blue muslin gown with embroidered flowers on the net overlay.

"Are you not required to go into mourning since Sir Charles only just died?" Lily asked.

Emilia dropped her hand and replied, "Lady Roswell doesn't think it is necessary since I didn't know my father."

Lily eyed her curiously. "You seem awfully close to this Lady Roswell."

"We only just met yesterday," Emilia shared. "She is Lord

Chatsworth's sister-in-law. I had an unexpected run-in with him in Hyde Park."

"You met a lord?" Lily asked. "Is he handsome?"

Emilia nodded. "He is very handsome, and very kind. I didn't realize who he was when I initiated a conversation with him."

"You spoke to a gentleman without being properly introduced?" Lily tsked. "Do I know you anymore?"

She laughed. "It sounds worse than it was, but Lord Chatsworth offered to help me."

The humor left Lily's face. "Why would he do such a thing?" she asked.

"I know it sounds odd, but he is just doing it out of the goodness of his heart," Emilia replied. "I assure you that his intentions are honorable."

Lily frowned. "I would be leery of this Lord Chatsworth. Surely, he must be getting something out of helping you."

"He has asked for nothing in return."

"I still must question his motives," Lily said.

Emilia reached up and retrieved the pale blue gown. "Do not be such a naysayer. Lord Chatsworth was Sir Charles' godson and he feels it is his duty to help me."

Lily's frown deepened, skepticism etched on her features. "Men are not so different here than they are from our village. I wouldn't be so quick to trust this handsome lord."

As Emilia carefully carried the gown over to the settee, she knew that her friend meant well, but Lily didn't know Lord Chatsworth like she did. She had felt a kinship spark between them the moment she had sat down on that bench.

Lily followed her to the settee and said, "I apologize for my words, but I just don't want to see you get hurt."

"I won't," Emilia assured her. "Once you meet Lord Chatsworth, you will understand."

"Lady's maids do not mingle with lords and ladies," Lily pointed out.

Emilia removed her wrapper as she asked, "Who says?"

"I think that is a universal rule," Lily replied. "Regardless, we need to get you dressed and readied for the day."

After she was dressed, Emilia sat down at the vanity table. She removed the cap from her head and started brushing her hair.

Lily held her hand out and said, "I do believe my job is to style your hair. Which I am quite proficient at."

"You are right." Emilia handed her the brush. "I am just happy that you are here with me."

"Well, you are paying me quite nicely for the honor," Lily teased.

While Lily started pulling her hair back into a stylish coiffure, Emilia asked, "Do you think the girls will miss us at the school?"

"Some will, but I did grow tired of the pretentious girls that spoke down to us," Lily said. "They could be rather mean to us."

Emilia bobbed her head. "That they could be, and Mrs. Allston did nothing to chide their impertinent behavior. She was far too worried about offending their parents."

"Well, that life is behind you now," Lily said before taking a step back. "Do you like your hair styled this way?"

Emilia turned her head and briefly admired her hair. "It is beautiful," she acknowledged. "Shall we go have breakfast?"

"I still think it is best if I eat in the kitchen. You will just need to point the way," Lily said.

Rising, Emilia looped arms with her friend. "I command you to join me for breakfast, and if I command you, you must do it," she remarked. "Besides, I don't know where the kitchen is yet."

"I will go, only because you are being rather insistent about it," Lily responded.

Once they were walking down the corridor, Emilia asked,

"Do you think your mother will take issue with you not being a teacher anymore?"

"I don't think she will care as long as I keep sending money home," Lily replied.

"You are a good person to help your family," Emilia said.

Lily gave her a knowing look. "You would do the same thing for your family," she asserted. "Besides, my mother's arthritis has made it harder for her to take in work as a seamstress."

"I have now decided that I shall pay you three times what you were making as a teacher," Emilia declared.

"That is too much—"

Emilia spoke over her. "Regardless, I have spoken," she declared. "We both know that Mrs. Allston didn't pay us a fair wage anyways."

"Thank you," Lily said.

As they stepped into the entry hall, Dalby tipped his head to acknowledge her. "Miss Sutherland," he greeted.

Emilia came to a stop and gestured towards Lily. "Dalby, allow me to introduce you to Miss Lily. She has graciously agreed to become my lady's maid."

Dalby shifted his gaze towards Lily. "It is a pleasure to meet you, Miss Lily."

Lily dropped into a curtsy.

"We were on our way to breakfast," Emilia shared. "Will you kindly show us the way?"

If Dalby was surprised that Lily was joining her for breakfast, he didn't show it. Instead, he replied, "It would be my pleasure, Miss."

Emilia felt great joy that Lily was with her. Now she didn't feel as alone in this grand townhouse, despite it being filled with servants.

Fredrick stood outside of his mother's bedchamber as he tried to find the strength to enter. He never knew what to expect when he visited her. Would she remember him? It was emotionally exhausting to watch his mother's mind slip away as she withered away in bed.

But she was still here and he was going to take advantage of the time that they had together.

He knocked on the door and it was promptly opened by his mother's lady's maid. "Good morning, my lord," Nancy greeted.

"Good morning," he responded. "How is my mother this morning?"

With a glance over her shoulder, Nancy replied, "It is not a good day."

"Should I come back?"

Nancy shook her head. "I don't think that would make a difference," she replied, opening the door wide.

Fredrick stepped into the darkened room and saw his mother was sitting up in bed with a tray of untouched food next to her. She looked pale and fragile amidst the expanse of the bed, and her eyes looked tired. Much more tired than he had seen previously.

His mother looked at him, and there was no flicker of recognition in her eyes regarding who he was. "Hello," she said softly.

"Hello," he replied. "How are you faring today?"

"I am hungry."

Fredrick pointed towards the tray of food. "Then why don't you eat?"

"I don't want to eat that food," she replied. "I want pudding."

"Have you spoken to the doctor about this?"

His mother huffed. "I have, but he won't listen to me. Will you talk to him? He might listen to you."

"I would be happy to, but I doubt the doctor will change

his mind," Fredrick said. "Do you have any more dry sweetmeats that you can indulge in?"

His mother's eyes darted towards Nancy in the corner before she lowered her voice. "I have some, but I have to keep them hidden from people that want to steal them."

Fredrick nodded, pretending that he understood. "That is wise." His mother had grown more wary as her mind slipped and she claimed her lady's maid was stealing from her. Which was ludicrous. Nancy had been her loyal servant for many years.

"You look so much like my father," his mother said. "He was just here, you know."

"Who? Your father?"

His mother smiled. "Yes, and we had the most wonderful conversation. We are to return to our country estate after the Season. Which I am greatly looking forward to. I can't stand the stench of London."

Fredrick didn't have the heart to tell his mother that her father died many years ago, and the country estate that she grew up in now belonged to a distant cousin. So instead, he remained quiet, unsure of what he could say to help her.

"Are you one of my doctors?" his mother asked.

"No, I am your son, Fredrick," he replied, hoping she would remember. He didn't know why he kept trying, but he did. He wanted her to remember him, even if for a moment.

Her eyes flickered with regret. "I'm sorry, but I don't remember you."

Fredrick felt a stab of disappointment at her words. "It is all right," he said. "I am just happy to see you."

"Could you ask Jane to come in?" his mother asked.

"I'm sorry, but Aunt Jane can't come visit you today," Fredrick said. "I'm afraid she is rather busy at the moment."

His mother let out a yawn and her hand flew up to cover her mouth. "Pardon me, but I think it is time that I rest. I didn't sleep well last night."

Fredrick performed a slight bow. "I shall come back at another time."

"Thank you," his mother said before she placed her head on her pillow.

As he departed from the room, he felt a profound sadness sweep over him. How he wished he could go back in time and fix this. How was it fair that his mother was suffering, and he could do nothing to help her?

"How is Mother?" Roswell asked as he approached Fredrick in the corridor.

"She was asking for Jane again."

Roswell winced. "What did you say?"

"I just told her that Aunt Jane was busy," Fredrick replied. "I didn't dare tell her that her sister died nearly thirty years ago."

"That was the right thing to do."

"Was it?" Fredrick asked. "I don't know what the right thing is to do anymore when it comes to Mother."

Roswell placed a comforting hand on Fredrick's shoulder. "It is a good thing that you came home from the war to be with her. I know, deep down, she appreciates it."

Fredrick took in his brother's haggard appearance. His hair was slightly disheveled, and his clothes were wrinkled, which was in stark contrast to how he usually looked.

"Where have you been?" he asked.

"I was out looking for Caleb all night, but it was not in vain. I have a lead," Roswell revealed. "Someone directed me to a tavern, but it is in the rookeries."

"You aren't going by yourself, are you?"

Roswell dropped his hand and replied, "I am more than capable of chasing down a lead on my own."

"I don't dispute that but you look terrible." Fredrick scrunched his nose. "And you don't smell much better."

"That is even better for where I am going," Roswell said.

The last place that Fredrick wanted to visit was the rookeries, but he couldn't let his brother keep going on as he had been. He was working entirely too hard, and he had yet to find Caleb. He was afraid his brother might get desperate, and desperate people tended to make a mistake. A mistake that might cost Roswell his life. Could he live with himself if that happened?

"I will join you," Fredrick said.

Surprise flickered on Roswell's face. "I thought you didn't want to get involved."

"I don't, but Anette did volunteer me to help you. Besides, I can't just ignore that Caleb is still missing," Fredrick remarked. "We both know the longer he is missing, the less chance there is that he will be found alive."

"I will gladly take your help," Roswell said.

Fredrick could hear the relief in Roswell's voice, and he was sure that he had made the right decision.

The sound of a dog barking could be heard from further down the corridor and it was followed by Anette saying, "Mr. Fluffy."

The puppy charged towards them with a slipper in his mouth.

Roswell reached down and scooped the puppy into his arms. "What have you stolen, you troublesome pup?" he asked as he removed the slipper from Mr. Fluffy's mouth.

Anette came to a stop next to her husband. "Who knew that puppies took so much work?" she asked.

"I did," Roswell replied, "but you were insistent that you wanted a puppy."

"I do recall that Mr. Fluffy was my wedding present," Anette said. "This is entirely your fault that he has eaten two of my slippers."

Roswell handed the puppy to his wife. "I shall buy you more slippers."

Anette held the puppy up and stared at him in the eyes. "You will obey me, Mr. Fluffy," she ordered in a stern voice.

In response, Mr. Fluffy lunged forward and licked her on the lips.

"Yuck," Anette said. "Dog kisses."

Roswell leaned forward and kissed his wife on the cheek. "I just have one more errand that I need to complete with Fredrick, then I shall be home for the afternoon."

"Dare I ask if this errand involves going into the rookeries?" she asked.

"It does, but you need not worry."

"I always worry, but I trust that you will come home to me," Anette said as she repositioned the puppy in her arms. "Now Mr. Fluffy and I are going to have a very frank conversation about what he can and can't eat."

Roswell chuckled. "I wish you luck with that."

Fredrick felt the slightest twinge of jealousy at what his brother had with Anette. It was evident that they loved each other very much. But he didn't want a wife. At least that is what he kept telling himself.

Turning to face him, Roswell asked, "Shall we depart?"

They headed towards the entry hall and exited through the door that Carson held open. Once they were inside of the coach, Fredrick asked, "What lead are you tracking down?"

"One of my informants told me that he had met with Caleb the day before he went missing at The Rusty Anchor Tavern," Roswell shared.

"And you suspect someone might know something about Caleb's whereabouts?"

Roswell shrugged. "It is worth a shot."

"Very well," Fredrick said. "But you will need to prepare yourself that it might be a fools' errand."

"I have to at least try," Roswell asserted. "I can't sit back and do nothing while Caleb is out there somewhere."

"I understand."

Roswell leaned back in his seat and studied his brother for

a moment. "Do you?" he asked. "I can't imagine you are one that would enjoy working with a partner."

"I was forced to learn, and quickly," Fredrick admitted. "My comrades are the only reason why I am still alive today. After I was shot, I wanted to give up, feeling as if I had nothing else to live for, but I knew I couldn't ignore their plights."

Roswell's brow lifted. "Nothing to live for? You are an earl and will inherit Father's title and vast estate."

"I know I should be grateful for everything that I have been given, but I can't help feeling as if I let my comrades down by leaving them on the Continent," he shared. "The war still rages on, and I am here, doing nothing."

"You aren't doing nothing," Roswell argued. "You are helping Mother and Anette told me about the good thing you are doing for Miss Sutherland."

An image of Miss Sutherland came to his mind, but he quickly banished it. He had more important things to dwell on than her lovely face. And it was lovely.

Shaking off Roswell's praise, Fredrick said, "I am only helping Miss Sutherland because her father once helped me."

"I think there is more to it than that."

Fredrick didn't want to know what Roswell meant by that so he turned his attention towards the window. He saw- and smelled- the moment they started to venture into the rookeries. The buildings grew darker and appeared increasingly dilapidated. The air itself seemed to hold a mugginess, a pungent blend of excrement and an overwhelming sense of hopelessness.

The coach came to a stop in front of a tavern that held a crooked sign above it that identified it as The Rusty Anchor Tavern.

They exited the coach and stepped inside the tavern. The patrons in the dark, crowded hall barely gave them any notice as they drank while sitting around the round tables.

Roswell pointed towards a table in the corner and said, "Let's go sit down."

They made their way towards the table and a dark-haired young woman approached them. Her hair was pulled back into a tight chignon and she had an apron tied around her waist, concealing her worn green gown.

"What can I get you, gentlemen?" she asked.

"Two ales," Roswell replied, "and some information." He removed a gold coin from his waistcoat pocket and slid it towards her. "I need to know if someone was in here a few days ago."

The young woman regarded him with a solemn expression, yet her eyes betrayed a lingering sense of suspicion. "Why do you need to know?"

"My friend has gone missing, and I need to find him," Roswell replied.

"I can't help you," she replied. "But a word to the wise, I would leave here and not come back. You don't belong here."

Roswell lifted his brow. "And you do?"

"More so than you," the young woman replied before she turned to leave.

"Please," Roswell said. "Will you not at least hear me out?"

The young woman stopped and faced him. "Very well," she replied. "What do you wish to ask me?"

Leaning forward, Roswell replied, "I am looking for a gentleman that came through here less than a week ago."

"We don't get very many gentlemen here," the young woman said. "Can you describe him?"

"He has dark hair and would have been dressed in a similar fashion as me, despite being a gentleman," Roswell replied. "He wouldn't have caused any trouble."

The young woman pressed her lips together before saying, "I'm sorry." She placed her finger on the coin and slid it back towards Roswell. "As I said before, I can't help you, but don't give up hope. I'm sure your friend will come home soon."

Fredrick considered the young woman for a moment. Her speech and mannerisms marked her as a genteel woman, making him consider what hardships she had endured to end up being a serving wench at a tavern in the rookeries.

As the young woman walked away from their table, Fredrick leaned closer to his brother and asked, "Did something seem off about the serving wench?"

Roswell gave him a blank look. "I didn't notice anything."

That is when Fredrick realized that his brother wasn't thinking clearly, and that could get him killed.

Chapter Six

Emilia watched as Lily's eyes darted around the drawing room, and she wished there was something to do that might calm her friend's nerves.

"I shouldn't be in here," Lily said in a hushed voice.

"You have every right to be in here," Emilia asserted.

Lily pulled a needle through the fabric and sighed. "This place is too fancy," she said. "I feel as if I will dirty it just by my essence."

"That is ridiculous and not the least bit true."

Lowering the fabric to her lap, Lily remarked, "I need to learn how to become a lady's maid but I can't do that if I spend all my time with you."

"Do you want to leave?"

Lily looked unsure. "I think it would be best if I go speak to the housekeeper. She will tell me what my duties are, won't she?"

"I'm sure she will," Emilia assured her. "Mrs. Harvey has only been kind to me."

"Yes, but that is because you are the mistress of the house. I am just a lady's maid."

Emilia gave her friend a pointed look. "I hired you to be my lady's maid and to keep me company. You are a cross between a lady's maid and a companion."

"I wouldn't dare consider myself a companion," Lily said. "Companions are generally genteel women, not country bumpkins."

"You are not a country bumpkin, but I understand how you feel. I feel out of place here, too."

Lily glanced at the open door before asking, "How does it feel to be wealthy?"

Emilia hesitated before revealing, "It feels wonderful."

"You don't have to worry about working for your income, and you get to wear the most beautiful gowns," Lily said.

Emilia smiled. "I feel as if I am in a fairy tale."

"At least you don't have any evil stepsisters to contend with," Lily joked.

Dalby stepped into the room and announced, "Mr. Rymer would like a moment of your time. Would you care to receive him?"

Emilia always welcomed a visit from her solicitor. "Yes, please send him in."

Lily rose from her seat and said, "This would be a good time for me to go speak to Mrs. Harvey. Unless you would like me to stay."

"No, that won't be necessary," Emilia assured her.

After Lily departed from the room, Mr. Rymer stepped in and approached her with a satchel over his shoulder.

"Thank you for agreeing to meet with me," the solicitor said. "I do not intend to take up too much of your time."

Emilia felt like laughing at Mr. Rymer's innocent remark. All she had was time, and she was rather bored just sitting around the drawing room. She gestured towards a chair and asked, "Would you care to sit?"

Mr. Rymer moved to sit in the proffered chair and

retrieved his satchel. "I have a few things I wanted to discuss with you." He reached into the satchel and pulled out a piece of paper. "I need to draft your will."

"Pardon?"

Mr. Rymer gave her an understanding look. "It is commonplace for someone of your position to have a will on file in probate court. This will also ensure that your wishes are honored after your death."

"That does make sense, but it seems rather morbid."

"I assure you it is all innocent enough, and you can change it as often as you like, especially as your situation changes," Mr. Rymer said. "But for now, who would you like to name as your beneficiary in case of your untimely death?"

Emilia grew silent. The only two relations that she had were Calvin and Clarissa, and it would only be fair of her to leave them their father's fortune. At least until she had a family of her own.

Coming to a decision, Emilia said, "I would like to leave Lily ten thousand pounds, but the rest will be given to Calvin and Clarissa, to be divided up evenly."

Mr. Rymer's eyes widened slightly but he didn't dare contradict her. "Very good," he said. "That is most generous of you."

"I think it is only right since it is our father's fortune."

"I shall see to that. Do you have any requests that you would like honored?"

Emilia nodded. "I want to be buried by my mother," she replied. "A headstone would be nice, too."

"I will ensure you have a headstone, Miss," Mr. Rymer stated. "Anything else?"

"Not at this time, but I am sure I will think of something soon enough," Emilia said. "But I do have a question."

Mr. Rymer lowered the paper to his lap. "What would you like to know?"

"I saw documents for a boarding school in my father's desk. Did he intend to open this school for underprivileged girls?"

"Yes, that is right," Mr. Rymer said. "We already secured the building and were in the process of hiring the staff when Sir Charles grew ill."

"Would it be possible to proceed with the boarding school?"

Mr. Rymer gave her an approving look. "Yes, and I think your father would be proud of you for doing so," he said. "We already hired a headmistress but we still need a few more teachers. It is rather difficult to find women that are willing to work in the rookeries."

Lily's voice came from the doorway. "I'll do it," she volunteered. "I can work there during the day and as your lady's maid in the evening."

Emilia turned her attention towards Lily. "That is a lot of work for you," she said. "Are you sure?"

"Being a teacher is familiar and it is not as if you aren't paying me enough," Lily replied. "I would be happy to do it."

Mr. Rymer turned towards Lily. "I must assume that you are Miss Lily."

"I am," Lily confirmed.

"Well, if you are going to teach, it is only fair that I do so as well," Emilia said. "At least until we can hire enough staff."

Mr. Rymer frowned. "Are you sure you wish to do that? I only ask because the *ton* is not kind to people that work for an income."

"I won't be working. I will be volunteering," Emilia said.

"I'm not sure if the *ton* would distinguish that," Mr. Rymer remarked.

Emilia squared her shoulders. "I would like to open this boarding school as quickly as possible, and if it means that I must work as a teacher for that to happen, then so be it."

"I understand, Miss," Mr. Rymer said. "I will continue with the preparations. On a good note, we already have a list of girls that have been accepted. Your father handpicked them for the school."

"I am pleased to hear that."

"As for the name of the school…" Mr. Rymer paused. "Do you wish to keep the name?"

Emilia smiled. "I think it was a lovely tribute to my mother and she would have loved to see the school come to fruition."

"Out of all the decisions your father was forced to make for the boarding school, naming it was the easiest for him," Mr. Rymer shared.

Emilia found such comfort in those simple words. It confirmed to her that her father truly did care for her mother, in his own way.

Mr. Rymer stuffed the paper back into his satchel. "Will there be anything else?"

"I don't believe so, but I would like the boarding school to open as soon as it is feasible," Emilia said.

"It shouldn't be too difficult to open it in a few months from now."

"Why so long?"

"These things do take time, but I will see what I can do to speed things along," Mr. Rymer said, rising. "I will speak to Mrs. Anderson, who will act as the headmistress."

Lily spoke up. "Is Mrs. Anderson kind?"

"She seems like a pleasant enough woman," Mr. Rymer replied. "I have yet to hear a cross word from her."

Emilia knew her friend had a point. She didn't want a headmistress like Mrs. Allston. "I would prefer a headmistress who is kind to the girls and the staff."

"I shall convey your wishes to Mrs. Anderson," Mr. Rymer said. "I should note that her interview impressed your father, and he was not an easy man to win over."

"Well, that does give me hope," Emilia responded.

Mr. Rymer said his goodbyes. He had just departed when Dalby stepped back into the room and announced, "Lady Roswell Westlake has come to call, Miss. Shall I send her in?"

Emilia perked up. "Yes, thank you."

A moment later, Anette entered the study with a broad smile on her lips. "I have the most wonderful news…" Her voice trailed off when her eyes landed on Lily. "Oh, hello. I didn't realize you had company."

Gesturing towards Lily, Emilia said, "Lily is my lady's maid and my part-time companion."

"Interesting," Anette acknowledged. "It is a pleasure to meet you, Lily."

Lily dropped into a curtsy. "My lady."

Anette turned her attention back towards Emilia. "As I was saying, I have the most wonderful news. I was able to secure you a spot at the well-attended, highly coveted soiree at Lady Shorne's townhouse, and it is tonight."

"How were you able to do that?" Emilia asked.

A mischievous glint came into Anette's eyes. "How I did it is not important. It is more important that I did do it."

Emilia was still skeptical. "Do they even want me there?"

"They don't *not* want you there," Anette replied. "Frankly, it would make the night much more interesting if you came."

With a furrowed brow, Emilia asked, "Do you think I am ready to go out in public?"

"You need to be seen in public as often as possible," Anette replied. "The soiree tonight will be a good start."

"You don't intend to tell me how you got the invite for me, do you?"

Anette waved her hand in front of her. "I may have learned some information about Lord Shorne and I used that information to leverage an invitation for you."

In a hesitant voice, Emilia asked, "Are you referring to blackmail?"

"Perhaps, but that is a harsh way to look at it," Anette replied. "I like to think that what I did was give Lady Shorne a gentle push in the right direction."

Emilia didn't quite know what to think about Anette. Did she dare go to the soiree, knowing she wasn't truly invited- or wanted- there?

Anette came to sit down next to her. "I can tell you are conflicted about going, but you must go to the soiree. Once you get your foot in the door, you will start receiving invitations to social events on your own," she said.

"What if I don't make a good first impression this evening?" Emilia asked.

"That is not an option. You must show up, smile and prove to the *ton* that you do belong there," Anette said. "If you believe it, so will they."

"And if I get the cut direct?"

"No one will dare give you the cut direct when you enter the soiree on Fredrick's arm," Anette said. "To do so would be a great insult to one of the most powerful families in England."

Emilia started fidgeting with her hands in her lap. "And Lord Chatsworth agreed to this?"

"Not yet, but he will," Anette rushed to assure her. "Please say that you will come. We shall have such fun."

She lowered her gaze, grappling with the storm of emotions surging within her. The prospect of stepping into high Society, where every eye would be fixed on her, silently assessing her every move, filled her with terror.

On the other hand, there was Lord Chatsworth, in whom she placed her trust. He wouldn't abandon her. He would protect her. She was sure of that. For a man she hardly knew, she had immense faith in his character.

It was only a matter of time before she entered high Society so she might as well do it on her own terms, with a handsome lord by her side.

Emilia met Anette's eager gaze. "I will come tonight."

Anette clasped her hands together. "You shall take the *ton* by storm tonight." She jumped up from her seat. "I will see to all the preparations. Ensure you are at Lady Shorne's townhouse by nine tonight and do not exit your coach until Fredrick assists you out." She paused, only to catch her breath. "Now, I have a few suggestions for your ball…"

As Emilia listened to Anette speak in a rushed tone, she hoped that she was doing the right thing. But she didn't dare back out now.

Dressed in his finery, Fredrick waited in the drawing room, his impatience growing as he awaited the arrival of Roswell and Anette. They were preparing to attend a soiree this evening, a prospect that vexed him greatly. He couldn't quite fathom how Anette had convinced him to go, but her powers of persuasion were impressive.

He hated attending social events, especially since he had no desire to marry. The prospect of being hounded by scheming, matchmaking mothers who aimed to marry off their daughters filled him with irritation. The forced, unwanted conversations were something he had grown to dread.

The persistent assumption that he needed a wife baffled him. He was doing just fine on his own. But he couldn't even fathom his own lie. The truth was, he wasn't doing well, but a wife would just complicate his already tangled emotions.

Anette's gratingly cheerful voice greeted him as she stepped into the drawing room. "Good evening, Fredrick."

"Good evening," he responded. Why was she in such a pleasant mood? Didn't she realize they were going to a soiree?

Roswell appeared by his wife's side. "The coach is out front. Shall we depart?"

A Suitable Fortune

"Oh, before we go…" Anette started. "I have one more favor to ask of Fredrick."

Fredrick eyed her with trepidation. "Which is?"

"I think it is best if you escort Miss Sutherland into the soiree," Anette replied. "It is important that the *ton* knows that we are supportive of Miss Sutherland's entrance into high Society."

Fredrick wasn't quite sure how he felt about this. While he genuinely wanted to assist Miss Sutherland, he had reservations about the extent of his help. His mere presence wouldn't deter the relentless, gossiping busybodies of the *ton*. And what if their association led to the wrong assumptions about their relationship?

Just as he was about to voice his concerns, a different thought struck him. Could he really leave Miss Sutherland to fend for herself, fully aware of how out of place she was in high Society? She stood out like the brightest star on the darkest night, rendering everyone else dull in comparison.

"All right, I will escort Miss Sutherland into the soiree," Fredrick replied.

Anette arched an eyebrow. "That is it?" she asked. "You aren't going to argue with me?"

"I am a smart enough man to not do so."

"But I had a whole list of persuasive arguments," Anette said.

Roswell chuckled as he offered his arm to his wife. "Take this as a win and move on," he advised. "It isn't often that Fredrick relents so easily."

As Fredrick followed them to the coach, he hoped he was doing the right thing for Miss Sutherland and himself. He couldn't care less about what the *ton* said about him, but he had earned that right. But he was fearful for Miss Sutherland.

Once they were all situated in the coach, it jerked forward and merged into traffic.

Roswell turned to his wife and said, "You are looking especially lovely this evening."

Anette smiled. "You said that already."

"Well, it makes it no less true," Roswell responded.

Fredrick turned his attention towards the window as they made the brief journey to Lady Shorne's townhouse. He was pleased by the profound love demonstrated by Roswell and Anette. However, he couldn't help but find it a bit wearisome at times.

The coach came to a stop in front of a whitewashed townhouse and a footman hurried to open their door.

Fredrick waited until Roswell assisted his wife out of the coach before he went to stand by them on the pavement.

Anette pointed towards a coach that was further down the line. "I see Miss Sutherland's coach," she informed Fredrick. "Why don't you go assist her out of the coach?"

"Very well," Fredrick replied, knowing there was no reason to argue this point with his sister-in-law.

He headed towards the coach that Anette had pointed out, knocked, and opened the door, revealing Miss Sutherland.

Fredrick held his hand out and asked, "May I assist you out of the coach?"

Miss Sutherland stared at his hand. "Do you think this is wise?" she asked. "I can't help but feel that this is a terrible mistake."

"I have learned that the hardest journey begins with taking the first step," Fredrick advised.

"That is easy for you to say because you are a lord. I am just…" she sighed, "… a nobody."

Fredrick could hear the pain in her voice and he knew that she was struggling. "That is the most ridiculous thing I have ever heard. You are a magnificent somebody."

"I am only a 'somebody' because of what my father did for me."

He dropped his hand to his side as he said, "You owe no one anything. You don't have to justify your past, or your future. Embrace that you have different experiences than most members of high Society and use that to your advantage."

Miss Sutherland was quiet for a moment before asking, "I know I have no right to ask this of you, but will you remain by my side, at least until I find my own strength?"

Fredrick nodded. "I will," he replied, extending his hand towards her. "But I can't help you if you don't leave your coach."

He watched Miss Sutherland square her shoulders. And that gesture went to his heart, more than any words she had spoken.

After he assisted her onto the pavement, he moved her hand to the crook of his arm and asked, "Are you ready?"

"I am," she replied.

He briefly perused the length of her and admired her pale pink gown. He wasn't one to notice women's fashions, but he thought Miss Sutherland looked rather lovely this evening. She definitely looked the part of a lady, but now she had to act the part of one.

Fredrick led her towards the townhouse and saw that his brother and Anette were waiting for them in the entry hall.

Anette gave them both an approving nod. "Just remember to hold your head high and ignore any whisperings that you might hear."

Miss Sutherland smiled, but it didn't quite reach her eyes. "I do hope I won't embarrass any of you this evening."

"Just you being here is enough for us," Anette encouraged.

Fredrick patted her hand. "We will all walk in together," he declared. "Just breathe."

"I can do that," Miss Sutherland said.

As he guided her towards the parlor, he couldn't help but notice- and sense- the palpable tension that enveloped Miss

Sutherland. Not that he blamed her. She was about to be put on display, with the members of high Society poised to engage in their customary gossip. Yet, she was going through with it, facing her fears and insecurities head-on. He found that act of courage to be truly admirable.

The moment they stepped into the parlor, a hush fell over the room. Men and women turned to face them, their faces revealing a complex mixture of curiosity and disapproval. Several women swiftly unfurled their fans and shielded their expressions behind them as they vehemently whispered with their companions.

Fredrick paid little heed to the *ton*'s reactions, but he worried about Miss Sutherland. She didn't deserve the harsh treatment she was receiving. After all, she had committed no wrong.

A quick glance at her revealed that she was maintaining her composure, holding her head high with a resolute demeanor. The fear in her eyes had transformed into determination, and some of the initial tension seemed to dissipate.

"You are doing remarkably well," he whispered to her.

"Don't be deceived by my calm demeanor. I am shaking in my slippers."

As they navigated through the crowd, it felt as though the hordes of people willingly cleared a path for them, allowing them to reach the back wall. He couldn't help but notice a few young women batting their eyelashes at him and offering him coy smiles. It never failed to happen. Being an eligible bachelor was rather bothersome.

There was only one real solution, but he refused to fall prey to the parson's mousetrap.

Fredrick dropped his arm and said, "Well, we did it."

"Yes, but what exactly did we do?" Miss Sutherland questioned. "Everyone is still staring at me and I can practically hear their displeasure."

Coming to stand next to her, Anette said, "We expected

that to happen, but now everyone can move past this moment."

"I don't think it is that simple," Miss Sutherland remarked.

"Regardless, there is someone that I want you to meet." Anette went on her tiptoes and scanned the room. "There she is."

Miss Sutherland followed her gaze. "Who?"

"Lady Lizette," Anette replied. "I do believe she will be rather sympathetic towards your plight, considering she struggled entering high Society herself. Come along."

As Anette led Miss Sutherland across the dance floor, Fredrick said to his brother, "Your wife has been more than gracious in helping Miss Sutherland."

Roswell bobbed his head. "Anette enjoys helping others and it helps her avoid working on her needlework."

Fredrick had barely released a chuckle when his attention was drawn to something across the room. A young woman with brown hair sat on a chair, engaged in conversation with an older woman. There was an odd familiarity about her that he couldn't shake, a sense that they had crossed paths before.

As if in response to his gaze, the young woman turned her head and locked eyes with him, an unspoken challenge to see who would look away first. It was at that moment that realization struck. This elegantly dressed young woman with her fine gown and neatly coiffed hair was none other than the serving wench he had encountered at the tavern.

But that was impossible. Wasn't it?

Fredrick broke the gaze with the young woman and turned towards Roswell. "Do you see that lady across from us, the one sitting down?"

"You will have to be more specific," Roswell responded.

"The brown-haired one with pearls in her hair and a pale blue gown," Fredrick said. "She is speaking to an older woman."

After a brief moment, Roswell asked, "What about her?"

"Does she not look the least bit familiar?"

"No," Roswell replied. "Are you acquainted with her?"

"Not exactly, but I do believe it is the serving wench from the tavern."

Roswell stared at him in astonishment. "Surely you jest. What would a serving wench be doing at a soiree?"

"I am not one to forget a face, and I do believe it is her," Fredrick said.

It was as though fate conspired in his favor when he witnessed the young woman stand up from her seat and make her way to the refreshment table. This was the opportunity he had been waiting for, and he had no intention of letting it slip by.

Fredrick hastened his steps and came to a stop a short distance from her at the refreshment table.

Her eyes remained fixed straight ahead, showing no interest in glancing in his direction as they wandered over the glasses of lemonade. "Do you not know that it is impolite to stare?" she asked in a hushed voice.

"I am aware, but I can't help but wonder if our hostess knows that you work as a serving wench."

"I do not need to work for an income, my lord."

Fredrick reached for a glass of lemonade as he responded, "You know who I am, but I am at a disadvantage in not knowing your name."

"Who I am is not important," she replied.

Bringing the glass to his lips, he said, "No, but it would ensure that we are both playing by the same rules."

"There are no rules in this game."

"What game is that?" Fredrick asked.

The young woman retrieved two glasses of lemonade and turned to face him. Her eyes hinted at a keen intellect, yet her lips curled into a subtle smirk. "If you don't already know, I'm afraid I can't help you."

Before he could respond, she retraced her steps and returned to her seat, not bothering to glance back at him.

Curiosity about the young woman's identity gnawed at Fredrick, and he was determined to uncover the truth. This was far from over, he assured himself, as he continued to ponder the mystery surrounding her.

Chapter Seven

Emilia let Anette guide her across the hall as she tried to ignore the disapproving glances from the other guests. It shouldn't bother her, but it did greatly. Would she ever win the *ton*'s approval? It seemed like an impossible feat, considering the cold reception that she had just been given.

Anette came to a stop in front of a dark-haired young woman and a tall, broad-shouldered man who had a commanding presence.

"Lady Lizette. Tristan," Anette greeted. "Allow me the privilege of introducing you to my new friend, Miss Sutherland."

Tristan bowed. "It is a pleasure to meet you, Miss Sutherland."

Emilia dropped into a curtsy. "The pleasure is all mine, sir."

Lady Lizette smiled, and it seemed genuine, setting her at ease. "How are you faring this evening?"

"It has been rather daunting," Emilia admitted. "I fear that the *ton* hates me."

"Do not concern yourself with the *ton*'s reaction. I do

believe they hate everyone at first," Lady Lizette said. "They will move on once they grow bored. They always do."

Anette nodded. "I agree. Once you have your ball, this will all be behind you and the *ton* will adore you."

"I doubt that," Emilia said.

"You are an heiress," Anette remarked. "You are fortunate enough to be able to play by your own rules."

Tristan cleared his throat, drawing their attention. "I do not wish to contradict Anette, but you still must use some discretion."

"Yes, some, but you can still have fun," Anette stated with mirth in her voice.

Lady Lizette met Emilia's gaze and said, "I read about you in the newssheets and I find your journey here to be most incredible."

"It was rather exciting, but I do feel bad that my good fortune was at the expense of others," Emilia responded.

"Yes, but do not discount what you have had to endure to be here," Lady Lizette said.

A loud, booming voice interrupted their conversation and announced the musical performance was about to begin.

Anette looped arms with Emilia. "We should find our seats before the performance begins."

Emilia tipped her head at Lady Lizette and Tristan. "It was a pleasure to speak to you."

"If you have no complaints, I shall come to call so I can become more acquainted with you," Lady Lizette said.

"I would greatly enjoy that," Emilia responded.

Her words had just left her mouth when Anette started leading her away. "You don't want to wait too long to find your seat or else you could be sitting in the back," she advised.

As they walked towards the seats that were set up in front of the pianoforte, Lord Roswell and Lord Chatsworth approached them.

They claimed their seats near the front and Emilia sat

down between Anette and Fredrick. She was looking forward to the musical performance. She had never learned to play the pianoforte, due to her reduced circumstances growing up, but she loved hearing it being played.

The room grew silent as a short, black-haired lady came to stand in the front of the room. "Good evening," she greeted.

Anette leaned towards her and whispered, "That is Lady Shorne," she explained. "She is not a pleasant woman."

Lady Shorne smiled, but it felt too contrived. "Before we begin, it is customary for me to select a guest from the audience to come treat us to a song, whether played or sung," she said. "For this evening, I have selected Miss Emilia Sutherland to do us the honor."

Emilia's heart sank. There was no way she could go up there and perform in front of the *ton*. First of all, she couldn't play the pianoforte, which meant she would have to sing. Her singing had been reserved for her mother and the students at the boarding school, not for such a prestigious audience.

"Is Miss Sutherland here?" Lady Shorne's eyes roamed over the guests until they landed on Emilia. "Ah, there she is. Come on up, dear."

Anette frowned. "I can't believe she would do something so underhanded," she muttered. "I'm sorry."

Emilia could see the compassionate look that Fredrick was giving her, but he couldn't help her now. No one could. She would have to do this on her own.

She rose with deliberate slowness as she felt a tremor of fear, knowing that she had to do this or else she would not only embarrass herself but her friends.

As she made her way to the front of the room, she couldn't ignore the self-satisfied grin adorning Lady Shorne's lips. It was evident that Lady Shorne had contrived this situation with the intention of watching her fail.

Lady Shorne put a hand out towards her. "What shall you entertain us with?"

In a soft voice, she replied, "I will sing."

"Very good," Lady Shorne said as she dropped her hand. "What shall you sing?"

Emilia hesitated. What could she sing? It wasn't as if she could sing "God Save the King." Although, she could think of one song that might work.

"I will sing "Drink to Me Only with Thine Eyes," Emilia said.

Lady Shorne nodded. "I shall accompany you on the pianoforte, assuming you have no objections."

"I have none," Emilia responded.

With every step that Lady Shorne took as she made her way to the pianoforte, Emilia's heart seemed to sink deeper into a pit of dread. Lady Shorne took her seat and raised her fingers to the keys, then asked, "Are you ready?"

No.

But she didn't dare admit that.

Emilia tipped her head in acknowledgement before she turned to face the audience. She took a deep breath as she listened to the music and waited for her turn to start singing.

As fear began to swell within her, her gaze fell upon Fredrick, and the genuine concern in his eyes strengthened her resolve. He was unmistakably anxious on her behalf. In that moment, a wave of calm enveloped her. She decided to sing for him, imagining the room empty and allowing his compassion to be her guiding light.

When the time was right, she parted her lips and let the song flow forth. Her voice started with a hint of hesitation but gained confidence with each passing word. With every note, she poured her heart and soul into the music, hoping that her performance would be sufficient to captivate and impress the discerning audience of the *ton*.

She sang the last word of the song and hoped that it had been enough. That *she* had been enough.

A Suitable Fortune

As Lady Shorne's last note resonated through the room, a wave of applause swept over the crowd.

Emilia smiled as Lady Shorne approached and stood beside her, patiently waiting for the applause to subside.

"Well done," the lady offered her praise, but there was no warmth to her words. "You may return to your seat now."

She dropped into a curtsy before she made her way back to her chair. As she took her seat, Fredrick turned towards her with an incredulous expression and said, "You can sing."

Her lips twitched. "I can sing."

Anette leaned closer to her and whispered, "You sing superbly. I had no idea you could sing so well."

"I do not enjoy performing in front of others," Emilia admitted. "I was terribly nervous."

"You didn't appear nervous," Anette said as she reached into her reticule. "You have earned a biscuit."

Emilia looked at her in surprise. "You brought a biscuit to the soiree?"

"Octavia convinced me to do so, especially since performances can be long and rather boring," Anette said, extending her a biscuit. "But not your performance. It was perfect, and I especially enjoyed the look of disbelief on Lady Shorne's face when she realized you could sing."

As Emilia accepted the biscuit, Fredrick said, "I must agree with Anette. You did sing superbly."

"Thank you," Emilia responded. For some reason, she was especially pleased that he had enjoyed her performance.

"Where did you learn to sing like that?" Fredrick asked.

"My mother," Emilia shared. "She taught me from a young age, and we used to sing to each other when we were working on embroidery."

Fredrick's eyes held approval. "Frankly, I don't think I've heard a lovelier voice at these soirees."

"You flatter me, my lord," Emilia said.

"It is merely the truth," Fredrick remarked. "Had I known

you were so talented, I wouldn't have worried about you standing up there."

Emilia watched as a young woman approached the pianoforte and took her place on the bench. The pianist's hands danced across the keys with a captivating ferocity that held Emilia's attention. It was a delightful diversion to be entertained by such a skillful performance.

Fredrick looked down at her biscuit. "You do realize that there is a refreshment table just on the other side of the room."

Anette interjected, "Let her eat her biscuit in peace."

Emilia smiled at her friend before asking Fredrick, "Would you care for half?"

"If you are offering," Fredrick replied.

She broke the biscuit in half and extended it towards him. "I hope you enjoy it, my lord."

After she took a bite from her biscuit, Emilia realized that she was genuinely enjoying herself. She hadn't embarrassed herself when she had performed her song, and she was enjoying time with her friends. At least she considered them her friends.

Emilia snuck a glance at Fredrick and briefly admired his handsome face. He was so different from what she thought a lord would be. His warmth and kindness put her at ease while in his presence. But she didn't dare become too familiar. He was helping her enter Society, and nothing more.

So why did her heart seem to race in her chest every time he directed his gaze towards her? This would not do. Falling for a lord would do her no good.

With the morning sun streaming into his bedchamber, Fredrick rested his shoulder against the window frame, gazing out at the vast gardens. He had every reason to be happy, but he wasn't. He was miserable. And every day, it grew worse.

The weight of guilt hung heavily on him for not being with his comrades on the Continent, where they fought for their lives, while he attended soirees with the *ton*. How could he turn a blind eye to their plight? They had seen each other at their worst, yet their mutual respect and appreciation remained unwavering.

He understood the reasons behind Wellington's decision to send him home, but he couldn't help wishing for a different outcome. Now, he found himself trapped in a relentless cycle with no apparent escape. He didn't want to return to the life he'd had before the war because he was different now.

The door opened and his valet stepped into the room, holding a pair of polished boots. "Carson informed me that breakfast has been set out, my lord," Rickard said.

Fredrick pushed off the wall and went to retrieve the boots. "I suppose I should eat before my ride."

"I saw Lord Roswell escorting his wife down to the dining room so you won't be alone," Rickard shared.

After he sat on the bed, Fredrick put his boots on and let out a groan.

"Is your wound hurting you?"

Fredrick shook his head. "No, I was expressing my discontent with these boots. They haven't been properly broken in yet."

Rickard studied him for a moment before asking, "You still miss the war, don't you?" It was phrased as a question, but it was delivered more like a statement.

"Don't you?"

With a shake of his head, Rickard replied, "Do I miss fighting every day to just stay alive? No. I do not miss the war."

Fredrick rose. "I just feel like a failure."

"A failure?" Rickard asked. "No, my lord, you are a hero.

You saved many lives through your strength and determination."

"I don't feel like a hero, especially after what I did to Timmy."

"That was not your fault—"

Fredrick cut him off. "Whose fault was it?" he demanded. "I took the shot."

"Yes, but our scout told us that there were enemy soldiers there and we—"

"Took their word for it," Fredrick said, finishing his thought. "How could we have been so stupid?"

"Our scouts were not incompetent," Rickard defended. "They were right more times than not."

"Well, they were wrong that time."

Rickard pressed his lips together. "I disagree. Those soldiers were trying to kill us and we were just trying to protect ourselves."

"We should have tried harder."

"My lord…"

Fredrick had had enough of this conversation. He refused to sit there and listen to his valet attempt to justify their behavior. What he had done was an atrocity, and he didn't deserve the medals that he had been awarded by the war office.

Approaching the door, he turned the handle and entered the corridor. He was aware that his valet was attempting to assist him, but the efforts were proving futile. Rickard couldn't very well rewrite history.

He was a blasted lord and he was expected to carry on with a stiff upper lip. Yet, he was exhausted from pretending that all the grandeur and formality in London held any real significance. What truly mattered was what was transpiring on the Continent.

Fredrick made his way towards the dining room, offering a nod to Carson as he passed through the entry hall. Upon entering the dining room, he saw that Roswell and Anette were enjoying their breakfast and they were engrossed in a conversation.

Roswell looked up and acknowledged him. "Good morning, Brother."

He responded in kind before he shifted his gaze towards his sister-in-law. "Anette," he greeted.

Anette smiled. "Our dear Miss Sutherland made the newssheets."

"Interesting," Fredrick muttered. "What was said of her?"

Picking up the newssheets, Anette shared, "Miss Sutherland has the voice of an angel and captivated the audience at Lady Shorne's soiree." She placed the paper down. "Isn't that promising?"

"I suppose it is," Fredrick said.

"There is no 'suppose' about it," Anette declared. "Miss Sutherland is slowly winning over the *ton*, just as I thought she would."

Fredrick reached for a cup of tea. "She still has a long way to go before the *ton* will accept her."

Anette regarded him with a curious gaze. "You are being a naysayer this morning, especially since last night was such a triumph."

"I won't argue with you on that," Fredrick replied, "but I also don't want to raise your hopes, or Miss Sutherland's for that matter."

Carson stepped into the room with a silver tray in his hand. "A letter was delivered for you," he said, extending the tray towards Roswell.

Roswell retrieved the letter and unfolded it. His eyes scanned the note before he crumpled it in his hand and tossed it onto the table.

"What did it say?" Anette asked.

"Kendrick wants to see me," Roswell hesitated, "and Fredrick."

Fredrick leaned to the side as the footman placed a plate

of food in front of him. "Why does Kendrick want to see me?"

"He says that he has some information that you might find interesting," Roswell shared.

"Why didn't Kendrick come himself?" Fredrick asked.

Roswell looked amused by the question. "Kendrick is not one to leave his office, unless absolutely necessary."

Fredrick had no desire to meet with the spymaster, but he was curious as to why Kendrick wished to meet with him. He hoped it wasn't merely an attempt to recruit him as an agent. He didn't want that life, at least not here in London. If he was still under Wellington, he would gladly continue working as a spy.

"I will meet with Kendrick, but only because I consider it a professional courtesy," Fredrick said, rising.

"You want to go now?" Roswell asked, looking at the plate of untouched food in front of him.

Fredrick nodded. "I am not really hungry."

Roswell leaned over and kissed his wife on the cheek. "This shouldn't take too long, my love."

"You always say that, my love biscuit," Anette joked.

Fredrick should leave well enough alone, but he had to ask. "Why do you call Roswell 'love biscuit'?"

"That is simple," Anette said. "I love Roswell and I love biscuits. It is only natural for me to combine them."

Well, he had asked. He shouldn't have, but he had. And now he knew the answer and he felt dumber because of it.

Roswell came around the table. "We should go. The sooner we get there, the less temperamental Kendrick will be."

Fredrick followed his brother towards the entry hall. He directed Carson to have the coach brought around front.

It was a short time later that they were traveling in the coach down the road.

Roswell's gaze remained fixed on the open window, his brows furrowed in deep concentration.

Fredrick had to assume that Roswell's deep worry was primarily due to Caleb's situation, especially given their lack of any leads on his whereabouts. "We will find Caleb," he assured him.

"I am beginning to question if that is true," Roswell said, meeting his gaze. "Caleb has never disappeared for this long. I just can't help but think he is in trouble, and I am doing nothing about it."

"You are doing everything you can."

"Which isn't enough," Roswell said, his voice rising. "It is not as if I can search all the rookeries looking for him. It is an impossible feat."

Fredrick wanted to lie to his brother and tell him that everything would be all right, but he knew Roswell would see right through him. They both knew the odds of Caleb being found alive with every day that passed were becoming dire.

The coach came to a stop in front of a brown brick building situated on the outskirts of the fashionable part of Town. The exterior appeared in need of a fresh coat of paint, and the cracked, disheveled windows added to its overall state of disrepair.

Fredrick lifted his brow. "This is where Kendrick operates from?"

"Our last building was compromised so we were forced to relocate," Roswell explained as he stepped out of the coach.

As he went to stand by his brother on the pavement, Fredrick remarked, "This place looks abandoned."

"Trust me," Roswell said.

Fredrick trailed behind Roswell as they made their way to the main entrance and entered a dimly lit hall. A lone guard was positioned against the back wall, his gaze fixed on them with mild curiosity.

"Who is this bloke?" the guard asked.

Roswell smiled. "He is my brother."

"Ah, so he is utterly useless as well," the guard joked. "I don't think the agency is prepared for two of you."

"Kendrick requested Fredrick's presence," Roswell explained.

The guard sized Fredrick up and nodded. "Very well," he said, opening the door. "Stand down, men."

Fredrick cast a quick glance around, curious about the men the guard was referring to, but it became apparent that they were not alone.

After they stepped through the door, Fredrick noticed that desks filled the long, rectangular hall. Agents were seated at the desks, engrossed in reviewing documents, paying little attention to them as they walked by.

Roswell approached a door and knocked on it.

"Enter," came a gruff reply.

His brother opened the door and said, "After you, Fredrick."

Fredrick walked through the door and saw that Kendrick was sitting behind his desk. The silver-haired spymaster had numerous piles of papers in front of him and an air of weariness surrounded him. It was evident not only in his eyes but also in his overall demeanor.

"Chatsworth, I am glad that you came," Kendrick said. "I have some information that I think you will find particularly interesting."

Moving to sit down on a chair, Fredrick asked, "What information is that?"

"We discovered how Mr. Barnard entered our shores and was able to cause havoc on your family," Kendrick shared.

Now Kendrick had his attention.

Kendrick continued. "We have since learned that Lord Drycott has been smuggling items out of France, including passengers who are willing to pay, and are depositing the goods in his so-called factories in and around London. We have confirmation that Mr. Barnard was one of those passengers."

Roswell stepped forward and asked, "Who were the other passengers?"

"That is what we are trying to determine," Kendrick replied. "We suspect that they might be French spies, as well."

"Do you have enough information to arrest Lord Drycott and force him to tell you?" Fredrick asked.

"Not yet, and we don't want to let him know that we are onto him," Kendrick explained. "Caleb's assignment was to find the proof that we need to bring down Lord Drycott's entire operation. I was hoping you would work with Roswell to identify the other passengers. Although, I should warn you that you are not the only agents working on this. It's a matter of high priority at the moment."

Fredrick frowned. Did he truly want to return to the life of a spy? It wasn't that he couldn't handle the peril, but his heart wasn't fully invested in it.

"In uncovering the identities of these other passengers, I do believe you will eventually locate Caleb," Kendrick remarked.

Roswell turned to Fredrick and asked, "What do you say, Brother? I could use the help, and not just because Anette volunteered you."

Fredrick knew his brother was not one to ask for help, and he hesitated. He could do one more assignment. He would help track down Caleb, uncover any potential French spies in England, and then be done with this life.

"I will do it," Fredrick said. "But this will be my only case."

Kendrick nodded his head in approval. "I had a feeling you might say that," he said, extending Fredrick a piece of paper. "This is all that we have to go on."

Fredrick accepted the paper and looked at it in disbelief. "This is all that you have?"

"That is more than enough for a seasoned agent such as you," Kendrick replied. "Good day, gentlemen."

Roswell went to open the door. "Let's get to work," he encouraged.

As he rose from his seat, Fredrick hoped he had made the right decision. He was all too aware of how this job had a tendency to pull you back in and never let go. But he needed to find Caleb, and quickly.

Chapter Eight

Emilia sat in the drawing room as she labored on her needlework. Her housekeeper had secured her various copies of *Ackermann's Repository*. In the periodicals, there were depictions that showed needlework patterns she could replicate on her own. It was a luxury that she could scarcely afford when she worked at the boarding school.

It was rather pleasant to be wealthy, she thought. While she might not have earned the admiration of the *ton*, she didn't have to worry about her next meal. The most challenging aspect of her new life was grappling with the persistent feelings of inadequacy, knowing that she didn't truly fit into this world. She wanted to believe she did, but it was proving to be quite a struggle.

Lily sat across from her on the settee and she was reading a book. She lowered the book and asked, "Are you terribly bored yet?"

"I am not," Emilia said. "I could work on embroidery all day long."

"Yes, that is true. It is a vexing little habit of yours," Lily teased.

Emilia lowered the fabric to her lap. "I do not wish you to be bored. Would you care to play a card game?"

"No," Lily sighed. "I shouldn't complain to you. After all, I am sure there are many of my duties that I am overlooking right now."

"You are entertaining me and that is sufficient."

Lily leaned forward and lowered her voice. "I do think your staff finds it rather odd that we spend so much time together. I do not think that is normal for a lady's maid."

"It might not be, but I do not care."

Turning her head, Lily asked, "When is your teacher coming to instruct you on how to play the pianoforte?"

"This afternoon," Emilia replied. "Every genteel lady is expected to play the pianoforte, and I have no excuse since I own a rather grand one."

"I wish I had seen Lady Shorne's face when you started singing. I bet she was furious."

Emilia smiled. "She definitely did not seem pleased."

"Good, it serves her right," Lily said. "She was just hoping to embarrass you and she failed spectacularly."

Dalby entered the room and Emilia perked up. She was hoping his presence indicated that Lord Chatsworth or Lady Roswell had come to call.

"Mr. Calvin Livingston and his sister, Miss Clarissa Livingston, have come to call," the butler informed her. "Are you receiving callers?"

Emilia blinked. What were they doing here? Did she want to speak to them? The last time they had spoken, it had not gone well.

Lily regarded her with curiosity. "Are you going to meet with them?"

She pondered the question before responding, "I don't rightly know. Should I?"

"Aren't you the least bit curious as to what they want?" Lily asked.

A Suitable Fortune

Emilia had to admit that Lily did have a point. Calvin and Clarissa had made the effort to travel from Cheapside to visit with her. The least she could do was meet with them.

Turning her attention towards the butler, Emilia said, "Please send them in."

"Very good, Miss," Dalby replied before he departed from the room.

While waiting for them to enter the drawing room, Emilia couldn't help but wonder if she had made the right choice in agreeing to see them. She held no animosity towards them, but she suspected that they might harbor resentment for the way she had disrupted their lives.

Calvin entered the room first and bowed politely. "Miss Sutherland," he greeted. "Thank you for agreeing to meet with us."

A moment later, Clarissa stepped into the room, her expression marred by a frown. "Yes, thank you," she said, her words carrying a trace of animosity.

Emilia had risen when they had come into the drawing room and she dropped into a curtsy. "The pleasure is all mine."

An uneasy silence settled between them, and Emilia struggled to find the words that could break it. She was uncertain about their purpose for visiting, and the situation felt rather awkward.

Rising, Lily said, "I should let you speak to your guests in private, but I will just be in the entry hall if you need me."

Once Lily had stepped out, Clarissa went over to the pianoforte and ran her fingers along the side of it. "Do you even know how to play the pianoforte?"

"I do not," Emilia replied. "But I hope to learn soon."

"What a waste, then," Clarissa muttered.

Calvin cast a look towards his sister, one that silently implied she should behave. "We did not come to quarrel with

Emilia, but rather to sit down and become more acquainted with one another."

Clarissa moved towards an upholstered armchair and asked, "May I sit?"

Gesturing towards the chair, Emilia replied, "Yes, please. Would you care for a cup of tea as well?"

"No, I would not," Clarissa replied.

Emilia returned to her seat. "Are you hungry?" she asked. "I can have some cucumber sandwiches sent up. It would only be a moment."

Clarissa's frown only seemed to deepen. "I am not hungry." She glanced around the room. "I hope you don't have any designs on redecorating this room."

"I do not. I think it is lovely as it is," Emilia said.

Her response didn't seem to appease Clarissa, but she doubted anything she said would. Emilia turned her attention towards Calvin. "May I get you some tea?"

"Tea would be nice, thank you," Calvin replied.

Emilia leaned forward in her seat, reaching for the teapot. She poured a cup of tea and extended the cup and saucer to him.

Calvin accepted the tea and sat down next to his sister. "You must be wondering why we came to call."

"I do find myself rather curious," Emilia admitted.

"Initially, we were rather consumed by anger that our father disowned us and left you the bulk of his fortune," Calvin started. "However, after some time, we came to the realization that you weren't at fault, and you are the only family that we have left."

Calvin continued. "We are here to make amends and apologize for how terribly we treated you when we visited last."

Emilia was genuinely taken aback by Calvin's words. Perhaps he may feel that way, but she harbored doubts that Clarissa shared the same sentiment. Nothing in Clarissa's demeanor or actions suggested any remorse for her previous behavior.

After taking a sip of his tea, Calvin lowered the cup to his lap. "I do hope you will find it in your heart to forgive us," he said. "Whatever happens between us, we are still family. And that means something to us."

Pressing her lips together, Emilia wasn't quite sure how to respond. She wanted to believe them, but she questioned their true intentions. What did they want from her?

Calvin exchanged a look with Clarissa, prompting her to say, "Yes, I second what my brother said." Her words sounded rushed and lacked sincerity.

Emilia knew she had two options. She could be gracious and overlook the fact that Clarissa still disliked her. Or she could ask them to leave her home, a home that had been their residence just a few days prior.

She decided that it was best to treat them with kindness, something that they hadn't bestowed upon her.

"I accept your apology," Emilia said. "I know that couldn't have been easy for you, for both of you, given the circumstances."

Calvin smiled. "You are most generous," he said. "Is she not generous, Clarissa?"

Clarissa pursed her lips and muttered, "Yes, she is a blasted saint." Her tone conveyed a degree of sarcasm.

"I do apologize for Clarissa but it has been rather a difficult time for us, I'm afraid," Calvin attempted. "Not only were we disowned, but we were declared illegitimate."

Emilia raised her hand in a calming gesture. "I understand. You do not need to explain yourself. I can only imagine how trying it has been for you both, and for what it is worth, I am sorry."

"Are you sorry enough to return what is rightfully ours?" Clarissa snapped.

Calvin cast his sister a disapproving look. "That is not fair of you," he chided. "Emilia did nothing wrong."

Clarissa crossed her arms over her chest and rolled her eyes, making it evident that she disagreed with her brother's sentiments. But at least she was quiet now.

"I was wondering if there was anything that you are in need of," Calvin started. "We would be happy to render any assistance that you require."

"That is kind of you to offer, but I am making do on my own," Emilia said.

Clarissa perused the length of Emilia before asking, "Where did you get that gown? It isn't as awful as the one you arrived in."

Emilia couldn't be entirely certain, but there seemed to be a subtle undertone of both curiosity and critique in Clarissa's words. "Lady Roswell let me borrow some of her gowns while the dressmaker creates a new wardrobe for me."

"What dressmaker did you use?" Clarissa asked.

"Madame Auclair," Emilia replied.

Clarissa's mouth dropped open. "She is the premier dressmaker in all of London. How were you able to secure an appointment on such short notice?"

Emilia had been informed of this by her housekeeper, but she took a secret pleasure in Clarissa's reaction. "Mrs. Harvey set it up for me."

"Of course she did," Clarissa grumbled. "You are quite fortunate. It took me months before I was able to see Madame Auclair."

"Madame Auclair has promised me a ballgown before I host my first ball in a few days," Emilia shared.

"She never worked that fast for me," Clarissa remarked.

Calvin interjected, "I do hope your ball will be a rousing success and you bedazzle the *ton*."

"Thank you," Emilia said.

Clarissa let out a huff of air. "Do you require any

assistance in preparing for the ball?" she asked, feigning annoyance with her own question.

Emilia understood that it must have been difficult for Clarissa and she had no intention of holding her lackluster behavior against her. "That won't be necessary. Lady Roswell has been helping me."

"Lady Roswell is competent, but I do believe I can assist you in ways that she cannot," Clarissa said. "To begin with, I have decorated numerous ballrooms and I know this townhouse inside and out, including the best place to situate the orchestra for ideal sound in the ballroom."

"I don't…" Emilia started.

Calvin spoke over her. "We are trying here. Will you not meet us halfway?" he asked, his eyes imploring hers.

Emilia didn't particularly want Clarissa's help, but it would be rude to refuse it. On the other hand, she could always use another hand when it came to planning the decoration of the ballroom.

Summoning a smile to her lips, Emilia replied, "I will gladly accept Clarissa's assistance."

"Wonderful," Calvin said as he leaned forward and placed his nearly full teacup onto the tray. "Clarissa shall return tomorrow to help with the preparations."

Clarissa abruptly rose, causing her brother to awkwardly stand. "We should go," she insisted. "We do not want to overstay our welcome."

Calvin tipped his head. "It was a pleasure, Emilia." He paused. "May I call you that?"

"Yes, we are family as you pointed out earlier," Emilia replied.

Turning towards his sister, Calvin held his arm out. "Shall we depart?"

Annoyance flickered in Clarissa's eyes as she placed her hand on his sleeve and let him guide her out of the drawing room.

Emilia sank back against the settee, letting out a sigh. What fresh torment could she expect from Clarissa when she came to call tomorrow? Emilia resolved to ensure that Anette was present during the visit, in hopes of deflecting some of Clarissa's hostility.

Lily's voice came from the doorway. "She hates you."

"Clarissa?" she asked. "Yes, she most certainly does."

"Yet you agreed to let her help plan the ball?" Lily inquired.

Sitting up straight, Emilia replied, "I thought it was the right thing to do."

Lily didn't look convinced by her words. "Well, regardless, it is time to change into a different gown."

"What is wrong with the gown that I have on?"

"A lady only spends a few hours in each gown and then you move on to the next," Lily said. "At least, that is what Mrs. Harvey told me."

Emilia reached for her teacup and brought it up to her lips. "I think I shall stay in this gown for the rest of the day."

Lily ventured further into the room. "Shall we play a card game before you rest from your taxing morning?" Her words were laced with humor.

"That sounds delightful," Emilia said.

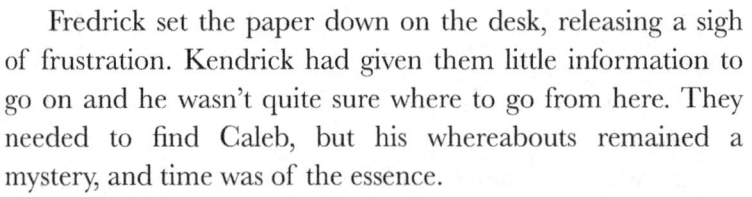

Fredrick set the paper down on the desk, releasing a sigh of frustration. Kendrick had given them little information to go on and he wasn't quite sure where to go from here. They needed to find Caleb, but his whereabouts remained a mystery, and time was of the essence.

He harbored a sincere hope that Caleb was still alive. But with each passing day that Caleb failed to return home,

Fredrick couldn't help but wonder if he would ever see him again.

Rising, he walked over to the window and looked out. He had agreed to take on this assignment in part because he wanted to hold Lord Drycott accountable for allowing Mr. Barnard onto English soil. Mr. Barnard had nearly killed Roswell and Octavia, and that could not go unanswered.

The sun had nearly set and Fredrick contemplated if life would get better for him. He had everything that he could ever want, but nothing that he truly wanted. He just wanted to feel something again.

Anette entered the room and announced, "I have invited Miss Sutherland for dinner this evening and she should be arriving soon."

Botheration. He had no desire to entertain house guests this evening, even though, secretly, he was pleased that it was Miss Sutherland. He just couldn't let Anette know that. He was well aware that if he showed any sign of enjoying the company of Miss Sutherland, Anette would suspect there was more to it, which there wasn't. But it might lead to more unwanted questions- questions he had no desire to answer.

Miss Sutherland was nothing more than a friend- no more, no less. It didn't matter that when she smiled, it felt as if his very soul lifted, even if only for a brief moment.

Turning to face his sister-in-law, Fredrick asked, "Didn't we just see Miss Sutherland last night at the soiree?"

"We did, but I thought it might be a nice gesture," Anette said. "Besides, we need to plan the ball that is being held in her honor."

"I have no desire to help plan a ball."

"Nor would I expect you to," Anette remarked. "While you and Roswell have a glass of port after supper, Miss Sutherland and I will discuss the particulars."

Fredrick glanced down at the paper on his desk, aware that he couldn't afford to waste any time. He had important work that he had to see to, but could he resist the opportunity to spend more time with Miss Sutherland?

Knowing that Anette was still waiting for a response, Fredrick inclined his head and replied, "Very well."

A bright smile graced Anette's lips, as if she were privy to a secret. He couldn't help but wonder what she was up to. Surely, she wasn't that delighted that he had agreed to the dinner with Miss Sutherland?

Carson stepped into the room and announced, "Miss Sutherland has arrived, and she is in the drawing room."

"Thank you," Anette acknowledged.

After the butler departed from the study, Anette asked, "Will you go greet Miss Sutherland? I'm afraid I grabbed the wrong gloves for dinner."

"Your gloves look fine to me," Fredrick remarked.

Anette waved her hand dismissively. "I'll only be a moment." Without uttering another word, she left the room.

Fredrick didn't mind greeting Miss Sutherland. In fact, he found her not only pleasant but rather captivating. As he'd gotten to know her better, he'd discovered an inner strength in her that he deeply admired, and he suspected she didn't fully realize her true worth.

He departed his study and headed towards the drawing room. As he stepped into the room, it appeared that Miss Sutherland's eyes brightened at the sight of him, or maybe he was merely imagining it. Perhaps it was the play of light in the room that had deceived his eyes.

Fredrick bowed. "Good evening," he greeted.

She dropped into a curtsy. "My lord," she said.

"Anette and Roswell will be down shortly," Fredrick informed her, unsure of what else to say. Why was he suddenly nervous? He never got nervous.

He took a moment to admire Miss Sutherland. She was adorned in a pale blue gown that emphasized her graceful figure, and her dark hair was elegantly arranged atop her head. A string of pearls adorned her neck. There was no denying her beauty, but each time he saw her, it seemed to be even more enchanting.

Miss Sutherland's eyes left his and roamed over the room. "This is a lovely drawing room," she acknowledged.

"My grandmother decorated it but my mother added a few touches here and there."

Her gaze met his with a depth of compassion. "I heard about your mother and I wish to offer my deepest condolences. It is never easy to watch someone that you love grow progressively worse."

The way she spoke, he suspected that she had firsthand experience with such a situation. "Is that how your mother died?"

She nodded. "I was a stranger to my mother in her final days. She seemed to be living out her life when she was younger. It was difficult, but I wouldn't trade anything for those final days with her. She was all I had."

"You had no other family?"

"None that my mother spoke of," Miss Sutherland replied. "And I never knew my father's…" Her voice trailed off. "I suppose that makes sense since he wasn't truly my father. Sir Charles was."

Fredrick walked further into the drawing room, but still maintained a proper distance. "I'm sorry you didn't get to know Sir Charles. He was a good man. A bit misunderstood, but he always did the right thing."

"Speaking of family," Miss Sutherland started, "Calvin and Clarissa came to visit me."

"What did they want?"

"Nothing, per se," Miss Sutherland replied. "Clarissa even offered to help me with decorating the townhouse for the ball."

For some reason, that revelation did not sit well with him.

Clarissa and Calvin weren't exactly known for their selfless behavior.

"I would be cautious around Clarissa and Calvin," he advised.

Miss Sutherland grinned. "I intend to. I want to believe they are being genuine, but I couldn't help but wonder why the sudden change of heart."

"Good," Fredrick said. "You must trust what your heart is telling you."

"Is that what you do- trust your heart?"

Fredrick shook his head. "No, I am much too pragmatic for that. I go off instinct and it has yet to lead me astray."

"My mother always encouraged me to follow my heart, but I didn't have time to do something so foolish. After she died, I had to find a way to survive without her. Which I did, but it took a lot of hard work."

"It is impressive that you found your own way."

"Not impressive," Miss Sutherland said. "The way I lived before I came to London was not something anyone would be envious of, especially someone in your position. It took me nearly three years to save three pounds, and I oftentimes went without to accomplish such a feat."

Fredrick held her gaze. "You are wrong. You took what you had been given, and you found a way to push forward, despite the obstacles in your way." He paused. "I find that to be remarkable."

"You are kind, but wrong to say so. There is nothing remarkable about me. I am utterly unremarkable."

"Why do you sell yourself short?" Fredrick asked. "You are so quick to deflect praise, and yet you are worthy of it."

Miss Sutherland began to fidget with her hands, a sure sign that she was nervous. "I suppose I am not used to people complimenting me."

"Then perhaps you should start." Fredrick took a step

closer to her. "I will help you learn how to take a compliment."

She eyed him curiously. "How are you going to do that?"

"I will compliment you, and you will accept it graciously," he replied. "Shall we begin?"

Miss Sutherland grew determined but her eyes betrayed her hint of hesitation. "Yes, I suppose so."

Fredrick smiled and said, "You are looking especially lovely this evening."

"Thank you, but—"

He cut her off. "No buts. You say 'thank you,' and perhaps even offer a coy smile in return."

A line in her brow appeared. "I am supposed to flirt with everyone who offers me a compliment?"

"You misunderstood me. I never said you had to flirt with anyone, but rather acknowledge their compliment with more than just words," Fredrick explained. "Let's try again."

Miss Sutherland opened her mouth to no doubt object, so he spoke first. "You have a lovely singing voice. It is without a doubt one of the finest I have ever heard."

"Truly?" she asked.

Fredrick raised an eyebrow. "It is the truth, but what do you say in response to my compliment?"

"Thank you," she replied.

He waited to ensure there was no "but" following her words. Satisfied that there wasn't one, he said, "Well done. You have made remarkable progress in such a short period of time."

Miss Sutherland's lips twitched. "I had an excellent teacher."

"Shall we try another one?"

"I think we have done enough for one day," Miss Sutherland said. "After all, I wouldn't wish for all this flattery to go to my head."

Fredrick chuckled. "Very well, but we will keep practicing."

Anette's voice came from the doorway. "What were you practicing?" she asked as she walked further into the room with Roswell.

"Miss Sutherland's ability to accept a compliment," Fredrick replied. "For some reason, she believes she is not worthy of praise."

"That is utterly ridiculous. Of course, Miss Sutherland is worthy of praise," Anette declared.

"I agree, wholeheartedly," Fredrick said.

Roswell came to stand next to his wife and remarked, "Regardless, that is an odd thing to practice."

Miss Sutherland spoke up. "It is something that I have always struggled with. I never quite know when someone is being genuine with their compliments."

"Well, just assume from now on that we are," Anette said.

Carson stepped into the room and announced, "Dinner is served. If you will kindly make your way to the dining room."

Fredrick turned towards Miss Sutherland and offered his arm. "May I escort you?" he asked.

"Thank you, kind sir," she said, placing her hand on his sleeve.

As they trailed behind Roswell and Anette to the dining room, Fredrick remarked, "You really do look lovely this evening."

"Thank you." She hesitated before adding, "You are looking rather dapper yourself." Her words were followed with a smile.

Amused, he asked, "Was that a compliment or are you attempting to flirt with me?"

Her eyes went wide, and she hastily responded, "Compliment you, my lord! I would never, ever flirt with you. That is a preposterous idea."

"Why?" he asked. "Do I repulse you?"

"Heavens, no!" she exclaimed. "You are a lord, and I am just…" Her words trailed off.

"A what?" he pressed.

Miss Sutherland pressed her lips together. "I am not worthy of your notice."

Fredrick came to an abrupt stop and turned to face her. "You are worthy of my notice, and I will not tolerate you questioning otherwise," he said. "Quite frankly, you are more than just an acquaintance to me. I consider you a friend."

"Do you?" Miss Sutherland inquired.

"Will you stop doubting whether or not you belong in this world?" he asked. "You are the daughter of a baronet and an heiress. Whether you want it to be, this is your life now, and I hope you embrace it."

Miss Sutherland's eyes searched his, as if she were gauging his sincerity. "You are right, but I just find it hard to believe I am worthy of such an honor."

"Very few people are, but I can state with certainty that you are one of them," Fredrick affirmed.

"I am grateful to have you as a friend, my lord."

Fredrick placed a hand on her sleeve. "I would be honored if you called me by my given name, Fredrick."

Her face softened. "I would like that very much, assuming you do the same."

"I would like that, Emilia," he said. He couldn't quite explain why saying her name felt so right, but it did.

When he said her name, Emilia smiled and it spilled into her eyes, making it nearly impossible to look away.

But he had to. For his own sake. Forming any type of attachment to Emilia would be a terrible mistake, and it was one that he could not afford.

Chapter Nine

Emilia walked into the dining room on Fredrick's arm, wondering how he had the ability to make her feel so special. He had never judged her for her upbringing. Instead, he had encouraged her to embrace her unique perspective.

How could she not help but harbor small, minute feelings for this man? They wouldn't amount to anything, but she couldn't quite seem to help herself. Perhaps she only felt this way because he had been so kind to her.

No.

It was more than that. He stirred up feelings that she didn't think she would ever have. If fortune hadn't smiled upon her, she would have likely become a spinster. She had accepted that long ago, but now everything was different. She was an heiress, and she could marry for love.

As she settled into her chair, she snuck a glance at Fredrick. Why wasn't he married? He was certainly handsome enough. The kindness that emanated off his person was enough to make any woman swoon.

Emilia may be rich, but she shouldn't dwell on things she couldn't have, with Fredrick being one of those things. He considered her a friend, for which she was most grateful. Her feelings may be unrequited, but she still wanted him in her life. He made everything better simply by being a part of it.

A footman placed a bowl of soup in front of her and she reached for a spoon. She wasn't in a talkative mood, and she hoped that the conversation would flow around her.

But she was not so lucky.

Lord Roswell met her gaze and said, "I would love to know more about you, Miss Sutherland. Your upbringing is far more interesting than mine."

"I disagree. It was just different," Emilia said. "I would have rather eaten off a golden spoon and ridden in carriages."

"Is that what you imagined our childhood was like?" Fredrick asked. "I only ask because I've never eaten off a golden spoon before."

Emilia smiled. "To be honest, I am not quite sure how nobility raises their children. I must assume you had a nursemaid or two."

"We did," Fredrick confirmed, "but my mother was very attentive to us. She would come in every night and read to us."

"Is that a rarity amongst the *ton*?" Emilia asked.

Lord Roswell nodded. "In most households, children are meant to be seen, not heard. But that was not the case in ours. We had dinner as a family."

Emilia lifted her brow. "All of you?"

"Yes, and it was loud and chaotic… and perfect," Fredrick replied. "We never had to question if our parents loved us. We just knew they did."

"I love that," Emilia said. "My mother was very attentive to me as well, but that is because we lived in a small cottage. We had no choice but to interact with one another."

"Were you educated at home?" Anette asked.

Emilia wiped the sides of her mouth with her napkin before replying, "I was fortunate enough to attend a boarding school near my village, but my mother encouraged me from a young age to be a voracious reader."

"You must have had an impressive library then," Lord Roswell mused.

Emilia smiled, finding his comment humorous. "No, we didn't own any books. I would make do by borrowing one book at a time from one of my mother's clients. Once I finished, I would return the book and select another one."

Fredrick gave her a knowing look. "I would imagine that you are in heaven with Sir Charles' library. He had many first editions in there."

"I am well aware, and it is exactly like the library I used to dream of," Emilia admitted. "I bet my mother is smiling down from heaven, knowing my dream came true."

"You must learn to dream bigger," Fredrick remarked.

Emilia was about to reply when she saw peacock feathers out the window. "Do you own a peacock?"

Fredrick groaned. "Freddy is the bane of our existence, but we don't dare get rid of my sister's pet. Although, I am tempted now that Octavia will be residing at her own residence."

"Your sister has a pet peacock?" Emilia asked.

"It is true, and it is an ornery little thing," Anette said. "But Freddy leaves me alone when I go into the gardens."

Lord Roswell shook his head. "Yes, and I have seen nothing like it. Freddy will observe her with his black, beady eyes but then he will walk away. It is almost as if they have an understanding."

Anette smirked. "He must know I carry a pistol in my reticule, and I am not afraid of using it."

"Or it could be that Freddy does not like the sound of Mr. Fluffy's incessant barking," Lord Roswell mused.

"Mr. Fluffy does not bark any more than a normal puppy," Anette defended. "He is just trying to figure things out."

"I daresay Mr. Fluffy wasn't the brightest one in the litter," Lord Roswell said.

Anette frowned. "Just because Mr. Fluffy gets frightened easily doesn't mean he isn't intelligent."

"He is afraid of boots," Lord Roswell shared. "And do not get me started on when Mr. Fluffy sees slippers under the bed."

Emilia found herself enjoying the soup and the conversation that was going on around her. She hadn't grown up with any siblings and this is what she imagined it would be like.

Fredrick leaned closer to her and whispered, "Sometimes they get lost in their own conversation and they forget there are other people in the room."

"I think it is sweet," Emilia remarked.

"It is not. Sharing a townhouse with newlyweds is awful." Fredrick shuddered to emphasize his point.

Lord Roswell's voice interrupted their conversation as he addressed his brother. "Perhaps you should get yourself a wife."

"No, thank you," Fredrick asserted. "I need a wife like I need to be shot again."

Emilia stared at him in disbelief. "You have been shot before?"

"That is a casualty of being in war, I'm afraid," Fredrick replied. "The enemy has no qualms about trying to kill you."

"How many times have you been shot?" Emilia asked.

Fredrick held up two fingers. "Twice, but one was merely a flesh wound. A sniper shot me but luckily his aim wasn't very good."

Emilia couldn't explain why it bothered her that Fredrick had been shot, but it just did. The thought of him being hurt both terrified and saddened her.

"I have been shot at as well," Lord Roswell admitted. "But I was smart enough not to get hit."

"Well done, my love biscuit," Anette teased.

A Suitable Fortune

Love biscuit? Emilia turned her questioning gaze towards Fredrick, but he just shrugged it off. First a pet peacock and now an unusual token of affection. She was beginning to wonder if the wealthy had too much time on their hands.

As the footmen came around and collected their bowls, Fredrick turned towards her and asked, "Have you started to receive any invitations to social events?"

"Not yet," Emilia replied.

Reaching for her glass, Anette said, "I wouldn't give it much heed. Once you have had your ball, everyone will be vying for your attention."

Emilia watched as a footman placed a tray full of venison onto the center of the table. Fredrick rose and started serving the meat to them.

Once Fredrick returned to his seat, Emilia picked up her fork and knife and shared, "Between the planning of the boarding school and the ball, I intend to be rather busy for the next few days."

"What boarding school?" Anette asked.

"My father had planned on opening a boarding school in the rookeries to honor my mother but it was delayed by his death," Emilia replied. "I intend to move forward with the project."

Anette exchanged a concerned look with Lord Roswell. "Do you think that is wise?" she asked. "It is a noble feat, but you have just entered high Society. I worry that people might think less of you for embarking on such an undertaking."

Emilia bobbed her head. "I would rather do what my conscience dictates than earn the approval of the *ton*."

Fredrick surprised her by saying, "I think it is a grand idea."

"You do?" Emilia asked.

"Just think of how you will impact those girls' lives that attend your boarding school," Fredrick replied. "It is admirable and should deserve our praise."

Emilia sat up straighter in her seat, feeling touched that Fredrick was so approving of her idea.

Anette waved her fork in front of her. "My apologies. I do not wish to be a naysayer. Of course I shall support this endeavor."

"Thank you," Emilia responded. "Right now, we are working on hiring more teachers. Until then, I will be teaching the girls embroidery."

"I take back my support," Anette said. "You can't be in earnest. I understand that you want your boarding school to succeed, but you can't go back to being a teacher."

Lord Roswell leaned closer to his wife. "You aren't being very supportive, my dear."

"I just want Emilia to understand that there will be consequences to her actions. Genteel women do not go into the rookeries, for any reason," Anette stated.

"I do believe you visited the rookeries once," Lord Roswell remarked.

Anette rolled her eyes. "That was through no fault of my own. I was abducted."

With wide eyes, Emilia asked, "You were abducted?"

"Yes, but it was ages ago," Anette said dismissively. "I was able to free myself and save the day. End of story."

Lord Roswell chuckled. "I recall the events rather differently."

"Regardless, we are focusing on Miss Sutherland now," Anette stated. "I am just afraid for her reputation once the *ton* finds out."

"The *ton* is always going to find a way to criticize others. Why not let Emilia make a contribution to Society, however small?" Fredrick asked.

Anette put her hands up in defeat. "I can see that I am outnumbered and I *might* be wrong."

"That must have been very difficult for you to admit," Lord Roswell teased.

"It doesn't happen very often," Anette bantered back.

Fredrick shifted in his seat to face Emilia "Tell us more about the boarding school."

"My father drafted all the plans before his death, but the building is secured. Furthermore, the headmistress and a few teachers have been hired," Emilia shared. "My father had already selected the girls who will be attending."

"And this is what you want to do?" Fredrick asked.

"It is," Emilia confirmed. "What is the point of having all this money if I can't use it to help other people?"

"Well, I would caution you to take at least four footmen whenever you travel to your boarding school," Fredrick said. "How deep in the rookeries are you going?"

"I was told that the school was just a few blocks in," Emilia responded. "It is a nice two-level red brick building that has been spruced up for our tenancy."

Anette interjected, "May I teach at your boarding school?"

Lord Roswell looked bemused by his wife's request. "You can't be serious?" he asked.

"I could teach them how to shoot a pistol," Anette replied. "It is a skill that every young woman should possess."

Emilia thought it might be best to proceed cautiously, considering Lord Roswell's reaction. "The girls would be lucky to learn from you, but perhaps you are more of a guest teacher."

"That sounds reasonable," Anette said.

The butler stepped into the room with a tray in his hands and approached Lord Roswell. "My lord, a missive just arrived for you."

Lord Roswell accepted the note and unfolded the paper. He read it and then crinkled it in his hand. "Ladies, I'm afraid we are going to have to cut this dinner short. Fredrick and I have important business that we must see to."

Fredrick pushed back his seat and rose. "Good evening,

Miss Sutherland," he said before he followed Lord Roswell out of the room.

Anette smiled, not appearing the least bit concerned by her husband's abrupt departure. "Shall we eat before our food grows cold?"

Emilia's eyes shifted towards the door and she couldn't help but wonder where Fredrick had gone to so suddenly. Whatever it was, it must have been important.

Fredrick gave his brother an expectant look as they sat in the darkened coach. "Where are we heading?" he asked.

"One of Lord Drycott's factories in the rookeries," Roswell replied. "One of my informants claims that he saw Caleb."

"Can this informant be trusted?"

Roswell nodded. "He can, considering I pay him enough for his loyalty."

"Let's hope this is not a fool's errand."

"It won't be," Roswell asserted.

Fredrick knew that his brother was anxious by the way he was tapping his right foot. Roswell had been searching the rookeries for Caleb but he had found no sign of him. He hoped for Roswell's sake that this informant hadn't led them astray.

"Dare I ask what is transpiring between you and Miss Sutherland?" Roswell asked.

Fredrick gave him a blank look, having no idea what his brother was talking about. "Pardon?"

"You and Miss Sutherland seem to be getting rather close," Roswell pressed.

"That is because we are friends."

Roswell smiled. "Ah, friends. I was just 'friends' with Anette as well."

With a frown, Fredrick replied, "No, Emilia and I are just friends, nothing more."

"You are calling her by her given name?"

Fredrick realized his misstep and he rushed to correct it. "She gave me leave to, but only because we are friends. I daresay you are reading too much into this."

"Or perhaps you are not reading enough into it," Roswell countered.

"You are infuriating," Fredrick muttered.

Roswell chuckled. "I will leave you be, but I would be blind if I didn't notice the growing attraction between you and Miss Sutherland."

"I have no desire to take a wife," Fredrick said.

"I never said anything about marriage," Roswell remarked.

Fredrick turned his head towards the window, hoping this line of questioning would come to an end. Did he find Emilia to be intriguing? Yes. But that didn't mean he had any interest in pursuing her. They were just friends. Why couldn't his brother be satisfied with that response? He most certainly was.

A silence descended over the cab as they ventured further into the rookeries. Fredrick's gaze fell upon the desolate figures shuffling along the narrow pavements, clad in ragged attire and bearing faces that were marked by dirt and despair.

The coach came to a stop and Roswell opened the door. After they stepped onto the uneven pavement, Roswell said, "Follow me. The factory is only a short distance away. I didn't want to give our presence away by arriving in a coach."

Fredrick walked alongside his brother as he attempted to ignore the putrid odors emanating from the destitute people they passed. An animal carcass lay before them, forcing them to carefully detour around the unsightly spectacle.

It wasn't long before they arrived at a looming, darkened

factory, its imposing two-level brick structure standing recessed from the road. No light came from within, which wasn't surprising for the late hour.

Roswell came to a stop and said, "I hope this isn't a waste of time." His voice held a weariness to it.

Fredrick placed an encouraging hand on Roswell's shoulder. "Don't give up hope. We will find Caleb."

Roswell gave a solemn nod, his countenance etched with unwavering resolve. His brother's reaction didn't surprise Fredrick. The life of a spy allowed no room for self-doubt. It required relentless determination, regardless of the odds stacked against you. One single misstep could be the difference between life and death.

Lowering his hand, Fredrick followed his brother towards Lord Drycott's foreboding factory. Upon reaching a nondescript side entrance, Roswell reached for the handle and muttered, "Locked."

Roswell crouched down and withdrew two long metal pins from his jacket pocket. With calculated precision, he inserted them into the lock and, after a few tense moments, they both heard the unmistakable click of the door unlatching.

Rising from his crouched position, Roswell reached for the handle and gently turned it. The door creaked open, and they stepped into the building, with the only illumination coming from the moon's pale beams filtering through the grimy windows.

They walked further into the hall and Fredrick observed crates of all sizes haphazardly stacked along the walls. Fredrick moved closer to one of the crates and noticed that the markings on the outside were from a renowned French company.

"Roswell," Fredrick said in a hushed voice. "These crates must have been smuggled from France."

His brother walked over to stand next to him and replied, "This is further proof that Lord Drycott is smuggling goods but Kendrick is more concerned with *who* he has transported in."

"What is this factory supposed to be?" Fredrick asked.

"According to Kendrick, it is used for cloth weaving, but it is nothing more than a workhouse. The people are paid only ten shillings a week, and I doubt that covers more than very sparse meals for them."

Fredrick's heart ached for the laborers toiling in these harsh conditions. How were they able to survive on such meager wages? With the average wage ranging from twenty to thirty shillings a week, it appeared that Lord Drycott was indeed taking advantage of his laborers.

The sound of approaching footsteps echoed through the dimly lit hall, signaling the presence of an intruder or a guard. In the shadows, Fredrick and Roswell stood frozen, their hearts pounding. They couldn't afford to reveal themselves. Lord Drycott mustn't learn of their investigation into his smuggling operation.

As the tall, broad-shouldered figure came closer to where they were hiding, Fredrick retrieved his pistol that was tucked into the waistband of his trousers. He hoped he didn't need to use his weapon, but he was determined to be prepared for any situation.

The clouds must have shifted because a beam of moonlight streamed through the windows, revealing the man's face. Caleb. They had found him, and he was alive.

Roswell stepped out from the shadows and demanded, "Where in the blazes have you been?"

Caleb's face took on a stunned expression, clearly not expecting to encounter them in the darkened factory. "Roswell?" he asked.

"Yes, and Fredrick is with me," Roswell replied.

Caleb's face broke out into a big smile. "It is about time that you found me," he said. "I had almost given up hope."

"What are you doing here?" Roswell asked.

"Isn't it obvious?" Caleb asked, holding up his hands. "I am guarding the place."

Fredrick moved to stand next to his brother and inquired, "Dare I ask why?"

Caleb grew solemn. "I was tasked with proving that Lord Drycott was smuggling, but then I realized that it was much bigger than that."

"Kendrick informed us of this. Apparently, Lord Drycott has transported French spies onto English soil," Roswell said.

"It is true, and now I am trying to track down where the spies are, all while keeping an eye on Lord Drycott's operation," Caleb remarked.

"So you got hired on as a guard?" Fredrick questioned.

Caleb's expression turned wry. "It has been the perfect cover, but the pay leaves much to be desired. I have survived on stale bread and watered-down ale since I got the job."

Roswell placed a reassuring hand on his friend's shoulder. "We are relieved to see you safe. I feared the worst since we haven't heard from you in some time."

"I'm sorry that I worried you, but I had to see this assignment through," Caleb explained.

"I understand," Roswell said, removing his hand. "To ease your parents' worry, Anette told them that you traveled to Scotland to your hunting lodge."

Caleb bobbed his head. "How is Anette?"

"She is beside herself with worry," Roswell replied. "She even offered to help look for you in the rookeries."

"That doesn't surprise me in the least," Caleb said.

Fredrick spoke up. "We're glad you are safe, but you should have notified Kendrick of your progress on the assignment. He was worried about you as well."

Caleb gave him a disbelieving look. "Did Kendrick say that?" he asked. "I only ask because Kendrick isn't worried about anyone."

"In so many words," Fredrick said. "Kendrick tasked us

with finding you. Where are you even staying when you aren't at work?"

"At a boarding house just up the street. It is safe, for the time being," Caleb assured them. "But I am glad that Roswell is here. I could use his lock picking skills to break into Lord Drycott's office."

"Where is his office?" Roswell asked.

"Follow me," Caleb replied as he spun on his heel. "Be careful of the rats. They outnumber the workers three to one."

The echoing scurrying of rats filled the air as they ventured further down the lengthy corridor.

It wasn't long before they arrived at a door and Caleb informed them, "This is Lord Drycott's office."

Roswell bent down, retrieving the pair of metal pins and skillfully inserting them into the lock. With a methodical twist, he cautiously rotated them until a satisfying click resonated. "We are in," he proudly announced.

They all filed into the cramped, square office, which emanated a musty odor.

As Caleb proceeded to light a candle, he said, "It is much too dark in here. Besides, no one else is here so there is no need to move around in the dark."

Fredrick made his way to the desk, noticing it was cluttered with stacks of papers and books. It was apparent that organization was not among Lord Drycott's top priorities.

Roswell opened the top drawer of the desk and retrieved a bundle of additional papers. "It seems like we'll be spending some time here, gentlemen."

With a stack of papers in hand, Fredrick began to carefully peruse the documents, hoping to find any clues regarding the identities and whereabouts of the French spies.

After what felt like hours of diligent searching, Roswell's voice broke the silence as he raised a piece of paper and announced, "I think I've got something."

"Thank heavens," Fredrick muttered as he dropped the papers in his hand.

Roswell continued. "It is a manifest for one of Lord Drycott's ships. It lists the contents of what was being shipped, the crew and notes two passengers."

"Did they list the passengers' names?" Caleb asked.

Roswell shook his head. "No, it just identifies them as passenger one and two. There is no other distinction."

"So those two passengers could be anyone?" Fredrick questioned.

"It would appear so," Roswell said.

Caleb leaned his shoulder against the wall, his brow furrowed. "I suspect that one of those passengers is a woman."

"Why would you suspect such a thing?" Roswell inquired.

"I overheard a conversation that I wasn't supposed to hear, and Lord Drycott kept referring to a woman," Caleb shared. "I could be wrong, but we might want to consider the possibility."

Roswell exchanged a worried glance with Fredrick before asking, "Did Lord Drycott recognize you?"

Caleb huffed. "I am dressed in tattered clothing and I haven't bathed in weeks," he replied. "Lord Drycott didn't even acknowledge my presence when I stumbled upon their conversation."

As Fredrick took a moment to study Caleb, he couldn't help but notice the sorry state that the man was in. Caleb's worn clothes barely clung to his tall frame, and his jacket appeared too short for his long arms. His face was smudged with a layer of dirt, and his disheveled hair only added to his worn appearance.

"We will consider all possibilities when it comes to the gender of the French spies," Roswell acknowledged. "But, for now, we need to put everything back exactly how we found it so as not to alert Lord Drycott of our presence here."

They went about carefully returning everything to its proper place. Once satisfied that they had left no trace of their presence, they extinguished the candle's flame and silently retreated from the office.

Once Roswell locked the door behind them, he said, "If that manifest is to be believed, we only have two French spies that we must contend with."

"That manifest may have been doctored," Caleb mused.

"Precisely my worry," Fredrick said. "And are we certain that we were even looking at the right manifest?"

Roswell shrugged. "It showed that a shipment of goods arrived nearly two weeks ago," he said. "It would be a reasonable assumption that that was the ship that brought the spies with it."

"I don't work in assumptions," Fredrick remarked.

They made their way through the factory and arrived back at the side entrance. Caleb went to open the door and said, "I'll keep working on this front, and you see what you can find out on your end."

"Remain vigilant," Roswell urged.

Caleb nodded, his resolve unwavering. "Inform Anette that I am doing well, and I shall return when this assignment is over."

Once Fredrick departed from the factory, he waited for Roswell and, together, they made their way towards their waiting coach.

"I am worried about Caleb," Roswell confessed.

"As am I," Fredrick said.

Roswell kept his gaze straight ahead, his demeanor revealing his deep concern. "Let's resolve this case quickly so Caleb can return home," he declared.

Fredrick could sense his brother's determination and he had no qualms about doing so. With Caleb located, they could now focus on finding the two French spies. But that was much easier said than done.

Chapter Ten

Emilia had just concluded breakfast with Lily and couldn't help but notice the curious glances exchanged among the footmen in the dining room. It might have been considered unusual to dine with one's lady's maid, but she didn't care. In her own home, she would do whatever she so desired.

"Shall we adjourn to the drawing room?" Emilia suggested.

Lily leaned closer and spoke in a soft voice. "Do you think that is wise?"

"Is something amiss?"

Casting a wary glance at the footmen, Lily hesitantly responded, "I don't rightly fit in here, and I find myself in a delicate situation. I overheard a few of the maids implying that it wasn't right for me to be spending so much time with you."

Emilia reached for her friend's hand. "You and I have been friends since we first started at the boarding school. I will not abandon you now."

"I'm not asking you to, but perhaps I don't dine with you, at least for every meal," Lily suggested.

Making a face, Emilia replied, "I don't like that option. There is nothing less enjoyable than dining alone."

Lily withdrew her hand. "You are an heiress and need to keep up appearances."

"But in my own home?"

"I think it is for the best," Lily replied.

Dalby entered the room and announced, "Mr. Rymer has come to call, Miss. I have shown him into the drawing room."

"Thank you," Emilia acknowledged before she shifted her gaze back to Lily. "You should come since Mr. Rymer wishes to speak about the boarding school."

"Very well," Lily said.

Emilia rose gracefully and made her way towards the drawing room. She didn't quite like the idea of not spending as much time with Lily. She understood the difficult position that Lily was in but she didn't know of a way that she could fix it. She had no desire to go about her day on her own.

As she stepped into the drawing room, Mr. Rymer bowed and greeted her. "Good morning, Miss Sutherland."

"Good morning," she replied.

Mr. Rymer's gaze traveled over her shoulder and acknowledged Lily. "It is good to see you looking so well, Miss Lily."

Lily came to stand next to Emilia. "Are you here about the boarding school?"

The solicitor grinned. "Yes, I am and I have brilliant news," he said. "Please take a seat and we can discuss the particulars."

Walking over to the settee, Emilia sat down on it and Lily chose an upholstered armchair. "Please proceed, Mr. Rymer," Emilia encouraged.

Mr. Rymer sat across from them and reached for his satchel. "The building has been furnished and Mrs. Anderson has moved in, alongside one teacher and a cook. I took it upon myself to hire a laborer who will be responsible for the care of the building."

"I think that is a brilliant idea," Emilia praised.

Mr. Rymer leaned forward, his eyes dancing with enthusiasm as he said, "I haven't even gotten to the best part yet." He paused for a moment, savoring the anticipation. "If all goes well, the boarding school should be ready to open by the end of the week."

Emilia's eyes widened in surprise. "That is just three days away."

Mr. Rymer nodded. "Indeed, but we've already started gathering the girls, and as long as there are no unexpected setbacks, the actual instruction will begin the following week."

Clasping her hands together, Emilia responded, "This is wonderful news!"

"I was hoping you would say that," Mr. Rymer stated. "This is also under the assumption that you both will be teaching for the foreseeable future. Mrs. Anderson does not anticipate having too much trouble finding teachers, but these things do take time."

Lily spoke up. "May I teach philosophy and geography?" she asked. "That is what I taught at my previous school."

"I do not think that will be an issue," Mr. Rymer replied.

"And I shall teach needlework," Emilia said.

Mr. Rymer removed some papers from his satchel. "Mrs. Anderson wanted me to give you the budget that she came up with. Once you sign off on the amount, I can release the funds to her."

Emilia accepted the papers and glanced over the minimal amounts. "I do not see an issue with any of these numbers."

"I do believe Mrs. Anderson was rather conservative in her budget, but it shouldn't increase too much," Mr. Rymer said. "This is a step in the right direction. If you would like to tour the boarding school…"

Clarissa's voice interrupted Mr. Rymer's explanation, her disapproval evident. "You cannot be in earnest?" she asked, walking further into the room. "You aren't truly opening a boarding school, are you?"

Emilia focused her attention on Clarissa and answered with determination. "Yes, I am. It will be in honor of my late mother."

"But poor people attend boarding schools," Clarissa stated. "Anyone of importance employs a governess."

"The girls that have been selected for the boarding school can't afford anything, much less a governess," Emilia said. "My hope is that we can educate the girls from the rookeries so they can have a chance to find employment after they graduate."

Clarissa looked dumbfounded. "Who would hire someone from the rookeries?" she asked.

Anette's voice came from the doorway, breaking the tension. "I would," she declared.

Turning to face Lady Roswell, Clarissa asked incredulously, "Why would you hire someone that is so beneath you?"

"That is simple. I believe everyone deserves a chance, no matter where they start from," Anette replied.

"They will rob you completely and you will be left with nothing," Clarissa stated.

Anette ventured further into the room. "At first, I was skeptical about the boarding school, but I was wrong to be so. I think it is a fine idea what Miss Sutherland is attempting to do."

Clarissa, her hand defiantly placed on her hip, dismissed the idea with an air of disdain. "This is preposterous. My father would be furious if he knew that his money was going to a bunch of misfits."

"Actually, it was Father's idea," Emilia revealed in a calm and resolute voice. "He had already started the process to open the boarding school."

"Impossible!" Clarissa shifted her disbelieving gaze

towards Mr. Rymer. "Tell them, Mr. Rymer. Tell them that my father would never finance something so uncouth."

Mr. Rymer, maintaining his composed stance beside his chair, gently refuted Clarissa's disbelief. "Miss Sutherland is right. Your father had entrusted me with the duty of overseeing the boarding school several months before his death."

"I don't believe you," Clarissa declared. "I will not stand here and let her just waste my father's money."

"I'm afraid you have little choice in the matter," Mr. Rymer said, coming to Emilia's defense. "Miss Sutherland has the right to spend her money as she sees fit."

Clarissa stuck up her nose haughtily in the air. "The *ton* will mock you for this, and you will never be in their good graces."

"I understand, but I must do this," Emilia said. "If you would like, you may tour the boarding school with us."

"Good heavens, no!" Clarissa exclaimed.

Emilia extended the papers back to Mr. Rymer and said, "Please issue the necessary funds to Mrs. Anderson at once. Inform her that I shall visit the school tomorrow at my earliest convenience."

Mr. Rymer tipped his head. "It shall be done, Miss." He stuffed the papers back into his satchel. "Good day, ladies."

Once the solicitor departed from the drawing room, Emilia asked, "Would anyone care for some tea?"

Anette bobbed her head. "I would greatly enjoy some."

"I also had the cook send up some biscuits since I know how fond you are of those," Emilia said.

"That is most kind of you," Anette acknowledged as she sat in the chair that Mr. Rymer had just vacated.

Clarissa huffed. "Am I the only one that thinks the boarding school is a terrible idea?"

"Yes," Anette promptly replied.

In a display of exasperation, Clarissa theatrically rolled her eyes before advancing closer to the group. "I just worry that Emilia hasn't thought through the repercussions of her actions."

"It is her choice, and we must respect that," Anette remarked.

"You are married to the son of a marquess. How can you go along with this madness?" Clarissa asked.

"I do not consider it madness," Anette replied.

"Well, it is," Clarissa declared as she gracefully lowered herself onto a chair. "It is utter madness and it could very well ruin my father's good name."

Emilia poured two cups of tea, extending them graciously to her guests. "Shall we discuss the particulars of the ball?"

Clarissa, taking a sip of her tea, responded after a pause, "Very well. I shall go to the boarding school. However, my intention is to prove the absurdity of the idea."

"The boarding school is situated in the rookeries," Anette interjected.

With a determined set of her jaw, Clarissa acknowledged, "I know, but if this is the only way to prove that I am in the right, then so be it."

Emilia exchanged an apprehensive look with Anette, uncertain of Clarissa's sudden change of heart. Did she want Clarissa to visit the boarding school with her if all she was going to do was criticize everything?

"You may come, but you mustn't be mean to the girls," Emilia said. "I will not tolerate such behavior."

Clarissa brought a hand to her chest. "I would never be mean to innocent children."

Emilia doubted that but she kept her opinion to herself. "We shall depart tomorrow after breakfast."

"Will *she* be coming with us?" Clarissa asked, her critical gaze directed at Lily.

"Yes, Lily will be coming since she will be a teacher at the boarding school," Emilia said.

Glancing down at her tea, Clarissa scrunched her nose. "This tea is awful. Did Mrs. Crowe quit?"

"No, it is the same tea that she always prepares," Emilia replied.

Clarissa leaned forward and placed her teacup down. "I have a few ideas about the ball, particularly the decorations."

"What do you suggest?" Emilia inquired.

"You shall need a chalked dance floor, and may I suggest my father's crest... er... our father," Clarissa corrected.

Anette nodded in agreement. "A chalked dance floor is all the rage right now."

"You also must ensure that the chandelier and sconces have been properly polished," Clarissa said. "Nothing is more embarrassing than an unkempt ballroom."

Emilia still wasn't quite sure why Clarissa had agreed to help her, but she remained cautious around her. However, if there was even a chance that Clarissa wanted a relationship with her, she was going to accept it. She had never had a sister before and she quite liked the idea of having one.

Fredrick had just begun to descend the stairs when he saw that Anette was in the entry hall. A look of relief came to her face when she saw him. "Good, you are ready," she said.

"Ready for what?" Fredrick asked.

Anette's lips curled into a frown. "Roswell was supposed to tell you," she replied. "We are going on a ride with Miss Sutherland."

Fredrick stepped down onto the marble floor. "I am unable to do so. I am rather busy at the moment."

Anette glanced around the room before she lowered her voice. "The French spies can wait, but Miss Sutherland cannot," she remarked. "This is the first time she has taken a ride through Hyde Park and I thought it would be best if we were there to support her."

"A ride through Hyde Park is hardly difficult," Fredrick said.

"No, but she was not raised with horses as we were," Anette argued. "Fortunately, she knows how to ride a horse, but she is not very experienced."

Fredrick enjoyed his time spent with Emilia, but he couldn't relent too easily. If he did, then Anette might suspect he had developed some feelings for Emilia, just as Roswell had wrongly assumed. While Emilia was undoubtedly a delightful and charming young woman, he harbored no feelings for her but considered her a cherished friend.

As he opened his mouth to continue arguing, Roswell's voice came from behind him. "There is no point in arguing with Anette. She always wins."

With a sigh of defeat, Fredrick raised his hands up in surrender. "I suppose I can make time for a ride through Hyde Park."

Anette smiled broadly. "You made the right choice," she said. "I saw to our horses and they are out front."

Roswell approached his wife and kissed her on the cheek. "Hello, Wife," he greeted her with affection. "You were up rather early this morning."

"I was, partly because I have been seeing to the planning of Miss Sutherland's ball," Anette revealed. "It should be spectacular."

"I have no doubt about that," Roswell responded, extending his arm.

Fredrick followed them out of the townhouse and accepted the reins of his horse from the footman.

His heart ached momentarily as he thought about the stallion he had been forced to leave behind on the Continent. Wellington had assured him that his stallion would be on the next ship back to England, and he hoped that he would be reunited with his beloved horse soon enough.

Until then, he was forced to ride one of the other horses in the stables. They were all fine horses, but he preferred his stallion. He always had.

After Fredrick mounted his horse, they set off towards Hyde Park. They grew closer to the south entrance and he saw Emilia, sitting atop her horse. She seemed a bit rigid and unsteady, her riding hat obscuring her expression. Two grooms sat astride on their horses as they were set back from Emilia.

Emilia mustered a smile when she acknowledged them, although it appeared somewhat forced. "Good morning," she said.

Anette put her hand up in greeting. "Good morning," she responded. "How are you faring?"

Emilia winced. "Not well," she admitted. "I fear that this horse has a mind of its own."

With a gentle laugh, Anette said, "You will get the hang of it soon enough." She held her hand up. "Shall we proceed on our ride?"

"I suppose so," Emilia muttered.

Fredrick moved to position his horse so he was riding alongside Emilia. "I take it that you did not ride horses much in the countryside."

"Not very often," Emilia admitted. "And when I did, I rode astride."

"You rode astride?" Fredrick asked, a hint of surprise in his voice, finding it hard to imagine Emilia engaging in such a scandalous activity.

Emilia adjusted the reins in her hand. "Very few people I knew owned side saddles. They were more for the wealthy."

"Would you care for some advice then?" Fredrick asked.

"Yes, please," Emilia rushed out.

Fredrick gave her a pointed look before saying, "Sit up

straight and tall, relax your back, hold the reins gently and hold your balance to keep control of your horse."

Emilia sat taller in her saddle and loosened her hold on the reins. "Is that better?"

"Yes, but try not to look so petrified," Fredrick teased.

"I feel rather unbalanced being on this horse," Emilia said.

"What if the horse rears up and upends me?"

"That is unlikely to happen." Fredrick glanced over his shoulder, noting that Anette and Roswell were engaged in their own conversation a short distance away. Not that he minded. He preferred to speak to Emilia privately.

Fredrick decided Emilia was overthinking things and was just in need of a distraction. What could he ask her that would get her talking? He rather enjoyed listening to her speak passionately about various topics. Her eyes seemed to sparkle with excitement. It was just one of the many things that he noticed about her.

"What were you like as a child?" Fredrick asked.

Enthusiasm lit up Emilia's eyes and he knew that he had asked the right question. "I was an inquisitive child, much to my mother's chagrin," she shared. "I would ask lots of questions, sometimes not even bothering to wait for the answer. That is why I enjoy reading so much. Many of my questions are answered in the pages."

"What books do you enjoy reading?"

"Anything I can get my hands on," Emilia replied. "I know young women are supposed to avoid certain books, but that piques my curiosity even more. Not that I would share my opinions with anyone."

Fredrick shifted in his saddle before asking, "Why not?"

"Even I know that young women must avoid some topics, such as politics and religion," Emilia said. "No gentleman wants to hear a woman's opinion on those."

"Perhaps you are not spending time with the right gentlemen," Fredrick argued.

Emilia laughed. "You and Lord Roswell are the only gentlemen that I am acquainted with. Well, besides Calvin."

Fredrick looked at her curiously. "You are acquainted with Calvin?"

"Remember, I told you that he called upon me, along with Clarissa, and hoped to repair our relationship, considering it did not begin well," Emilia shared.

Having been distracted by the Caleb disappearance, he had completely forgotten about what Emilia had told him earlier. He couldn't shake off the unease that settled within him. He wasn't quite sure why that bothered him, but Calvin's sudden interest in Emilia seemed rather suspect. Calvin only seemed to care for himself so why had he called upon Emilia? What did he hope to gain from that meeting? The questions swirled in Fredrick's thoughts as they continued their ride through Hyde Park.

Emilia continued, unaware of his thoughts. "I do hope that Calvin and Clarissa are sincere because they are the only family that I have left."

"I would be leery of them," Fredrick counseled.

She nodded. "I am, partly because I am slightly afraid of Clarissa," she said. "She is rather vocal in her disdain for things."

"It has been that way since she was a little girl," Fredrick shared.

"I did get her to agree to go to the boarding school and meet the students. I am hoping that her heart might soften once she sees the girls."

Fredrick shook his head. "I doubt it, but Clarissa is no different than most young women of high Society. You are the anomaly."

"I just feel like an outcast, more than anything," Emilia sighed. "I fear that no one will come to my ball and all of Anette's hard work will be for naught."

"Do not fret. I have no doubt that your ball will be a *crush*."

Emilia offered him a weak smile. "I wish I had your confidence, or even a portion of it. Perhaps I should just pretend."

"True confidence starts from within," Fredrick said. "Pretending to be confident may impress others, but you will know the truth."

"I just can't help but wonder what I would be like if I had been born into this life," Emilia said.

Fredrick grew quiet. He rather liked the fact that Emilia wasn't like most girls of the *ton*, partially because she possessed a rare sense of humility and a distinctive perspective on life.

"Do not try so hard to fit in," he counseled. "You may think that will solve all your problems, but it will just create new ones."

Emilia glanced over at him and asked, "Do you ever worry about fitting in?"

He smirked. "I am an earl, and my father's heir. I have no need to fit in to anyone's perceived notions about me."

"That must be nice," Emilia murmured.

"But I will need to rally support when the time comes for me to take my seat in the House of Lords," Fredrick admitted. "My father may be a powerful man in Parliament, but I have much still that I need to learn from him."

Emilia bit her lower lip. "Can you tell me more about my father?"

"What would you wish to know?"

"I know so little about him, other than what has been told to me," Emilia replied. "I know he was kind to the servants, and to you. For some reason, I still struggle with why he never came to visit me. Do you think he was embarrassed by me?"

Fredrick met Emilia's gaze, and the vulnerability in her eyes tugged at his heartstrings. He suspected she was asking what she already believed to be true. "Why would Sir Charles ever be embarrassed by you?"

"I grew up poor and I lack the sophistication that people possess in high Society," Emilia said, her gaze downcast.

"You are, and always will be, someone who is worthy of your father's notice. I cannot speak as to why he kept himself from you, but he chose to leave *you* his fortune, not Clarissa and Calvin," Fredrick asserted. "In the end, he chose you."

Fredrick hoped that his words would offer reassurance and support to Emilia. He couldn't explain why Sir Charles had made the choices that he had, but he genuinely meant what he said. Sir Charles had cared for Emilia enough to change her life for the better, and he wanted her to realize her true worth.

Emilia's expression softened. "You are right. He chose me." Her words seemed to lift the weight from her shoulders, and the uncertainty faded from her eyes. "I just hope I can live my life in a way that will make him proud."

"You already have," Fredrick informed her. "Opening up the boarding school is admirable, and your father would have been proud."

A bright, genuine smile graced her lips, one that Fredrick wanted to etch into his memory forever. It was the epitome of true happiness. "Thank you," she said. "That means a lot to hear you say that."

"It is merely the truth," he responded. "But you asked about what your father was like."

"I did," she replied.

Fredrick felt his lips curve into a smile as he shared, "Your father was a good man. He had a commanding presence about him that would make lesser men shake in their boots. Although he was not one to easily smile, given his serious nature, there was a kindness about him that only a select few acknowledged. His acts of goodwill were discreet, performed in private to avoid drawing attention to his good deeds."

"Do you suppose that is why he named the boarding

school after my mother so as not to draw attention to himself?"

"I cannot speak on that, but everything he did was done for a reason," Fredrick replied. "He was a man of few words, but his heart was always in the right place."

Emilia grew silent. "He sounds honorable."

"He was, and I consider him my mentor. I owe part of who I am to him."

"Thank you," she murmured. "I have been trying to get a sense of who my father truly was, but I was afraid to ask."

"Never be afraid to ask me anything. You may not like what I tell you, but it will always be the truth," Fredrick remarked.

"I am most grateful for that," Emilia said.

As they continued along the path, Fredrick realized that he was in no rush to return home. Yes, he had to track down two French spies but, for the time being, he would cherish this precious moment with Emilia.

Fredrick realized that he hadn't been this content in a long time, and he suspected it had everything to do with Emilia.

Botheration.

Deep within him, something stirred, and he had a sinking suspicion that it might be feelings for Emilia. Which was an inconvenient notion, for developing such feelings for her would undoubtedly lead to complications. Complications that he had no desire to act upon. No, it would be best to keep Emilia at arm's length from now on.

Chapter Eleven

Emilia sat atop her horse, desperately attempting to look graceful but she knew she was failing miserably. It was rather difficult to ride sidesaddle, but it had to be done. She couldn't simply ride astride in the middle of Hyde Park; such behavior would be far too scandalous.

Glancing at Fredrick, she noticed that his jaw was clenched, his focus steadfastly directed forward. Something had shifted between them, but she didn't know what it was. One moment, Fredrick was engaging and poignant, and the next, he appeared aloof.

She questioned herself if she had done something wrong. It was entirely possible that she had said or done something that had upset him. She was well aware that she lacked the refinement of the young women he was accustomed to.

As she racked her brain on what she could have done, Fredrick spoke up, drawing back her attention. "It is a fine day, is it not?"

"Yes, quite fine," she replied, thankful for the conversation, even if it revolved around such a mundane topic as the weather. At least he was speaking to her, which was a start.

"Perhaps we should head back," he suggested.

Emilia felt a stab of disappointment at his words. She didn't want to return home, at least not yet. She rather enjoyed being in Hyde Park with Fredrick, despite the discomfort of riding sidesaddle. But what could she say that would engage him in conversation once more?

"Before we go," she started, "will you tell me about…" Her voice trailed off. What did she want to know? She could ask him anything, literally anything, but her mind went blank. The only thing that came to her mind was the one thing she blurted out, "Cheese."

Fredrick looked over at her with a bemused expression. "Cheese?" he asked.

She felt her cheeks burn with embarrassment, but she couldn't just pretend she hadn't asked about cheese. "Yes, I am quite fond of cheese and I was wondering your thoughts on it."

Good heavens, could she have asked a more pointless question? What must he think of her?

"I also enjoy cheese," Fredrick replied. "But I am no expert on it."

"Yes, well, cheese comes in all types of varieties, but my favorite must be cream cheese," Emilia rambled on. "I have heard good things about Stilton cheese. I have yet to try it though."

Fredrick's lips twitched. "Are you attempting to engage me in polite conversation?" he asked.

"I am. Is it working?"

"No," Fredrick replied with a shake of his head. "Even though I do enjoy talking about a good cheese, there are far more preferable things to talk about."

Emilia decided to just be honest with Fredrick and hope he wouldn't chide her on her impertinence. "I wasn't ready to return home so I was trying to distract you."

"By speaking about cheese?" he asked with mirth in his voice.

Her gaze turned downcast. "It was the first thing that came to my mind," she shared.

"I would prefer you were just honest with me, and speak your mind," Fredrick said. "I can tarry for a little longer in Hyde Park."

Bringing her gaze up, Emilia responded, "Thank you. Riding in Hyde Park is much more preferable to sitting around my townhouse. It is rather lonely."

"What of Miss Lily?" he asked. "Is she not your lady's maid and companion? Does she not keep you company?"

"She does, but she feels uncomfortable spending so much time with me," Emilia explained. "She doesn't truly fit in anywhere, upstairs or downstairs, and I know it causes her some distress. I do think she will be much happier when she is back to teaching at the boarding school."

Fredrick nodded. "It must have been quite the adjustment for Miss Lily to leave her old place of employment to come to London to be a lady's maid."

"It was, which is why I am truly grateful for her sacrifice," Emilia said. "It has been nice to have a familiar face here."

"Well, you have Anette and me now. We are your friends, too."

Emilia smiled. "Thank you. That means a lot to me," she declared. "I still can't believe that I am friends with an earl. It just seems strange to me."

"Why is that?"

"Earls are important men who do important things," Emilia replied. "They don't have time to lollygag or speak about cheese."

Fredrick chuckled, just as she had hoped he would. "I daresay that your perception of earls is rather distorted. We are just men."

"Yes, but men with extraordinary power," Emilia asserted, holding up a fist to emphasize her point.

With a shake of his head, Fredrick stated, "With that

power comes great responsibility, and I hope I will live up to what is expected of me."

"You will," Emilia assured him.

"How can you be so certain?" Fredrick asked.

Emilia held his gaze as she replied, "You are a good man, perhaps the best man that I know. If you can't succeed, then who can?" She truly meant her words. Fredrick had shown her kindness with no expectation in return. If that wasn't the mark of an honorable man, then what was?

She watched Fredrick's face as he pondered her words. There was something in the way he looked at her that stirred her emotions.

"Thank you, Emilia," he said, his voice reflecting his sincerity. "Your trust means a great deal to me, and I will do my best to live up to your kind words."

They continued to gaze at one another, and she felt a deeper connection forming between them. The way he spoke, the intensity of his gaze, it made her heart race. She realized that Fredrick was not just a friend. No, he was more than that, but what he was, she couldn't figure out. But one thing was certain, he was someone who could make her believe in herself. She trusted him, wholly and completely.

Fredrick turned his gaze away and cast a glance over his shoulder. "I suppose it's time to head back unless you're eager for another round of my cheese expertise," he said with a wink, playfully signaling that he was teasing.

Emilia laughed. "I think I've had enough cheese wisdom for one day," she replied.

As they turned their horses and began the journey back to the townhouse, she watched Anette and Lord Roswell engage in conversation as they rode ahead of them.

"Anette seems very happy with Lord Roswell," Emilia remarked.

"They both have loved each other for a long time, but

neither made it easy for them to come together," Fredrick shared. "They both were entirely too stubborn."

"True love should never be taken for granted," Emilia said.

Fredrick gave her a curious look. "Do you intend to marry for love now that you are an heiress?" he asked.

Emilia hesitated and then winced. "I am not quite sure if I want to give up the freedom that my father so graciously bestowed upon me. If I did wed, everything that I have would belong to my husband."

"My mother was in a position similar to yours," Fredrick shared. "She had been given a large inheritance from her maternal grandmother and she was determined to make it on her own."

"What changed?"

"My father," Fredrick replied. "He swooped in and convinced her that love was indeed worth the risk. They have loved each other fiercely ever since then, and I have never met another couple that was so devoted to one another."

"I love that," Emilia admitted.

Fredrick sighed deeply. "When my mother inevitably passes, I don't know what will become of my father. I fear that he won't last long without her by his side."

Emilia could hear the pain in his words and she wished there was something that she could do to ease his concerns. But she was at a loss to do so. Perhaps she could distract him by asking a question of her own.

"Do you intend to marry for love?" Emilia asked.

That got a reaction out of Fredrick. He huffed in an indignant fashion. "I do not intend to marry, for any reason."

Fredrick's response took Emilia by surprise. She couldn't help but press him. "Don't you require an heir?"

"Roswell is my heir," Fredrick answered, his tone firm.

Emilia knew that it was none of her business, but she had to ask, "What about love, Fredrick?"

His eyes grew reflective, shadows of regret lurking within their depths. "I don't know if I'm deserving of love anymore. Not after what I have done."

"What have you done?" Emilia inquired.

Fredrick grew silent, and she was afraid she had gone too far in her line of questioning. Finally, he spoke. "War changed me. And not for the better. The man I was before I left doesn't exist anymore, leaving behind a shell of a man."

"Nothing you have done could have been that terrible," Emilia said.

"Why, because you think you know me?" Fredrick demanded.

Emilia was taken aback by his harsh tone. Fredrick had never spoken that way to her before, and she found it unsettling.

Fredrick's shoulders seemed to slump as some of the tension drained from his frame. "I am sorry. I had no right to speak to you in such a fashion."

"It is evident that you are hurting," Emilia observed.

"Every soldier must deal with the repercussions of his actions. Why should I be any different?" Fredrick asked, a hint of resignation in his voice.

Emilia looked at him with sympathy. "I can help you."

"No one can help me," Fredrick promptly replied. "I am in a hell of my own making, and there is nothing that can be done for me."

"I don't know what happens during war, but surely there is someone that you can talk to about this," Emilia encouraged.

Fredrick's gaze remained fixed ahead of him as he replied, "There is no one. I left my comrades to die on the Continent."

She couldn't accept his words. That went against everything she knew about Fredrick. "That can't be true," Emilia insisted.

"Wellington sent me home on assignment and requested I

remain behind to attend to my ailing mother," Fredrick shared.

"Could you go back after she passes?" Emilia inquired.

"No, I would be more of a hindrance than a help," Fredrick said. "I just have to accept my days as a soldier are over. I am just an earl that has far too many regrets to quash the painful memories of my past."

Emilia didn't know what to say or do. She wanted to tell him that everything would be all right, but she didn't know what the future held for him, or her.

While she tried to find the right words to provide some sort of comfort to him, Fredrick abruptly brought his horse to a halt and turned his gaze towards the woodlands.

"Did you see that?" he asked.

"I saw nothing," Emilia replied.

Fredrick's eyes scanned over the woodlands. "I saw a light shining through the trees. There, I saw it again." He dismounted and offered his horse's reins to the groom. "I will be back. Wait here."

"Are you sure that is wise?" Emilia asked.

Lord Roswell had dismounted as well and was approaching Fredrick. "Did you see that?"

"I did," Fredrick replied. "Shall we go investigate?"

As the gentlemen walked towards the woodlands, Anette moved her horse closer to Emilia. "They will be back shortly. Until then, what shall we talk about?"

"Cheese?" Emilia quipped.

Anette gave her an odd look. "Cheese?" she asked. "Is that what you and Fredrick were discussing?"

Emilia grinned. "It was just one of the many things that we spoke about."

"Well, surely we can find something that is more interesting than cheese," Anette responded.

The gentlemen stepped into the cover of trees, vanishing

from her sight, leaving Emilia to wonder what they were truly investigating.

As Fredrick ventured into the woodlands, he retrieved his pistol, an unsettling feeling in his gut. Someone had signaled them, but he didn't know who or for what purpose. It could very well be a trap.

Every one of his senses were heightened as he glanced over at his brother. The same uncertainty and wariness were etched on Roswell's face, and it was clear they were both walking into the unknown.

Fredrick halted abruptly, his breath catching as he laid eyes on the last person he'd expected to find in the woodlands. It was the dark-haired lady who had once pretended to be a serving wench, or was it the other way around? Confusion swirled around her identity, but there was no doubt that she stood before him, clad in a simple blue gown with her hair elegantly arranged in a chignon.

The young woman dispensed with pleasantries and got right to the point. "I see that you got my signal," she remarked with a steady demeanor.

"We did," Fredrick responded, his tone edged with impatience. "What is it that you want?"

"Caleb is in trouble," the young woman informed them. "You need to go help him."

Roswell stepped forward and asked, "How do you know that?"

"Lord Drycott learned of his identity and intends to kill him," she shared. "You must go save him before it is too late."

Fredrick wasn't ready to blindly accept her claims just because she said so. "Why should we trust you?"

Annoyance flickered in her eyes as she responded, "I am

not asking you to trust me. I am merely informing you that Caleb needs your help, and quickly."

Roswell frowned, echoing Fredrick's doubts about trusting her too quickly. "How do you know all of this?"

"How I learned it is not important, but just know that I do," she asserted.

"That isn't good enough for me," Roswell said.

The young woman pursed her lips. "Are you two daft?" she asked. "You need to go help Caleb before he is killed."

With a lift of his brow, Fredrick asked, "What if this is a trap?"

"If I wanted you dead, you already would be," she said. "I am just trying to do the right thing here, and you two are making it incredibly difficult to do so."

"We don't even know your name—" Fredrick started.

The young woman cut him off. "Would that truly make a difference?" she asked.

"It would be a start," Fredrick responded.

She stared at him, disbelief etched across her face, as if she couldn't quite fathom his response. He sensed her frustration, but he wasn't ready to trust her. Trust had to be earned, and it was not something he handed out freely.

"I don't have time for this," she declared, her voice laden with exasperation. "If you want to save Caleb, he is at the factory, but I would hurry."

The young woman began to walk away, but Fredrick couldn't let her leave, not without answers. He had too many questions, and he needed to know more. Raising his pistol, he commanded, "Stay where you are."

An amused expression crossed her face. "You intend to shoot me?" she questioned. "The honorable war hero that served right alongside Wellington. You would shoot an unarmed woman?"

"How do I know you aren't armed?" Fredrick asked.

She took a step closer to him, despite having a pistol being pointed at her. Her eyes showed no hint of fear. "I am armed, my lord, but I see no reason to draw my weapon. I know you won't shoot me."

Fredrick tightened his hold on the pistol. "You don't know that for certain."

"Don't I?" she asked. "I have made it a point to learn as much as I could about you." She shifted towards Roswell. "About both of you."

"Why?" Roswell asked.

"It is best that you don't know," she replied. "Quite frankly, we shouldn't even be having this conversation. But I can't, in good conscience, let Caleb die."

Roswell observed her intently and inquired, "Why can't you save him?"

Something resonated deep within her eyes that Fredrick couldn't quite decipher. Regret? Pain? Whatever it was, it seemed oddly familiar.

"I have said enough," she said. "Good day, gentlemen."

The young woman showed no hesitation as she started to walk away, turning her back on them. She had called his bluff. He hadn't intended to shoot her, especially since she didn't pose an immediate threat, but he had hoped for more cooperation.

To his surprise, she suddenly stopped and turned back around. "My name is Simone," she informed them before resuming her departure.

Once she had disappeared into the woodlands, Fredrick returned his pistol to its place and asked, "Should we trust her?"

"Do we have a choice?" Roswell asked.

"That is what I was thinking, as well," Fredrick replied. "We should hurry and go see if Caleb is in any danger."

After they emerged from the woodlands, Fredrick noticed that Anette and Emilia were engaged in conversation as they waited for their return.

A Suitable Fortune

Fredrick accepted the reins from the groom and addressed Emilia. "I do apologize, but Roswell and I have urgent business to attend to. Anette will see you home."

Emilia pressed her lips together as her eyes darted towards the woodlands, as if pondering a riddle. He knew she had questions, but they were questions he could not answer. Not now. Not ever. He couldn't risk Emilia getting involved in his world of espionage. It was far too dangerous for her.

Anette spoke up, assuring Emilia, "I would be happy to see you home."

Roswell mounted his horse and tipped his head at his wife. "I shall be home shortly."

"You better," Anette said. "You made a promise to me that you would always return."

With a warm smile, Roswell replied, "And I intend to honor that promise."

Fredrick knew he was being unfathomably rude to Emilia, but the urgency of the situation, assuming Caleb was indeed in danger, left little room for politeness. He kicked his horse into a run, only slowing once they had left Hyde Park behind.

Navigating through the bustling streets of London proved to be rather difficult, but they moved as quickly as they could. It was a short time later when they arrived at Lord Drycott's factory. In the daylight, the place appeared even more dismal, as if it were a destroyer of dreams.

They had just secured their horses when they could hear a commotion coming from a nearby alleyway. Not sure what they were walking into, they both removed their pistols and cautiously approached the alleyway.

In the dimly lit alley, Fredrick and Roswell came to a halt, peering into the shadows. They witnessed Caleb being held by two burly men, while a third man prepared to strike him again. Caleb's face, swollen and bruised, bore the signs of a severe beating, and he seemed unable to withstand much more of the punishment.

"Stop!" Fredrick ordered as he pointed the pistol at Caleb's attacker. "Let him go."

The assailant reluctantly lowered his fist and turned towards Fredrick. "This does not concern you, bloke."

"It does now," Fredrick asserted.

With a cocky smirk, the man taunted, "You only have two bullets and there are three of us."

Roswell's voice was firm as he interjected, "You're mistaken if you think we need these pistols to deal with you."

"We have a job that we need to finish," the man spat out.

Stepping closer, Fredrick declared, "That job ends now. Let him go and you can walk out of here with your lives."

The man eyed him with a dangerous glint. "I don't take orders from you."

"If you were smart, you would," Fredrick said.

Caleb's attacker studied Fredrick, attempting to discern the sincerity behind his words. Fredrick's resolve was unwavering, and this time, he wasn't bluffing. He had no intention of letting his friend be murdered before his very eyes. He found no pleasure in taking another person's life, but he was prepared to do so to defend Caleb.

The man waved his hand towards the other two attackers and grumbled, "Let him go. We can deal with him later."

The men released Caleb, and he crumpled to his knees, doubling over in pain as he emitted a groan.

Fredrick kept his pistol trained on the men as they filed past him, refusing to grow complacent and turn his back on them. He had little doubt that these men would kill him, and he wasn't about to make that mistake.

Once the men departed from the alley, Roswell lowered his pistol and rushed over to Caleb. "Are you all right?" he asked.

Caleb emitted another groan. "I will be. We need to leave before the men return."

"Can you walk?" Roswell asked.

"Yes," Caleb replied, his words lacking conviction.

Roswell crouched down and assisted him in rising. "Lean on me," he encouraged. "We need to get you to a doctor."

Fredrick exited the alley first, cautiously scanning for potential threats and confirming that the coast was clear. Once he was satisfied that they were alone, he returned to help Roswell support Caleb.

Caleb leaned heavily on them as they made their way towards their horses. It was evident that he was in significant pain with every breath, making Fredrick suspect that his friend might have broken ribs.

After they assisted Caleb onto Fredrick's horse, he took the reins and began to lead the horse away from the factory. They wouldn't be able to move very quickly at the pace they were going, but he knew that Caleb couldn't handle anything more than a walk in his current condition.

Fredrick remained vigilant as they made their way through the dirtied streets of the rookeries. Dressed as gentlemen with fine horses, they naturally stood out. But his mind kept straying to the mysterious young woman that had helped them.

How had Simone known that Caleb was in danger? And more importantly, who was she?

Chapter Twelve

Emilia sat alone at the grand rectangular table in the dining room. Lily had decided it was best if she didn't dine with her, and while Emilia understood her reasonings, she didn't have to like them.

Her gaze drifted down the length of the table and she reminisced about the enjoyable meals shared with the girls back at the boarding school. Their infectious excitement had been rather enjoyable, making her look forward to each and every meal with them.

How she hated to be alone.

Her eyes roamed over the lavishly decorated dining room until they landed on the two liveried footmen who were stationed there. They were both tall, but one had a lean frame, while the other appeared more stocky. They couldn't have been much older than she was, she thought.

The stocky footman's eyes met hers briefly before he quickly averted his gaze.

Before she knew what she was about, she asked, "What is your name?"

He seemed taken back by her question but he answered respectfully, "My name is David, Miss."

"Hello, David," she acknowledged. "How long have you worked here?"

"Three years," he replied promptly.

Sensing that David was somewhat ill at ease, Emilia shifted her attention to the lanky footman. "What is your name?"

The lanky footman straightened up, responding, "Matthew, Miss."

"And how long have you worked here?"

"Two years," he replied.

"Do you both enjoy working here?" she questioned.

The footmen responded in perfect unison, "Yes, Miss."

Emilia didn't have any expectations when conversing with the footmen; perhaps she simply desired a brief respite from her own thoughts.

Was this to be her life? She was surrounded by servants, but she had never felt more alone. This wasn't the life she had envisioned, merely waiting to be entertained. She craved something more, a chance to forge her own path, which was something that Fredrick had constantly encouraged her to pursue.

Fredrick.

An image of him came to her mind and she allowed herself to dwell on it. She never felt alone when she was with him. Just being in his presence lifted her spirits up and she couldn't help but wonder if she held a special place in his heart. He had an uncanny ability to read her in a way that no one had before, making him unlike anyone she had ever known.

She had developed these pesky feelings for him; feelings that would never be reciprocated. She may be an heiress, but he was an earl. Even if he ever decided to marry, despite his insistence on remaining unwed, it would never be to someone that courted scandal wherever she went.

Dalby stepped into the dining room and informed her, "Miss Clarissa Livingston is in the drawing room, Miss."

"Thank you," Emilia said as she rose. "Has the coach been brought around?"

"It has, and there are four footmen that will accompany you, per your request," Dalby replied. "Will there be anything else?"

"Not at this time," Emilia responded.

As the butler left the dining room, she took a deep breath as she tried to prepare herself. She had convinced Clarissa to accompany her on a visit to the boarding school today, even though she anticipated her half-sister's snippety remarks. Emilia hoped that by seeing the girls and comprehending their dire circumstances, Clarissa's heart might soften and she would become more empathetic.

Emilia made her way towards the drawing room and saw Clarissa was sitting on the settee. Her half-sister was adorned in a fancy gown, complete with an ornate hat embellished with peacock feathers. She looked as if she were headed to a social event with the *ton* rather than to the rookeries.

Clarissa's critical gaze immediately settled upon Emilia, who was wearing a modest green gown. Disapproval radiated from her half-sister's expression.

Feeling a need to explain, Emilia shared, "It is the simplest gown that I own."

Clarissa merely nodded and remarked, "Yes, quite simple."

"I didn't wish for the girls to be uncomfortable around me by wearing one of the gowns that Lady Roswell loaned me," Emilia explained.

"I am not concerned by that, but I do hope that the girls will keep their grubby fingers off of my gown. It is far too fine to be dirtied," Clarissa said haughtily.

Dalby stepped into the room with a tray. "A letter was just delivered for you," he announced.

Emilia approached him and accepted the letter. After she

unfolded it, she gasped as she read the contents of the message.

Rising, Clarissa asked, "What is wrong?"

She lowered the paper to her side and responded, "Lady Roswell won't be joining us today because she is tending to her brother who was attacked yesterday by a group of ruffians."

"We can't go into the rookeries, then," Clarissa declared. "If the streets of London aren't safe for a gentleman, they are utterly unsafe for ladies."

"We will have four footmen who will be accompanying us," Emilia said. "We do not need to fear, especially once we are inside of the boarding school."

"How long do you intend for us to stay at this boarding school? After all, you may be accustomed to living in squalor, but I am not," Clarissa remarked in her usual condescending manner.

Emilia worked to keep the displeasure off her face. She had no desire to tour the boarding school with only Clarissa, but she had no valid excuse to cancel the trip. Furthermore, she needed to meet the headmistress, Mrs. Anderson, and the girls. She simply hoped that Clarissa would behave on this outing, and refrain from belittling anyone.

"We shall stay as long as needed," Emilia said. "If you do not wish to come—"

Clarissa waved her hand dismissively in front of her, stilling her words. "I told you that I would come, and I meant it."

With a gesture towards the entry hall, Emilia asked, "Shall we depart then?"

"Not without you putting on a hat first," Clarissa replied. "A lady is never seen in public without a hat."

As if on cue, Dalby entered the drawing room with a straw hat and extended it towards her.

Emilia smiled. "Thank you," she acknowledged.

She placed the hat on her head and secured the string under her chin. "Good enough," she muttered.

They both exited the townhouse and stepped into the waiting coach. As the coach rocked forward, Emilia gazed out the window, unsure of what to say to Clarissa. They had never been alone with each other before, and the situation was somewhat unsettling. Did she dare ask about their accommodation in Cheapside?

Emilia wished that Lily was here, but she had gone ahead to the boarding school.

Clarissa's voice interrupted her thoughts. "I am glad that we got a moment alone because I wished to speak to you about something."

With a hint of hesitation, Emilia inquired, "Which is?"

"My dowry," Clarissa replied. "My father informed me that I would receive a dowry of twenty thousand pounds, but the solicitor didn't mention this amount during the reading of the will."

"Did you speak to Mr. Rymer about this?"

Clarissa shook her head. "No, but Calvin did," she replied. "Mr. Rymer instructed him to discuss it with you."

Emilia wasn't entirely certain how to respond, lacking all the facts. "I will discuss this matter with Mr. Rymer at once."

"I do appreciate that since my dowry is the only chance at securing a respectable match," Clarissa said with a hint of bitterness. "Ever since I was declared illegitimate, the doors that were once open to me have now been firmly shut."

Now the conversation turned awkward, and Emilia didn't know what she could say or do to appease the situation.

After a long, uncomfortable moment, Clarissa spoke up. "I'm sorry. That wasn't fair of me to say since it wasn't your fault that our father did that to me."

Emilia wasn't without compassion for Clarissa's predicament, understanding how difficult it must have been for her to leave behind her former life of privilege. While Emilia's status had been elevated in high Society, Clarissa had been cast aside as an outcast. However, she wasn't about to feel guilty for the inheritance she'd received. Her father's dying wish was to right a wrong.

The coach came to a stop in front of a nondescript two-level red brick building. A footman exited his perch and approached the main door to inform the headmistress of their arrival.

The door opened, revealing a slender, brown-haired woman. Her hair was neatly tied in a tight chignon at the nape of her neck, and she wore a brown dress that did little to enhance her figure. Her back was rigid, and her face was one of solemnity.

"That is the headmistress?" Clarissa asked.

Emilia frowned slightly. "I believe so."

The footman opened the door and assisted them onto the recently swept pavement.

Approaching them, the woman asked, "Miss Sutherland?"

"Yes," Emilia confirmed.

A warm, welcoming smile lit up the woman's face, completely transforming it and putting Emilia at ease. "It is so wonderful that you decided to visit us today. The girls have talked about little else since they heard the news. They have never had the chance to meet a real lady before."

The woman continued. "My apologies. Introductions are in order," she said. "My name is Mrs. Anderson and I am your headmistress."

"It is a pleasure to meet you," Emilia responded before gesturing towards Clarissa. "This is Miss Clarissa Livingston."

"You are most welcome, Miss Clarissa," Mrs. Anderson gushed as she led them inside.

The entry hall was modest, and the ivory-papered walls were adorned with a floral design. A set of stairs was positioned along one wall, leading to the upper level.

Mrs. Anderson led them into a room adjacent to the

entry hall, which was set up as her office. A desk occupied the center of the small, square room, with two chairs facing it.

The headmistress took her seat behind the desk and gestured towards the two chairs. "Please, have a seat. We have much to discuss," she said.

Emilia settled into one of the chairs and noticed that Clarissa looked deucedly uncomfortable as she sat down. "How are the girls?" she asked.

That was the right thing to ask because the smile returned to Mrs. Anderson's face. "They are just delightful. Your father selected girls that truly need our help. Many of them came to us with tattered clothing and very few possessions. We have since clothed them and fed them."

"That is wonderful to hear," Emilia said.

"You are truly making a difference in these girls' lives and I am grateful to be part of it," Mrs. Anderson responded. "Your father would be very proud of what you are accomplishing here."

Clarissa rolled her eyes. "I daresay you are overexaggerating Emilia's importance here, considering all she is doing is taking these poor girls off the street."

If Mrs. Anderson was taken aback by Clarissa's remark, she didn't show it. Instead, she replied calmly, "Miss Sutherland is doing much more than that. She is giving these girls hope for a brighter future. Once they complete their studies, they could become a lady's maid or possibly a housekeeper. She has opened doors that once were closed for these girls."

Upon hearing the headmistress' words, Clarissa fell silent, appearing to contemplate the significance of what had just been spoken.

With a glance at the wall clock, Mrs. Anderson asked, "Would you care to join us for our midday meal?"

"I would like that very much," Emilia replied.

Rising, Mrs. Anderson said, "I should warn you that the

girls can be rather talkative during meals but I wouldn't have it any other way."

"Neither would I," Emilia agreed as she also rose from her seat.

Noticing that Clarissa hadn't risen, Emilia questioned, "Is everything all right?"

Clarissa looked up at her with a bemused look on her face. "Yes, I was just thinking, which is never a good thing." She let out a light laugh, but it didn't sound particularly convincing. "Shall we go meet the girls?"

"Yes, assuming all is well with you," Emilia responded.

With a haughty tilt of her chin, Clarissa stated, "You do not need to concern yourself with me. Nothing is wrong with me, and you will be wise to remember that."

Emilia couldn't help but wonder why she bothered trying to decipher Clarissa's ever-changing moods. She thought she had glimpsed something, perhaps a crack in her haughty façade, but it appeared she had been mistaken.

But one thing was for certain- being at this boarding school felt a bit like being home. She would do whatever it took for this boarding school to succeed.

With the morning sun streaming in through the windows, Fredrick sat at his mother's bedside as she slept. He was a coward. It hurt him not to be recognized by his own mother. So he had waited until she was asleep to visit. Which was becoming much more often. Her body was withering away, right in front of him, and he knew he could do nothing about it.

It wasn't his mother's fault that her mind was slipping, but he wished he could have one conversation with her that wasn't clouded in confusion. It would have been different if he had returned home sooner from the war, but he was doing what his conscience had dictated. He had fought with a purpose until he did something that was unthinkable. Unforgivable.

The image of Timmy came to his mind, and he tried to banish it. But he was unable to do so. Timmy's eyes seemed to bore into his mind, reminding him of what he had done. How could he have killed someone so young? He had stripped Timmy of his future.

The door opened and Roswell stepped into the room. In a hushed voice, he said, "I just received word that Caleb is awake."

Fredrick rose and approached his brother. "Let's go," he said. They had much they needed to discuss with Caleb, and he wasn't getting much done here anyways.

After they departed from their mother's bedchamber, Roswell asked, "How is she?"

"The same, I suppose," Fredrick replied as they started walking down the corridor. "She was asleep the entire time I sat by her bed."

Roswell frowned. "She is sleeping more and more now. I can't help but wonder if the end is near."

"The doctor believes so, but I am not quite ready to say goodbye," Fredrick said.

"Neither am I, but I am just a stranger to her now," Roswell admitted.

"As am I."

Roswell's eyes held compassion. "It is a terrible feeling to be forgotten, but I have reconciled with the fact that it is not Mother's fault."

"I just wish I had come home from the war earlier," Fredrick said.

"No, you don't," Roswell countered. "Sometimes, I feel that your heart is still with the war effort on the Continent."

Fredrick grew quiet. "You aren't wrong. I miss my comrades," he admitted. "I am doing nothing of importance here, while my friends are risking their lives to keep England safe. I feel like a failure."

"I daresay that Caleb would disagree with you since you saved him from certain death yesterday," Roswell remarked.

They started descending the stairs when Fredrick admitted, "I don't know where I belong right now. I feel lost, alone, and all I feel is misery."

"You need a wife."

Fredrick looked heavenward at that ridiculous remark. "I need no such thing. In fact, that would only complicate matters."

Stopping in the entry hall, Roswell turned to face him. "I used to be where you are and Anette helped me through the pain. She gave me a second chance at life, and I do not intend to take it for granted."

"I appreciate what you are trying to do, but I do not want to take a wife," he asserted.

"You need an heir."

With a shake of his head, Fredrick responded, "You are my heir."

"No offense, but I do not want to be a marquess. I would prefer if you settled down and had a bushel of children."

Carson entered the entry hall and announced, "The coach is out front, my lords."

They left the townhouse and entered the coach. It was only a short distance to Caleb's townhouse and it wasn't long before they were standing in front of the main door.

The door was opened, and the butler greeted them politely. "Good morning," he said, opening the door wide.

"Where is my wife?" Roswell asked.

"She is in the parlor with her brother, Mr. Bolingbroke," the butler informed them. "If you wait here, I will announce you."

"That won't be necessary," Roswell responded, as he started towards the parlor.

Fredrick followed his brother into the room, attempting not to react when he noticed Caleb sitting on a settee. His face was terribly bruised and swollen.

Anette had risen from the settee when she saw Roswell. "My love biscuit," she greeted. "I see that you got my message."

"I did," Roswell said as he warmly greeted his wife with a kiss on her cheek.

Fredrick approached Caleb and asked, "How are you faring?"

Caleb shifted in his seat, appearing uncomfortable. "I will survive."

"You look awful," Fredrick remarked.

"I feel awful," Caleb groaned. "I am just grateful that you both arrived when you did. If you hadn't, I would be dead." He paused. "How did you know I needed your help?"

Fredrick exchanged a look with Roswell before revealing, "Simone told us that your situation was dire."

Caleb gave him a blank look. "Who is Simone?"

"You don't know?" Roswell asked. "We just had assumed you were acquainted with her."

"I am not," Caleb responded.

Fredrick crossed his arms over his chest. "Do you know how Lord Drycott discovered your true identity?"

Caleb shook his head. "No. I have been racking my brain all morning, but I don't remember making a misstep."

Their conversation came to an abrupt halt when Lady Oxley entered the room. "Fredrick. Roswell. What are you doing here?"

Roswell turned towards Lady Oxley. "We just came to speak to Caleb."

"Caleb is in no condition to have visitors," Lady Oxley said. "Besides, the doctor will be returning shortly to examine him. I must insist that you let Caleb recover."

Anette spoke up. "They were only here to offer encouragement."

Lady Oxley's demeanor softened. "My apologies," she said. "I'm afraid I am a little uneasy ever since Caleb returned home in such a state. The streets of London are far too dangerous and I can't believe how close we came to losing Caleb."

"You have no reason to apologize, my lady," Fredrick acknowledged. "We will come back later after Caleb has had some rest."

"Thank you," Lady Oxley said.

Roswell slipped his arm around Anette's waist. "If you don't mind, I believe I will stay with my wife for a little longer."

"Not at all," Fredrick responded. "I have work that I must see to anyways."

Fredrick departed the townhouse and stepped into the coach. As he traveled back to his own townhouse, he noticed that they were approaching Emilia's townhouse.

On an impulse he couldn't quite explain, he pounded on the top of the coach with his fist and the coach came to a stop. He exited the coach and approached the main door of Emilia's townhouse, where he knocked. The door was promptly opened.

"Good morning, my lord," the butler greeted.

"Is Miss Sutherland available to receive callers?"

The butler nodded and held the door open wide. "Please come in, and I will announce you."

Fredrick stepped into the entry hall, suddenly feeling rather foolish. Why had he come to call on Emilia? He needed to review the accounts and he didn't have time to lollygag. So why had he thought this was a good idea?

Perhaps he should leave before the butler announced him.

As the butler walked towards the drawing room, Fredrick called out after him. "Wait," he ordered.

The butler halted and turned back around. "Yes, my lord?"

"I've changed my mind," Fredrick informed him. "I'm afraid I must depart at once."

The butler's expression remained stoic, seemingly unaffected by Fredrick's indecision. "Very well."

Emilia appeared in the doorway of the drawing room, wearing a puzzled expression. "Do you not wish to at least say hello?" she asked.

Fredrick felt like an utter fool. What was he doing here? But he already knew the answer. He had wanted to see Emilia.

He bowed. "I apologize for the intrusion, but I forgot that I must tend to the accounts immediately," he explained.

Emilia approached him and smiled. And that one simple smile seemed to brighten his very soul. "Well, it was good to see you, even if only for a brief moment."

Fredrick knew that he should leave, but he remained rooted in his spot. What if he just tarried for a moment? That one thought had great appeal, but he had already given the pitiful excuse that he had to leave to work on the accounts.

"Have you heard how Caleb is faring?" Emilia asked.

"I just came from his townhouse and he is in bad shape," Fredrick responded. "But he will recover."

Emilia's expression revealed her concern. "When Anette sent word, I will admit that I have thought of little else," she said. "To think he was attacked by ruffians. What a senseless act."

"It was," he agreed. "Did you have a chance to visit your boarding school yesterday?"

The smile returned to Emilia's lips. "Yes, and everything was just perfect. Even the headmistress, Mrs. Anderson, exceeded my expectations."

"Did Clarissa accompany you?"

"She did," Emilia confirmed, but her words trailed off. "However, Clarissa was rather quiet after we left the boarding school. I'm not sure what happened, but something about the tour seemed to affect her."

Fredrick wasn't quite convinced of that. Clarissa was not known for her selfless actions. But what she hoped to obtain from Emilia, he couldn't say.

Emilia put her hand up. "I know what you are going to say," she said. "I am being cautious around Clarissa. Although, I hope she is being genuine."

"I just don't want to see you get hurt," Fredrick remarked.

"That is kind of you, but I can take care of myself," Emilia said. "I have been on my own for so long that I sometimes forget what it is like to be cared for."

Fredrick could hear the sadness in her voice, and it tugged at his heartstrings. He understood her feelings all too well, but he didn't want her to experience even a hint of sadness.

He took a step closer to her, though he still maintained a proper distance. "You aren't alone, not anymore. I am here."

She held his gaze, her eyes searching his. "For that, I am most grateful," she said in a soft voice.

As they stared at one another, Fredrick found himself entranced by her gaze. Her eyes were green, with intriguing brown flecks within them. They were unique, just as Emilia was.

Realizing the silence had gone on long enough, Fredrick blurted out the first thing that came to his mind. "Have you been to the Royal Menagerie yet?"

A slight furrow appeared between Emilia's brows. "No, I haven't."

"We should go together," Fredrick suggested. "I haven't been in quite some time, and you must go now that you are in London."

"I would like that, very much," Emilia stated.

Fredrick nodded. "This afternoon, then?" he asked as he took a step back.

"Yes, that would work nicely."

"Good, good," Fredrick muttered. Why couldn't he stop talking? He prided himself on maintaining his composure even in the most challenging situations, yet a simple conversation with Emilia seemed to reduce him to a blathering idiot. "I should go."

Emilia grinned and he marveled at how effortlessly she could smile. "I shall see you later today, my lord."

"Yes, you most assuredly will."

With those words, Fredrick made his exit from the townhouse, wondering what had just transpired. Why had he committed himself to taking Emilia to the Royal Menagerie? That was the last thing that he had time for. So why did he find himself looking forward to it?

Chapter Thirteen

Emilia wandered around the ballroom as she tried to envision how it would appear when the time came for her grand ball. The decorations had been ordered and the invitations had been sent out. It was only a matter of days now until she would see if anyone would actually attend.

Anette was insistent that people would come, but Emilia feared it was more for curiosity's sake than anything else. And she had no desire to be a public spectacle.

What if she tripped on the hem of her ballgown, which was currently being commissioned? Or what if she said something that was intolerably stupid?

Dalby entered the room and announced, "Mr. Rymer has arrived and I showed him to your study."

"Thank you," Emilia responded as she made her way across the ballroom.

Once she had arrived at the study, she saw Mr. Rymer was standing in the center of the room, reviewing a piece of paper.

"Mr. Rymer," she greeted. "Thank you for coming so soon."

He offered her a kind smile. "It is my pleasure."

Emilia went to sit on a settee and gestured towards a chair. "Please have a seat," she encouraged. "I wish to speak to you about Clarissa's dowry."

The solicitor's smile dimmed as he lowered himself onto the proffered chair. "I'm afraid she lost the dowry when she was disinherited by her father."

"She wasn't entirely disinherited because he did make some provisions for her and Calvin," Emilia said.

"Yes, but Miss Clarissa is, and always will be, illegitimate," Mr. Rymer remarked. "I doubt a dowry will help her find a suitable match."

"Clarissa is of the mind that she could make a respectable match, on the assumption that she had a dowry," Emilia said. "Was her dowry truly twenty thousand pounds?"

Mr. Rymer bobbed his head. "It was," he confirmed, "and Miss Clarissa had no shortage of suitors. In fact, there was a rumor that she had an understanding with Lord Lowesby."

"Why do you suppose my father didn't specify her dowry in the will?" Emilia asked.

"I can't say, but I do know that he was rather frustrated with Miss Clarissa and Calvin towards the end," Mr. Rymer revealed. "He felt they were entirely too spoiled."

Emilia sat back in her seat as she pondered Mr. Rymer's words. There was no denying that Clarissa was entitled, but she was also aware of the harsh realities faced by unmarried women. Emilia had been raised to fend for herself, but Clarissa hadn't. Everything had been handed to her. How was Clarissa supposed to navigate life without a husband to provide for her?

"I would like to provide Clarissa with a dowry," Emilia said.

Mr. Rymer's brow shot up. "If you do so, that money will come out of your own inheritance. You do understand that?"

"I do, but if there is even a chance that Clarissa can marry well, I want to give her that opportunity," Emilia explained.

"That is most kind of you, but I fear that your generosity would not have been reciprocated if the situation was reversed," Mr. Rymer remarked.

Emilia laughed. "I have no doubt it wouldn't have been reciprocated, but Clarissa and Calvin are the only family I have. That may not mean anything to them, but it does to me."

"I just hope that they don't take advantage of your generosity," Mr. Rymer said as he rose. "I will see to the necessary documents. Would you like me to inform Miss Clarissa, or will you see to that?"

Rising, Emilia responded, "I will inform her the next time we visit the boarding school."

"Miss Clarissa has agreed to go back?" Mr. Rymer asked in disbelief.

"She did," Emilia confirmed.

"Well, wonders never cease," he declared. "I wouldn't have thought Miss Clarissa would have gone anywhere near the boarding school."

"I do think there is more to Clarissa than she is letting on," Emilia said.

Emilia could sense Mr. Rymer's skepticism in his expression, but instead of arguing with her, he simply tipped his head. "Good day, Miss." With that, the solicitor headed back to his office, leaving her to contemplate her decision to provide Clarissa with a dowry.

She was sure that she was doing the right thing. Well, mostly sure.

Lily stepped into the room and said, "Dalby just informed me that Lord Chatsworth has arrived and is waiting for you in the drawing room."

Emilia felt her heart begin to race at the mere mention of Fredrick's name. She reached up and smoothed back her elegantly coiffed hair. "Do I look all right?" she asked. "Is anything amiss?"

Her friend gave her an understanding look. "You look perfect. Just perfect."

"Am I being silly?" Emilia asked. "Lord Chatsworth doesn't care what I look like."

"I think he does."

Emilia shook her head. "We are friends, even he has said so," she said. "I still find it quite extraordinary that I am friends with an earl."

Lily's lips twitched. "A very handsome earl."

"Is he handsome?" Emilia asked. "I haven't noticed."

"Then you would be blind," Lily joked.

Walking towards the door, Emilia said, "I mustn't keep Fredrick waiting for too long. He is a very busy man."

"Fredrick, is it?" Lily inquired.

Emilia could hear the teasing tone in her friend's voice but she didn't dare explain what she was feeling. In truth, she wasn't entirely sure herself. She held Fredrick in high regard, but it was preposterous to entertain the idea that he might feel the same about her. Besides, she didn't want to do anything that would risk their friendship.

"Yes, Fredrick gave me leave to," Emilia explained. "Now, if you will excuse me, I mustn't keep him waiting."

Lily laughed. "You can go. But do not think for a moment that this conversation is over."

Emilia assumed as much but she didn't feel the need for a response as she left the study. She had taken great care with her appearance in anticipation of her outing with Fredrick. She wore a lovely pale blue gown, its net overlay adorned with embroidered flowers. It was one of the finest gowns that Anette had graciously loaned to her. A coral necklace hung around her neck, and she even put a little rouge on her cheeks.

As she approached the drawing room, a mix of nervousness and excitement stirred within her at the thought of seeing Fredrick. This would not do. He was her friend, and she had no right to harbor feelings for him. But she couldn't quite convince her treacherous heart of this.

She entered the room and discovered Fredrick was not alone. Lord and Lady Roswell were standing next to him, engaged in conversation.

Emilia felt a stab of disappointment at seeing Lord and Lady Roswell. Not because she didn't enjoy their company, but she had been looking forward to spending time alone with Fredrick.

Fredrick turned his attention towards her and offered a courteous bow. "Miss Sutherland," he greeted.

She dropped into a curtsy. "My lord," she murmured.

Anette perused the length of her and said, "You look absolutely lovely. That gown suits you rather perfectly."

Emilia, holding out the sides of her skirt, expressed her gratitude. "I'm truly grateful for your generosity in lending me your gowns while mine are being commissioned."

"You are more than welcome. Besides, it was the least I could do," Anette remarked.

Fredrick cleared his throat and met Emilia's gaze, his eyes holding approval. "I must concur with Anette," he said. "You are looking enchanting."

And with those words, Emilia felt more beautiful than she had ever felt before.

Emilia worked hard to keep the blush from forming on her cheeks. It would do no good to show her emotions. She must hide them or else Fredrick would see right through her.

"Shall we travel to the Royal Menagerie?" Lord Roswell asked.

Anette nodded. "I think that is a lovely idea, Husband."

Fredrick approached Emilia and offered his arm. "May I escort you to the coach?"

With a gracious smile, Emilia replied, "Yes, I would enjoy that greatly." She hoped her eagerness to be close to him didn't appear too obvious.

They left the drawing room and made their way to the waiting coach outside. Once they were all situated, with Fredrick by her side, the coach merged into traffic.

Emilia couldn't help but inquire, "How is Caleb faring?"

Both Lord and Lady Roswell grew solemn at her question. "He is in pain, but he will recover," Lord Roswell explained. "He took quite the beating."

"I am sorry to hear that," Emilia said.

"I wasn't sure if I wanted to leave his side, but Fredrick was quite insistent that we join you at the menagerie," Anette shared.

Fredrick spoke up. "That is only because Caleb didn't need you to fuss over him. He has a mother that can do that."

Lord Roswell reached for his wife's hand. "Fredrick is right. It is a good thing that we are away, even if it is just for a few hours."

"I just worry about Caleb," Anette sighed.

"I know, my love, and that is why I love you so much," Lord Roswell remarked.

Emilia didn't quite know how she felt that Anette had shared that Fredrick had been insistent that they join them. Did Fredrick not want to spend time alone with her? Or was he just simply trying to help his brother and sister-in-law? Regardless of the reason, it seemed to be further proof that Fredrick harbored no romantic feelings for her.

A brief silence descended over their conversation before Anette shifted her gaze towards Emilia. "Do you want to hear something utterly terrifying?"

Her curiosity was piqued. "I do."

Anette gestured animatedly with her hands as she shared, "When I was younger, the menagerie had a monkey room, where the creatures roamed freely. On one occasion, the monkeys conspired against me and all threw their excrement at me. It was terrifying, and all Caleb did was laugh. It was awful."

In an amused voice, Lord Roswell interjected, "That does sound like Caleb."

Anette continued. "It took many baths before I felt clean again. Fortunately, the monkey room has since been shut down and good riddance."

"That is because the monkeys hurt someone. Not because they threw excrement at you," Lord Roswell clarified.

Turning towards her husband, Anette asked, "You would have protected me from the monkeys, wouldn't you have?"

Lord Roswell puffed out his chest. "The monkeys wouldn't have stood a chance against me."

"My hero," Anette gushed affectionately as she leaned into her husband.

Emilia thought it was sweet how much Lord and Lady Roswell appeared to be deeply in love. Their affection was evident, and they seemed to only have eyes for each other. It made her hope that one day she might find a love like that. If she did, she doubted that she would be as opposed to marriage as she was now.

She snuck a glance at Fredrick and noticed his stoic expression. She had seen him smile and even laugh before, but there was a sadness to him that she saw lurking within. How she wanted to help him, but it wasn't her place to do so. She may be his friend, but he still kept a part of himself hidden from her.

How could she get him to trust her, and perhaps, confide in her? Was that even possible? She truly hoped so because she cared for him far too much to let him continue suffering in silence. She would find a way to help him, even if it meant chipping away at the walls he had erected around his heart.

Fredrick led Emilia down the row of cages in the

menagerie. Her eyes would widen with amazement each time she spotted a new beast, and she gestured excitedly, her face lighting up with a bright smile. He found her genuine enthusiasm enchanting. Who would have guessed that Emilia had such a fondness for these exotic animals?

He glanced ahead and saw Anette and Roswell engaged in conversation with the guide, patiently waiting for them as they leisurely strolled past each cage. He had no intention of hurrying Emilia along; he was quite content to linger as long as she desired.

Emilia came to a stop in front of one of the cages, her eyes searching for the animal inside. When she spotted it, she gasped in delight. "It is a tiger!" she exclaimed. "I have only seen sketches of them before. I never thought I would see a real one up close."

She took a step closer to the cage, but Fredrick extended his hand to gently stop her. "I wouldn't go any closer," he cautioned.

"You are right, of course," Emilia said, her gaze remaining fixated on the magnificent creature. "I wish I had my sketchbook."

"Can you draw?"

Emilia nodded. "I can," she replied. "The boarding school was surrounded by woodlands, and on my days off, I would venture deep into the woods and sketch for hours."

"That sounds rather peaceful," Fredrick commented.

"It was," Emilia agreed before moving towards the next cage.

Fredrick clasped his hands behind his back. "What else did you do on your days off?" he asked, finding himself curious as to how she spent her time.

"I didn't get very many days off, mind you," Emilia began, "but sometimes I would travel to where my mother was buried just to tell her that I was all right."

He furrowed his brow. "Why would you tell her such a thing?"

Emilia turned to face him, her gaze sincere. "By saying it out loud, I hoped to convince myself of such a thing."

"Just by saying such a thing doesn't make it come true," Fredrick argued.

"True, but I do believe the more times you say something, the more likely it will become true," Emilia said.

"That is poppycock," Fredrick said.

She smiled. "I see that you are a naysayer."

"One cannot simply will oneself to be happy."

"I never said anything about happiness," Emilia said. "I can have everything that I need, but nothing that I want."

Fredrick tilted his head slightly. "What is it that you truly desire?"

Emilia averted her eyes, her fingers tracing the edge of her skirt. "Forget I said anything. It is not worth discussing."

He gently laid his hand on her arm. "I'm afraid you have me intrigued," he said. "What is it that you want?"

Emilia glanced up at him, her gaze vulnerable. "I want acceptance, to be loved. But it often feels like no matter where I go, I'm destined to fall short."

"What truly matters is that you accept yourself for who you are, and not concern yourself with how others perceive you," Fredrick advised.

"Says the rich lord," she joked.

He chuckled. "I see your point, but I do not agree with it," he said. "Are you at least enjoying yourself here?"

That was the right thing to say because a smile appeared on her lips. "I do not think I will ever tire of seeing the elephant."

"Yes, Chunee is rather popular amongst the visitors," Fredrick said. "He is often paraded in the streets just outside of the menagerie to attract guests."

"Can you imagine ever trying to ride an elephant?" she asked.

Fredrick shook his head. "I have no desire to ever ride an elephant and neither should you. It would be far too dangerous."

"I appreciate your concern, but I doubt I will ever be given such an opportunity," she said. "I can barely ride sidesaddle."

"You appeared to do just fine when we went on our ride through Hyde Park."

"That is because you seem to overlook what is right in front of you," Emilia said, her gaze turning to the many cages that lined the path.

Fredrick took a moment to appreciate her lovely face and the graceful curve of her neck. He had a feeling she might not fully grasp her own beauty.

Anette's voice came from up ahead. "Fredrick. Emilia," she called out. "The guide has agreed to show us the hippopotamus, but we must go now. If we wait too long, we will miss the feeding."

"I'm not quite sure what a hippopotamus is, but I am curious to find out," Emilia responded before she quickened her pace towards Anette.

Fredrick easily caught up with them and walked alongside Emilia. Her expressions and quick steps made it clear that she was excited to see the hippopotamus.

Once they arrived at the hippopotamus' enclosure, they watched from a safe distance as two handlers dropped an enormous amount of food into the cage from a tall perch.

Emilia stared at the massive, barrel-shaped beast in disbelief. "Look at its short legs but enormous mouth," she said, pointing at it. "It almost seems comical."

"Despite their size, hippopotamuses are incredibly agile in the water, and can even outrun a person on land," Anette shared.

"Truly?" Emilia repeated.

"Yes, which makes them incredibly dangerous," Anette said. "In fact, a hippopotamus' jaw can tear a person in half."

"Dear heavens. How do you know so much about hippopotamuses?" Emilia questioned.

Roswell interjected, a smile playing on his lips, "That is an excellent question."

"I researched everything I could get my hands on for the book I wanted to write," Anette shared. "Would you care to hear about their mating rituals?"

"No, she most assuredly would not," Fredrick stated.

Emilia laughed. "I must agree with Fredrick on this. I see no reason why I would need to know about their mating habits."

"Pity," Anette said.

They watched the hippopotamus for a short time before they continued on to the next enclosure.

Emilia grew silent for a long moment. "Do you think the animals are happy?" she questioned.

Fredrick considered the question before replying, "I doubt it. They are confined in cages, with no chance of escaping. It can't be much of a life."

"How awful," Emilia muttered.

As they continued walking side by side, both lost in their own thoughts, Fredrick found himself missing the sound of Emilia's voice.

"Are you enjoying the Season?" he asked.

"I suppose I am, but that is only because of your and Anette's efforts," Emilia replied. "If it weren't for you two, I wouldn't have left my townhouse yet."

"You are not giving yourself enough credit," Fredrick said.

Emilia looked at him with a thoughtful expression and asked, "May I ask you a question?"

"That is only fair since I asked you one."

"What is war like?"

Fredrick was taken aback. How did he answer such a question? He decided to offer an honest response, recognizing that Emilia meant no harm. "It is hell on earth," he admitted. He paused. "But I do not wish to talk about the war."

"Why is that?" she pressed.

"There is no good that comes from speaking of the war," Fredrick said, his voice growing tight. "People die, and we must move on until it is our turn to die."

Roswell's voice interrupted their conversation from behind them. "That is rather morbid, Brother. Is it not?"

Fredrick felt an unexpected wave of frustration. He hadn't realized that Roswell and Anette had been eavesdropping on their conversation, which only made him more annoyed. He didn't want to talk about the war, not with anyone, least of all Emilia. She was good and kind, and he was not. Quite frankly, he questioned why he even associated with her when she deserved someone better.

"No, it is all right," Emilia defended. "I was just curious. I shouldn't have asked."

Now Fredrick felt like a jackanapes. Emilia didn't deserve his ill treatment, and he cursed himself for it. The turmoil inside him only grew stronger, manifesting in clammy hands and shortness of breath. His chest pounded, and he couldn't seem to regain control.

Concern was evident in Emilia's eyes as she looked at him. "Are you well, my lord?" she asked as she stopped and turned to face him.

"No," he managed to respond in a shaky voice.

Emilia took a step closer, her voice soothing. "Focus on my voice and take deep breaths," she encouraged. "It will be all right. Trust me."

Slowly, his breathing returned to normal, and he felt much better, drawing comfort from Emilia's presence. "Thank you," he said.

"My mother used to get similar episodes," Emilia shared. "I learned at a young age how to soothe her."

"I haven't had one of those episodes since I found Timmy..." His voice came to an abrupt stop as the name slipped out.

"Who is Timmy?" Roswell asked.

In response, Fredrick's tone was unwavering, "No one I care to discuss."

Roswell seemed like he wanted to press the issue, but thankfully he dropped it. Instead, he suggested, "We should return home before it gets too late."

"That is a wise idea," Anette agreed.

"Fredrick?" Roswell questioned.

He nodded. "Yes, we do not wish to keep the ladies out too late," he said.

Emilia's eyes betrayed her worry. "Are you sure you are all right?" she asked. "We can stay longer."

"Do not fuss over me," Fredrick said, his words coming out harsher than he had intended.

A look of hurt flashed on her delicate features. "As you wish," she said, turning away from him.

Closing his eyes, Fredrick felt like a complete fool. He had been unkind to someone who had only tried to help. How could he have done such a thing?

But he knew why. He was broken, and he knew that nothing and no one could ever put him back together. Although he was deeply touched by Emilia's concern, he couldn't let her get any closer to the chaos that raged within him.

It was best for him to be alone. That way, he believed he couldn't cause harm to anyone else.

Roswell approached him and in a hushed voice chided, "That was poorly done on your part."

"I know," Fredrick said. He understood he couldn't defend

his actions. He was in the wrong, but that did not change his resolve.

His brother sighed. "Come on, then. We should hurry if we want to catch up to the ladies."

Fredrick trailed behind his brother, knowing that a life without Emilia in it would be miserable for him. But what choice did he have?

Chapter Fourteen

Emilia sat in bed, a book in her hands, though her thoughts were far from the pages in front of her. Her thoughts kept straying towards Fredrick and the events at the Royal Menagerie. She desired nothing more than to understand him better, to gain his trust and to help him.

The intensity of her emotions burned within her, and she couldn't help but feel as if he needed her assistance, even if he might never hold her in high regard. He was her friend, and that meant something to her, especially since she didn't have many of those in her life.

But how could she help him? That answer kept eluding her. She knew nothing about war and the devastating toll it took on its soldiers.

The door opened and Lily stepped into the room with a cheerful greeting. "Good morning! I see that you are finally awake."

"I have been awake for some time," Emilia responded.

Lily went to the wardrobe and retrieved a pale yellow gown. "I received word that some of your new gowns will be arriving in two days' time, including your ballgown."

"That is wonderful news," Emilia said.

"I thought you would approve of that," Lily stated. "Shall we dress you so I can depart for the boarding school?"

Emilia placed the book on the table next to the bed. "I do wish that you wouldn't go alone to the boarding school."

"No one gives me much heed," Lily responded. "Besides, I enjoy being at the boarding school far more than this townhouse." She stopped and winced. "I'm sorry. That came out wrong. I just tire of how the other servants look at me. I don't quite fit in anywhere."

With an understanding nod, Emilia said, "I know the feeling."

Lily approached the bed, holding up the gown. "Poor heiress," she teased with a smile.

Emilia returned her smile. "I know I have no right to complain…"

"No, you don't."

"… but I just wish I felt like I truly belonged somewhere." She sighed. "I must sound utterly ridiculous."

"You do, but I still claim you as my friend."

Emilia swung her legs over the side of the bed and stood up. "Perhaps I shall join you at the boarding school."

"There is no need, at least not yet," Lily said. "I am working with Mrs. Anderson as she makes the final preparations to open the school."

"Am I just to sit alone in the drawing room, waiting and hoping that someone decides to call upon me?"

"The plight of an heiress," Lily said, her smile growing. "What insurmountable burdens you must bear."

Emilia laughed. "I see your point."

"That is a shame because I prepared some more arguments."

"Save those for another time," Emilia said.

"Very well. Now, let's get you ready for the day."

Once Emilia was properly dressed, she sat at the vanity and started brushing her long brown locks.

Lily held her hand out. "I do believe it is my job to style your hair."

"I can brush my own hair," Emilia contended.

"You can, but you won't," Lily said.

Emilia put the brush aside and leaned back in her chair. "Once the boarding school is open, will you be leaving me?"

"I was hoping to spend more time at the school, assuming you do not have any objections," Lily replied. "I can ask a maid to fill in while I am gone during the day."

She wasn't entirely surprised by her friend's decision. Lily was a teacher at heart, and she didn't fault her for wanting to continue her work.

"I have no objections, and I will make do while you are gone," Emilia said. "The only reason I am agreeing to this is because I will see you at the boarding school when I teach."

Lily placed the brush down and hesitated. "About that…" Her voice trailed off. "Mrs. Anderson hired someone yesterday to teach needlework to the girls."

Emilia's heart sank. She knew Mrs. Anderson had been planning to hire a needlework teacher, but she hadn't expected it to happen so quickly.

"That doesn't mean you can't teach the girls needlework," Lily attempted. "After all, it is your school. You can do whatever you want."

She was wealthy and didn't need to work, but she missed teaching. It would have given her a sense of purpose and something to occupy her time. Quite frankly, she had far too much time on her hands since she had come into her inheritance.

Lily fashioned her hair into a stylish chignon before stepping back. "Are you upset?"

Turning in her seat to face her friend, Emilia replied, "No,

I am not. I am disappointed, but not with Mrs. Anderson. I feel as if that door has closed, and that part of my life is over."

"Is that necessarily a bad thing?" Lily asked.

"No… yes… I don't know," Emilia admitted. "Teaching was familiar."

Lily gave her an understanding look. "Don't try to hold on to your past; embrace your future."

A knock at the door interrupted their conversation, and Lily crossed the room to answer it. A maid entered the room and announced, "Mr. Calvin Livingston and Miss Clarissa have arrived, Miss. They are waiting for you in the drawing room."

"Thank you," Emilia said as she rose from her seat. "Inform them I will be down shortly."

The maid tipped her head before departing to do her bidding.

Lily remained near the door as she asked, "Would you like me to join you?"

"That won't be necessary," Emilia replied. "I can entertain Calvin and Clarissa on my own."

In a hushed voice, Lily said, "I heard that Miss Clarissa was rather haughty at the beginning of the tour at the boarding school."

"She had her moments," Emilia admitted.

"Mrs. Anderson said that Miss Clarissa seemed rather emotional when she met with the girls," Lily said. "I assured her that she was mistaken."

Emilia shrugged. "I don't know. It seemed rather genuine."

Lily didn't look convinced but she didn't attempt to argue with her. Instead, she said, "I should be going myself. The girls should have finished their breakfast at this point."

"Do you wish to take a coach?" Emilia offered.

"That won't be necessary," Lily said. "I am not a proper

lady like you are. People tend to leave me be on the pavement."

After Lily departed, Emilia headed towards the drawing room on the main level. She found that she wasn't dreading meeting Clarissa and Calvin. They were her family, and it would be best if they became better acquainted with one another.

She entered the drawing room and saw Clarissa and Calvin standing in the center of the room, engaged in conversation.

"Good morning," Emilia greeted.

Calvin promptly bowed. "Thank you for agreeing to meet with us."

Emilia waved her hand in front of her. "We are family, are we not?" she asked. "Shall I request some tea to be brought up?"

"Tea would be lovely," Clarissa replied. "I haven't had a good cup of tea since we moved to Cheapside."

"Allow me to inform Dalby," Calvin said before he went in search of the butler.

Crossing the room, Emilia sat down on the settee and asked, "Would you care to sit?"

Clarissa came to sit down across from her and asked, "How are the girls at the boarding school?"

"I am not quite sure since I haven't visited with them since we toured the school," Emilia replied. "I am hoping they are well."

A furrow formed on Clarissa's brow as she shared her impressions. "They didn't look at all how I perceived them to be."

"How was that?" she asked, slightly afraid of what the answer might be.

"Poor."

Emilia frowned. What could she say to that?

Calvin returned to the room and clasped his hands

together. "Dalby assured me that the tea would be up momentarily." His gaze shifted between Emilia and Clarissa. "Did I interrupt something?"

Clarissa responded with a tilt of her chin. "Not at all," she replied. "We weren't discussing anything of importance."

Emilia wanted to contradict that point, but she recognized the look in Clarissa's eyes, silently urging her to remain quiet.

Calvin's attention turned to Emilia. "Well, I was hoping tomorrow that we could all go on a carriage ride through Hyde Park, assuming you have no objections."

"I have many objections!" Clarissa exclaimed. "Did you forget that we were declared illegitimate? We are on the outskirts of high Society. Why would we draw attention to ourselves by going on a carriage ride in Hyde Park?"

Calvin appeared to consider his sister's concerns. "I understand what you are feeling, but it would be best if we were seen around Emilia, and often," he suggested. "If we are seen together, enjoying one another's company, the *ton* might see that we are united as a family."

"That is a big 'might,'" Clarissa argued. "Our friends have abandoned us, almost taking great pleasure in our downfall. Why would anyone wish to be seen with us now?"

"What say you, Emilia?" Calvin asked.

Emilia contemplated the situation, feeling the weight of her decision. She didn't want to let anyone down, and she was also aware of the challenges that Calvin and Clarissa were facing. They had lost everything when they were declared illegitimate. Shouldn't she at least try to help them when they asked?

"I will do it," Emilia announced.

Clarissa's face fell. "I do believe this is a terrible mistake. I have no desire to be a public spectacle of any kind."

"We will hardly be a public spectacle," Calvin countered. "As far as the *ton* is concerned, we are just one big happy family going on a carriage ride."

"But we are not a happy family, are we?" Clarissa demanded.

Calvin's expression grew stern as he responded, "I understand your anger, but I promise you, things will become clearer in time. You must trust me."

Clarissa narrowed her eyes and directed her anger towards Emilia. "Nothing we do will change the fact that the life we knew is over, and it is all because of our newfound sister." She pointed her finger at Emilia, her voice rising. "I don't know why I bothered trying to be friends with you. You ruined my life."

"Clarissa, that is uncalled for," Calvin chided.

Her mouth dropped. "You are siding with Emilia?" Clarissa asked.

Stepping closer to his sister, Calvin placed his hands gently on her shoulders. "Perhaps it's best for us to retire and allow you to rest."

Clarissa shrugged off his hands. "You are unbelievable, Brother. I shall wait for you in the entry hall."

After Clarissa stormed off, Calvin turned to Emilia, his expression apologetic. "I am truly sorry about what Clarissa said. She has just been overwhelmed lately."

"There is no need to explain Clarissa's actions because I find that I have great sympathy for her," Emilia said. "Everything she said was true, but I hope to change that by returning her dowry of twenty thousand pounds."

Calvin's eyes grew wide. "Are you in earnest?"

"I am," Emilia confirmed. "I had hoped to tell her myself, but I think it might be best if it came from you. I have already spoken to Mr. Rymer and he is seeing to the arrangements."

"Thank you," Calvin said.

"I hope that by restoring Clarissa's dowry, she may have a chance at finding a suitable match this Season, if that is what she desires."

Calvin beamed with gratitude. "I cannot thank you

enough, Emilia. With her sizable dowry, you have given her a chance for a brighter future."

"That was my intention," Emilia said.

He gave her a slight bow. "I am going to tell my sister the good news, but I do hope to see you tomorrow for our ride through Hyde Park."

"I shall be looking forward to it."

Once Calvin departed from the drawing room, Emilia walked over to collect her needlework, hoping that Anette or Fredrick might come to call on her today. She always welcomed their company, but more so, Fredrick.

His image came to her mind, and she allowed herself to dwell on it. She knew it would do her no good to hope for a future between them, but one could always dream. Surely there was no harm in that, was there?

Fredrick sat in the coach as it rumbled down the street, his gaze fixated on the window. The closer they got to Emilia's townhouse, the stronger the temptation to have the driver stop and call on her became. How easy would it be to alert the driver to come to a stop and call upon Emilia? But he wouldn't do it. He didn't want to know what Emilia meant to him, but these pesky feelings were becoming an unwanted distraction. He couldn't afford to risk his heart.

His mind, however, had other ideas. Despite his attempts to concentrate on more pressing matters, his thoughts constantly strayed back to Emilia. It was vexing, and not at all useful. Why wouldn't his mind cooperate?

Roswell's voice broke through his musings. "We could stop, if you would like."

"No, that won't be necessary...." His voice trailed off. "Stop where?"

His brother chuckled. "I daresay that it is rather obvious, is it not?" he asked. "Do you truly want me to say it?"

Fredrick sighed. "That won't be necessary."

"You did speak rather harshly yesterday to Miss Sutherland. Perhaps you would care to call upon her and apologize," Roswell suggested.

"We have more important matters to deal with, especially since Kendrick is waiting for us," Fredrick said.

"True, but I can't help but wonder if you are avoiding Miss Sutherland."

Fredrick should have expected that his brother would easily see through him, yet that didn't mean he had to persist with this line of questioning. "Can we discuss something else, anything else, really?"

Roswell's expression grew solemn. "Did you visit Mother this morning?"

"I did, but it was before she woke up. I didn't see a point in waiting," Fredrick replied. "She doesn't recognize any of us anymore. We are just strangers to her."

"She is still our mother," Roswell argued.

"That she is."

A heavy silence descended upon the coach as they retreated to their own thoughts. Fredrick knew his brother was right; he should visit his mother more. However, she seemed to be lost in her own world now. A world that didn't include him.

Fredrick's gaze once again returned to the window as he observed the street vendors striving to peddle their goods on the bustling pavement. All manner of goods were on display, and the aroma of savory meat pies wafted in through the open window.

It wasn't long before they arrived at the agency's headquarters on the outskirts of the fashionable part of Town. They both exited the coach and made their way into the dilapidated building where they were greeted by a guard.

"Hello, blokes," the guard said as he leaned his shoulder against the back wall, appearing unconcerned by their presence. "What can I do for ye?"

Roswell spoke up. "We are here to see Kendrick. He is expecting us."

The guard seemed to size them up. "Very well, but I have heard he is in a foul mood."

"When is he not?" Roswell joked.

With a chuckle, the guard opened the back door. "Go on, then," he encouraged. "But don't say that I didn't warn ye."

Fredrick trailed behind Roswell as they approached Kendrick's office. Once they arrived, Roswell raised his hand and rapped on the door.

"Enter," came Kendrick's gruff reply.

As they entered the small study, Fredrick's steps faltered when he laid eyes on the last person he expected to see.

Simone.

"You," Fredrick said.

Simone stood in front of a chair, dressed in a simple blue gown. A matching reticule hung around her wrist, enhancing her ladylike appearance. Her eyes flashed with something he couldn't quite decipher. Annoyance, perhaps?

Kendrick interjected, "I see that you are already acquainted with Miss Delacourt."

"We know her only as 'Simone,'" Roswell shared.

"Yes, well, shall we all sit down so we can continue this discussion?" Kendrick asked. "I don't have all day to watch you three stare daggers at one another."

Fredrick waited until Miss Delacourt settled into her chair before taking his own. He had so many questions, but he wasn't quite sure where to start.

Kendrick leaned forward in his seat. "Miss Delacourt is the other agent that I assigned to the case, and I thought it was necessary to bring you all together, considering we have two French spies somewhere on the loose in London."

"I don't need a nursemaid, or two," Miss Delacourt said, her tone dripping with disapproval. "I just need more time."

"Time is what we don't have, Agent," Kendrick remarked.

"I believe I have tracked the two spies to a boarding house in Chelsea and..." Miss Delacourt shared.

Kendrick put his hand up, halting her words. "How do you propose to apprehend two French agents single-handedly?" he asked.

"Easily," Miss Delacourt responded.

"Now that Caleb is injured, going at it alone is not a wise option," Kendrick asserted. "You need help."

Miss Delacourt huffed her discontent, but she remained quiet.

"For the sake of the Crown, I would like you three to work together," Kendrick said. "You will need to share what you know, and move forward, quickly."

Kendrick continued. "You may go now, and do not disappoint me on this."

After they had filed out of Kendrick's office, Fredrick had to increase his stride to keep up with Miss Delacourt. She hardly spared him a glance as they left the building and arrived on the pavement.

"Wait," Fredrick ordered. "We must speak with you."

Miss Delacourt stopped on the pavement and a deep frown marred her features. "What is it that you want?"

"Kendrick wants us to work together," Fredrick replied. "Don't you think we should at least attempt to do so?"

"I can handle this on my own. You can go back to entertaining Miss Sutherland," Miss Delacourt said, turning to leave.

Fredrick reached out and touched her arm. "I am not entertaining Miss Sutherland."

"I just assumed because you have been spending so much time with her," Miss Delacourt explained with a slight shrug of her shoulder.

Roswell drew closer and spoke in a hushed tone. "We need to talk, and this is not the place to do so," he said. "Since you seem to know so much about us, why don't we speak at our townhouse this evening?"

Miss Delacourt's expression wavered with uncertainty before she agreed, "Leave the window open in the study. I am not about to go through the main door and announce my presence."

"I am agreeable to that," Roswell said.

"Good." Miss Delacourt arched an eyebrow. "Are we done here?" she asked, challenging them.

Fredrick had many questions, but he knew this was not the time or the place to ask them. "You may go, but we will expect to see you tonight."

Miss Delacourt dropped into a low curtsy. "You are most gracious, my lord," she mocked.

As she started to walk away from them, Roswell called out to her. "Would you care to make use of our coach?"

"No, thank you," Miss Delacourt responded over her shoulder.

"Are you certain?" Roswell asked. "This part of Town is no place for a lady, and I cannot in good conscience leave you be."

Miss Delacourt paused on the pavement and turned around. "You are rather vexing, my lord," she said. "I am more than capable of finding my own way home."

Roswell gestured towards the waiting coach. "But there is no need. Allow us to escort you home."

"I am not going home, and even if I were, I would not wish to be seen with you two," Miss Delacourt said. "You two attract far too much attention for my tastes."

Fredrick had to admit that Miss Delacourt did have a point. They did attract attention wherever they went, partly due to his position as the heir to a marquessate. But could he, in good conscience, leave her here unaccompanied and defenseless?

Miss Delacourt watched as people brushed past them on the pavement before returning to address them. "I appreciate your concern, but if this arrangement is to work, you must refrain from treating me as you would any other lady."

Fredrick made one last attempt. "At least let us take you part of the way," he insisted.

She pursed her lips. "Did you not hear what I just said?"

"I heard you, but I cannot leave you defenseless on the street," Fredrick said.

Miss Delacourt let out a slight chuckle. "I am not defenseless, and if I didn't find that so humorous, I would be insulted," she remarked. "Good day, gentlemen."

They both watched Miss Delacourt's retreating figure until she was out of sight.

Roswell turned towards him. "We couldn't force her into the coach."

"No, but she is rather a stubborn thing," Fredrick said. "I am not quite sure how Kendrick expects us to work together."

"We will find a way," Roswell asserted.

After they stepped into the coach, it merged into traffic and Fredrick's eyes scanned the pavement for any sign of Miss Delacourt, but she was nowhere to be found. Where had she disappeared to?

Roswell followed his gaze. "I do hope Miss Delacourt is more cooperative this evening."

"I shall wait with bated breath," Fredrick said. "But it doesn't appear she wants to work with us any more than we wish to work with her."

A short time later, they arrived at their townhouse and they hurried inside. They were met by Anette with a bright smile on her face.

"Wonderful, you both are just in time," she announced.

"In time for what?" Roswell asked.

Anette looped arms with her husband. "We need to call upon Emilia and teach her the dance of love," she said, her eyes filled with amusement. "That is where Fredrick will come in."

"You wish for me to teach Emilia to dance the waltz?" Fredrick asked.

"Isn't that what I just said?" Anette pressed.

Fredrick put his hands up in front of him. "I'm afraid that is impossible. I have a lot of work that I need to see to. It is rather urgent."

Anette gave him a knowing look. "Emilia must dance the waltz and her ball is only two days away," she said. "If not you, then who will teach her?"

"Surely there is someone else," Fredrick contended.

A thoughtful look came to Anette's face. "You are right. I can ask another gentleman."

Fredrick hesitated, as that thought did not sit well with him. Emilia couldn't just dance with anyone. "Which gentleman?" he inquired.

"Does it matter?" Anette asked. "There are many gentlemen that would love to practice the waltz with an heiress."

Roswell chimed in. "I shall ask Lord William."

"No, you most assuredly will not," Fredrick swiftly objected. "He is a known rakehell. He shouldn't be anywhere near Emilia."

Anette arched her brow. "Then who do you propose?"

Good gads, there was not one gentleman that he could think of that was worthy to dance with Emilia. Perhaps he should just do it and be done with it.

"I will do it," Fredrick said.

"Good, let us depart, then," Anette responded. "We have much work to do."

Why did Fredrick have a feeling that he had been tricked

by Anette? But it didn't matter now. He agreed to dance the waltz with Emilia, and he couldn't go back on that.

The thought of holding her in his arms both terrified and excited him at the same time. He had resolved to keep her at a distance, yet the thought of her fitting perfectly in his arms began to chip away at his determination.

Chapter Fifteen

Emilia's eyes swept across the grand ballroom as she anxiously waited for her friends' arrival. When she received Anette's note, a wave of apprehension washed over her. What if Fredrick thought her to be a terrible dancer? She had learned most of the dances at the country balls, but she had never danced the waltz before. The opportunity had never presented itself, given her previous responsibilities as a teacher, leaving her little time for such frivolous things.

Her job was the only thing that had kept a roof over her head. Emilia couldn't believe how different her life was now. Her fortune was far more than suitable, and she found that for the first time, she could breathe.

Dalby entered the room and announced her guests. It was only a moment later when Anette stepped into the room on the arm of her husband.

"I cannot wait to see the ballroom after it has been decorated, including the chalked rendering of your family's crest," Anette gushed. "You shall be the envy of the *ton*."

"I doubt that," Emilia said.

Fredrick had followed Anette and Roswell into the ballroom and he bowed when their eyes met. "Emilia," he greeted.

Emilia dropped into a curtsy as she attempted to ignore her racing heart. "Fredrick," she said, pleased that her voice sounded steady.

Fredrick approached her, coming to a stop a short distance away. "I understand that you are not familiar with the waltz."

"I am not," she admitted. "I'm afraid the dancing master did not teach any of us the waltz since it was not performed at the country dances."

"Nor should it be," Anette chimed in. "The waltz is the dance of love."

Emilia's brow lifted. "Is that what it is called?"

Fredrick shook his head. "No one calls it that but Anette."

A group of musicians stepped into the ballroom with instruments in their hands, and they positioned themselves in the corner to warm up.

Emilia watched their preparations and then turned her attention to Fredrick. "I thought it would be best if we had some music to dance to. I hope that wasn't a wrong assumption."

Fredrick's eyes shone with approval. "I think that is a fine idea." He turned towards the musicians to address them. "When you are ready, you may begin playing."

As the music began to fill the ballroom, Fredrick took a step closer to her, and she was forced to tilt her head to look up at him.

"Are you ready to begin?" Fredrick asked.

She nodded.

Fredrick slipped his arm around her waist, and she inhaled sharply, causing his hand to pause. "Do you want me to stop?" he asked, his voice gentle.

"No," she replied.

With his other hand, he reached for hers and brought

them up. "Now, follow my lead and I promise I won't let you fall."

Fredrick started to lead her to the music and she found herself relaxing in his arms. She had never been this close to a gentleman before, but it felt as if she had always belonged in his arms. The world around them seemed to disappear, and in that moment, everything felt perfect.

Their eyes locked and she saw a deep intensity in his gaze. It made her wonder if maybe, just maybe, he held some affection for her.

Once the last note was played, Fredrick came to a stop but didn't release her right away. "You dance superbly," he praised in a low voice.

"It was only because I had the right teacher," Emilia said with a shy smile.

Fredrick's gaze briefly fell to her lips and he cleared his throat. "Yes, well, you will do just fine at the ball," he said in a hoarse voice.

Anette started clapping as she approached them. "That was perfect. Just perfect," she praised. "I do not think any more practice is necessary, do either of you?"

Fredrick released Emilia and took a step back. "I do believe that is sufficient," he agreed.

Turning towards Emilia, Anette said, "I spoke to my father-in-law, Lord Cuttyngham, and he has agreed to dance the first set with you, assuming you are agreeable."

"That is most kind of him," Emilia acknowledged.

"Now that we have that resolved, we will need to think of the ideal gentleman who will join you in the waltz at your ball —" Anette started.

Fredrick spoke up. "I'll do it."

Anette raised her brow. "I do think that is a mistake since the *ton* might speculate as to the nature of your relationship with Emilia," she said, her words cautious.

"She is a family friend," Fredrick said. "There is nothing more to it than that."

Roswell stepped forward and attempted, "I daresay that Anette has a point. You two seemed rather close as you danced the waltz."

"Is that a problem?" Fredrick asked.

A knowing look passed between Anette and Roswell. "No, but it might get the gossips' tongues wagging," he said.

"I will dance the waltz with Emilia." Fredrick paused for a moment and looked at Emilia with a searching gaze. "Unless Emilia has an objection."

Emilia's heart soared at the prospect of dancing with Fredrick again, especially the waltz. The thought of being in his arms again thrilled her, but she maintained her composure. "I have none," she replied, her voice steady.

Fredrick nodded, a hint of warmth in his gaze as his eyes lingered on Emilia. "It has been decided, then," he said.

Anette interjected, "I do have the most wonderful news. Most of the people we have invited to the ball have confirmed their attendance."

"That is very promising," Emilia remarked.

"I thought so as well," Anette said.

Emilia had a thought. "Did you invite Calvin and Clarissa to my ball?"

Anette hesitated. "I did not," she admitted. "I didn't think it was wise to invite them."

"Whyever not?" Emilia inquired.

Anette frowned. "You may have been quick to accept Clarissa and Calvin, but the *ton* is not so gracious. I doubt they would be well received at your ball."

"Shouldn't we at least give them the option to come?" Emilia asked. "It seems only fair, considering they are family."

Roswell winced. "They were declared illegitimate, making them social pariahs in the eyes of the *ton*."

Emilia turned her attention towards Fredrick, hoping he might agree with her. "What do you think?"

Fredrick's expression grew thoughtful. "I don't place much importance on what the *ton* wants. What does your heart tell you?"

"My heart tells me to invite them," Emilia responded.

"Then you have your answer," Fredrick concluded.

Emilia offered him a grateful smile. "Thank you."

"I didn't do anything. It was your decision to make, and only yours," Fredrick said.

Anette started pacing the ballroom. "I daresay that inviting Clarissa and Calvin might complicate things, but it isn't the worst thing," she stated. "Furthermore, there is a chance they might not even attend."

Roswell chuckled. "I fear that my wife might work herself into a frenzy."

"I am going on a carriage ride with Clarissa and Calvin tomorrow," Emilia revealed.

"For what purpose?" Fredrick asked.

"Calvin thinks it is a good idea for us to be seen together," Emilia replied.

"I'll accompany you," Fredrick said.

Before she could reply, Dalby stepped into the room and met Emilia's gaze. "Miss Clarissa Livingston was hoping for a moment of your time, Miss."

"Please show her to the drawing room," Emilia directed.

After the butler had departed from the ballroom, Anette stopped pacing and said, "Speak of the devil…"

Emilia sighed. "Clarissa is not as terrible as you may think," she contended. "There have been a few moments where she has been rather enjoyable."

"Only a few moments?" Anette joked.

"If you will excuse me, I shall hurry back," Emilia replied before she headed towards the drawing room.

Once she arrived, Emilia saw Clarissa staring out the

window, her hands clasped in front of her. "Clarissa," she greeted. "What a pleasant surprise."

"You should be in the drawing room, ready to receive callers," Clarissa advised as she turned to face her.

"I shall take that into account," Emilia responded.

Clarissa pressed her lips together before saying, "I wanted to apologize for my behavior earlier. I didn't want Calvin to know that I toured the boarding school with you."

"May I ask why that is?"

"Calvin was rather furious when I first told him about the boarding school. He thought that it would tarnish our family's good name," Clarissa explained. "I agreed with him, and I thought I could convince you of such. But I was wrong."

Emilia was taken aback by Clarissa's admission. "You were?"

Clarissa lowered her hands to her sides. "It was what that headmistress said about doors being opened to them. It made me realize that I am not so different from those girls." She took a step closer to her. "And then, Calvin told me about my dowry. I can't even begin to thank you."

"It is what Father would have wanted," Emilia said.

"I doubt that," Clarissa responded. "I wasn't always the most kind to Father. I made a lot of mistakes, and I'm beginning to see why things unfolded as they did."

Emilia could hear the sadness in Clarissa's voice and she felt a deep sense of compassion for her. "I hope with your dowry that you will find a love match."

Clarissa let out a disbelieving huff. "A love match?" she asked. "No, I just want to find a gentleman that will overlook the fact that I am illegitimate."

"You deserve so much more than that," Emilia said.

"Do I?" Clarissa asked. "I should have married the first gentleman that offered for me. That would have saved me a considerable amount of trouble."

"Would you have been happy if you had done so?"

Lowering her gaze, Clarissa replied, "Most likely not."

"I am hosting a ball in two days' time and I would like you and your brother to be in attendance," Emilia said.

Clarissa's gaze shot back up. "That is a terrible idea. The *ton* will be relentless in their gossip."

"I do not pretend to know how the *ton* will react, but I want you there," Emilia responded.

"Why?" Clarissa asked.

Emilia smiled. "Because we are family, whether you want to be or not."

Clarissa's face softened. "I would be remiss if I did not tell you that this ball is a horrible idea since you should be mourning our father."

"I hardly think I should mourn a man I didn't know."

"Fair enough," Clarissa responded with a wry smile. "I shall attend, and I will drag my brother along."

Emilia felt a tentative warmth between them, a spark of sisterly affection that she so desperately craved. "Should we hug? I feel as if we should hug."

Clarissa laughed softly, just as she had hoped. "I do not think we should get ahead of ourselves."

"No, of course not," Emilia responded.

With a glance at the tea service on the table, Clarissa said, "You have not asked if I wish for any tea yet. Were you raised in a barn?" Her words were light.

"No, a cottage," Emilia retorted. "It wasn't much bigger than this room."

Clarissa laughed again, the tension of the past seeming to fade away. "I should be going," she said. "But thank you."

"For what?"

The humor faded from Clarissa's face as she replied, "For not looking at me with pity in your eyes."

Emilia watched as Clarissa departed from the room, and she was glad that she had invited them to the ball. Her kindness was not conditional, and she very much wanted Clarissa in her life.

The moonlight streamed through the windows, casting a silvery glow across the room. Fredrick sat in an armchair, his patience wearing thin as he anxiously awaited Miss Delacourt's arrival. The late hour was making him increasingly frustrated, and he couldn't help but wonder where she was. He had more pressing matters to attend to, and this waiting was becoming unbearable.

But they waited, nonetheless.

Fredrick watched his brother take a sip of his drink, looking entirely too calm for his liking. Roswell's composure was almost maddening, given their current situation. "How much longer are we expected to wait?" he grumbled, his impatience getting the best of him.

Roswell merely shrugged. "I suppose we wait for as long as it takes."

"What if Miss Delacourt doesn't show?"

"Then we continue working the case on our own," Roswell reasoned.

Fredrick huffed. "That isn't going so well for us," he responded. "Besides, you heard Miss Delacourt, she's already tracked the French spies to a boarding house. We just need to know which one and we can end this."

Roswell gave him a knowing look. "What makes you so bothered by Miss Delacourt?"

"She is infuriating," Fredrick replied, not entirely certain himself why he found her so vexing. The mystery surrounding her grated on him, and not knowing was something he couldn't easily accept.

"Is she?" Roswell asked.

Fredrick didn't want to talk about this. Perhaps they should just sit in silence as they waited for Miss Delacourt.

Roswell leaned forward and placed his nearly full glass onto the table. "We could always discuss what transpired between you and Emilia today while you were dancing the waltz."

"Nothing transpired between us."

His brother raised his eyebrow inquisitively. "No?" Roswell asked. "It just seems that you two are getting rather close to one another."

Fredrick shifted uncomfortably in his seat, knowing his brother was being far too perceptive. "You would be wrong," he lied.

"I don't think I am," Roswell said. "Surely you know by now that Anette has been trying to push you and Emilia together."

"I had my suspicions."

Roswell cocked his head, his gaze thoughtful. "Was she wrong to do so?"

"Yes," Fredrick rushed to reply. "I have no desire to marry, and I do not wish to give Emilia false hope."

"Is that what you think you are doing?"

Fredrick stood up abruptly. "I do not wish to discuss this."

Leaning back in his seat, Roswell continued to press. "What is wrong with Emilia?"

"Nothing is wrong with her," he stated.

"Then why are you trying to push her away?" Roswell questioned. "It is evident that you have feelings for her."

Fredrick walked over to the mantel over the hearth and leaned against it. "It doesn't matter what I feel for her. I won't marry her. It wouldn't be fair to her."

"Emilia seems rather taken by you."

Fredrick sighed. "I do not presume to know what she is feeling, but she can have her pick of suitors. She doesn't need me."

"She may not need you, but I think she is precisely what *you* need," Roswell said.

He shook his head. "It doesn't matter. I do not want anyone to share in my misery. It is my burden to bear alone."

Roswell grew silent. "I kept Anette at arm's length because I didn't want her to be involved in my life as a spy. That, and a promise I made to Caleb. But I realized that I was wrong to do so. I am stronger with Anette in my life."

"I do not contest that, but you haven't experienced what I did on the battlefield," Fredrick argued. "War degrades a man, leaving him a mere shadow of his former self."

"You are still the same person," Roswell said.

"Maybe to you, but to me, I feel different. I feel alone."

Rising, Roswell approached him. "You are not alone. You have many people who care about you."

"What about the lives I took?" Fredrick demanded. "They had loved ones waiting for them, as well. But I took that from them."

Roswell placed a comforting hand on Fredrick's shoulder. "I do not mean to diminish what you have gone through, but you are home now. You are safe."

Fredrick closed his eyes as he felt tears forming in his eyes. He may be safe, but it didn't take away the haunting images of the people that he had killed, especially Timmy's. The memories seemed etched into his very soul, and he didn't think he would ever rid himself of those.

Miss Delacourt's voice came from the open window. "This is all very touching, but I'm afraid I don't have much time."

After she climbed through the window, she ran her hand down her pink gown and explained, "I had to wait until my companion retired for the evening before I could sneak out."

"You have a companion?" Roswell asked.

"I do," Miss Delacourt replied. "But that is not why I am here, is it?"

Fredrick turned to face her. "Perhaps we should become better acquainted with one another before we get started."

With a dismissive wave of her hand, Miss Delacourt replied, "That is not necessary. I know everything I need to know about both of you."

"That is what we thought you would say, which is why we decided to conduct a little investigation into you," Fredrick said.

"Wonderful," Miss Delacourt muttered. "I see that you wasted your time."

"We don't consider it a waste," Fredrick responded.

Miss Delacourt arched an eyebrow. "Very well. What did your little investigation uncover about me?"

Roswell spoke up. "Your father is Baron Hungerton and you are his only child. You are in your third Season, and by all accounts, you are regarded by many as shy and timid. Some even describe you as a 'wallflower.'"

"Impressive. You have uncovered precisely what I wanted you to learn about me," Miss Delacourt said in a sardonic tone. "My cover is to blend in, and not be conspicuous in any way. To the *ton*, I am just regarded as unremarkable in every way."

"But we know that is not true," Fredrick remarked. "How is it that you were recruited by Kendrick?"

Miss Delacourt frowned. "Kendrick caught me attending lectures at university, disguised as a man, and offered me a chance to work for him."

"Why would you do such a thing?" Fredrick asked. "Your reputation was at stake if you had been caught by anyone else."

"Men are not the only ones who wish to better themselves," Miss Delacourt stated.

"I don't dispute that, but women cannot attend university," Fredrick pressed.

"Why is that, my lord?" Miss Delacourt countered. "What

is it that men don't want us to learn? Are they afraid of what will happen when a woman gets educated?"

Roswell put his hand up. "We are not here to discuss whether or not women can attend university, are we?"

Miss Delacourt nodded. "You are right," she replied. "I do apologize. I'm afraid I can get rather passionate about topics that are dear to my heart."

"As we all can," Roswell graciously said. "Will you take a seat? We have much to discuss."

She effortlessly crossed the room and lowered herself down onto an upholstered armchair. "I am not sure what you know."

"Frankly, we know very little," Roswell admitted. "We know that Lord Drycott is smuggling goods, and on his last shipment, he brought back two French spies."

"That is all true, and I tracked those two spies to a boarding house, but I am unsure of their intention for being in England. That is the only reason why I haven't brought them in yet," Miss Delacourt said.

Fredrick did have a question. "How did you know that Caleb's cover had been blown?"

Miss Delacourt pressed her lips together. "I slipped into the factory as a worker, and I overheard the conversation between Lord Drycott and a group of burly men. All I know is that Lord Drycott knew of his identity and was ordering them to kill him."

"Why didn't you step in and warn Caleb?" Fredrick asked.

"If I did, my cover would have been blown and it would have done us no good," Miss Delacourt responded. "That is why I went and retrieved both of you. I knew you could help him, far better than I could ever have."

Roswell interjected, "Does Caleb know you were working this case alongside him?"

"No," Miss Delacourt replied. "Kendrick thought it would be best if we worked separately for the time being, but it wasn't hard to make him out as an agent when I worked as a serving wench at The Rusty Anchor Tavern."

"How is it that you are able to be a spy when you have a companion?" Fredrick questioned.

"With great care," Miss Delacourt replied. "My father hardly notices me anymore and Mrs. Fernsby tolerates me."

Fredrick heard her words, sensing an underlying sadness beneath her tone. Her admission seemed to have wounded her more deeply than she let on.

Miss Delacourt rose. "I intend to search Lord Drycott's study at his townhouse tomorrow. With any luck, he will have more information about the purpose of the French spies being here."

"We will accompany you," Fredrick insisted.

She looked unimpressed by his offer. "One person can easily go undetected in Lord Drycott's study, but three? Surely you cannot be serious."

"Then I shall go with you, just me," Fredrick remarked.

Miss Delacourt studied him, her eyes searching for something he couldn't quite discern. The seconds stretched before she finally conceded. "Fair enough," she said, her voice a mixture of resignation and determination. "Kendrick wants us to work together, so I suppose I should make an effort to do so."

Fredrick didn't know why, but he felt elated that he had secured that small victory.

"I shall meet you outside Lord Drycott's townhouse tomorrow at midnight. Do not be late," Miss Delacourt warned, making her way towards the window.

Roswell stepped forward. "You may leave by way of the main door if that is preferable."

"The fewer people that know I was here, the better," Miss Delacourt responded before she gracefully climbed out the window, disappearing into the darkness of the night.

Fredrick crossed his arms over his chest. "What do you make of Miss Delacourt?"

"I find her to be trustworthy, don't you?" Roswell asked.

"I do," Fredrick admitted. "But we are taking a huge risk by searching Lord Drycott's study. I hope it will yield some useful information."

Roswell walked over to the door. "If you will excuse me, I am going to join my wife in bed. It is late, and I am tired."

"Good night," Fredrick said.

After his brother departed from the study, Fredrick walked over to the settee and dropped down onto it. He should retire to bed, but he wasn't quite ready to do so. Instead, he found himself lost in thoughts of the waltz he had shared with Emilia. It was only then that he realized he was smiling.

Chapter Sixteen

Emilia sat at the dining table, her loneliness a familiar companion. She had initially decided to take her meals in her bedchamber, but for some reason, she kept finding herself drawn to the dining room. Perhaps a part of her hoped today would be different, that someone would join her.

How she hated to be alone. The loneliness weighed on her, a constant reminder of what she didn't have in her life. She should focus on the blessings that she had- wealth, security, and a bright future. Yet, her heart ached for the one thing she truly longed for: family.

How she missed her mother. Not a day passed without Emilia wishing for her mother's comforting embrace. Her father, too, was gone. The only two people she could still count as family were Clarissa and Calvin. And Fredrick had warned her to be leery of them.

Emilia wanted to believe that Clarissa and Calvin had genuine intentions, that they, too, yearned for a familial connection with her.

With a glance at the footmen, she let out a sigh. She had tried to talk to them before and it did not end well.

Dalby stepped into the room and announced, "Lord

Chatsworth has arrived. Would you care for me to show him to the drawing room?"

Emilia had a thought. "Might you ask him to join me for breakfast?"

The butler tipped his head. "Yes, Miss."

Moments later, Fredrick stepped into the room, sharply dressed in a deep blue jacket, buff trousers and Hessian boots. He was undeniably handsome, but she saw him as so much more than that. He was a man of great kindness, consideration, and he had a smile that caused her to lose rational thought.

Emilia gestured towards one of the chairs. "Please, have a seat."

She was pleased when Fredrick pulled out a chair next to her and sat down. "How do you fare this morning?" he asked.

She decided to be honest with Fredrick, feeling that he deserved the truth. "I am lonely," she admitted.

Fredrick nodded in understanding. "I am well acquainted with that feeling."

"Do you not have a house full of family?"

"Just because you have those things doesn't mean you can't feel alone at times," Fredrick replied. "Sometimes, I feel the loneliest when I am surrounded by people."

Emilia glanced down at her nearly full plate. "I do miss Lily. She has been spending more time at the boarding school, and I do not fault her for that. She doesn't seem well-equipped for a life as a lady's maid."

"I do not know what to say to that," Fredrick said.

She smiled. "Just you being here is enough," she responded. "I tire of having breakfast by myself every morning."

Fredrick returned her smile. "I am glad that I am here then. I was afraid that I would arrive too early."

"I wake up at an early hour. I'm afraid it is a habit that

started when I was young and I had to collect the eggs from the chickens."

"You and I have led such different lives," Fredrick acknowledged.

"We have," she agreed. Perhaps she had been too honest with him.

Fredrick leaned to the side as a footman placed a cup of tea in front of him. "What other chores did you have when you were young?"

"Too many to count," she said with a laugh. "I always seemed to be busy with one task or another."

"Did you not have time to sketch?"

Emilia bobbed her head. "During quiet times, I used to go outside on our porch and sketch whatever I saw, be it people or animals. It didn't matter to me. I just wanted to capture the moment," she shared. "When I showed my mother the sketches, she always praised them and displayed them on our walls. My mother was my greatest supporter."

Overwhelmed with emotion, she fought back the tears welling up in her eyes, not wanting to cry in front of Fredrick. What would he think of her?

Fredrick placed his hand gently on her sleeve. "It is all right to cry," he reassured her. "Heaven knows that I have shed a tear or two for my mother."

"You cry?" she asked. "I'm afraid I do not see it."

He chuckled softly. "I do not do it often, mind you, but there is a time and a place for it. Crying over one's mother is the perfect excuse to do so."

Emilia used her hand to brush away her tears. "I'm sorry. My mother died many years ago but sometimes it still feels like yesterday."

"You do not need to apologize," he assured her, reaching into his jacket pocket to retrieve a handkerchief, which he then extended towards her.

With a grateful heart, she accepted the handkerchief and murmured, "Thank you."

Fredrick dropped his hand and reached for his teacup. "Will you tell me more about yourself?"

"That is rather a vague question," she teased. "What would you wish to know?"

"What are your likes, or dislikes?"

Emilia gestured towards the cup of chocolate on the table. "I find that I love drinking chocolate. That is an extravagance I never had before I moved here. Chocolate was far too expensive for us to afford."

"Octavia loves chocolate as well," Fredrick remarked. "I find that I am not tempted by it."

"Are you close with your sister?"

Fredrick's eyes grew reflective. "I adore my sister, but she is quite the hoyden."

"I hope to meet her one day."

"You shall, at least once she returns home from her wedding tour," Fredrick said. "She married a fine man, and I played a part in bringing them together."

Emilia's lips curved. "You are a matchmaker, as well. Is there no end to your talents, my lord?" she asked.

"I must admit I have my flaws. Arithmetic is not my strong suit, but do not tell my father," he joked. "I have managed to maintain the illusion this long."

"Do you not handle your accounts?"

Fredrick's eyes lit up with mirth. "I am more than capable of keeping a ledger balanced."

"Perhaps you can help me, then?" she inquired. "Not only am I expected to run a household, but I must understand the particulars of running an estate."

"I will gladly assist with that." Fredrick glanced down at her plate and asked, "Are you not hungry?"

"I must admit that I am feeling rather anxious about the carriage ride with Calvin and Clarissa," she shared.

Fredrick's eyes held compassion. "You need not fear. I will be by your side the entire time."

Emilia bit her lower lip. "You seem to believe that Calvin and Clarissa's intentions are not genuine. Why is that?"

"It is just a feeling that I have."

"I hope you are wrong, because it would be nice to be a part of a family again."

Fredrick reached for her hand and encompassed it. "I truly hope I'm mistaken, as you deserve the very thing you are longing for."

He spoke his words with such sincerity that she believed them.

Dalby stepped into the room and Fredrick quickly withdrew his hand. "Mr. Livingston and Miss Clarissa Livingston have arrived. They are assembled in the drawing room, Miss."

"Thank you," Emilia acknowledged.

Fredrick rose and offered his hand. "Allow me," he said.

Emilia took his hand, appreciating his thoughtfulness. "You are most kind," she said before releasing his hand.

They walked side by side towards the drawing room, and Emilia found herself at a loss for words. Fredrick came to a stop by the open door and gestured for her to enter first.

Stepping into the drawing room, Emilia saw Calvin and Clarissa were waiting for her, as the butler had indicated.

Calvin smiled broadly, but it dimmed as Fredrick came to stand behind her. "What is Lord Chatsworth doing here?"

Turning towards Fredrick, Emilia replied, "He has kindly agreed to accompany us. Isn't that wonderful?"

"Yes, that is delightful news." Calvin's response was less than enthusiastic, clearly displeased by the unexpected turn of events.

Clarissa curtsied. "My lord, it is a pleasure to see you again."

"My lord?" Fredrick asked with a raised eyebrow. "When did you start addressing me as such?"

A smile came to her lips. "Fredrick," Clarissa said. "I didn't wish to presume since our fortune has changed."

Calvin, however, seemed less at ease. He clasped his hands together. "Shall we depart for Hyde Park?"

"I brought my finest coach for the occasion," Fredrick said. "It is waiting out front."

"There is no need. Our circumstances may have been reduced, but we still have a carriage," Calvin said, his voice curt.

Fredrick graciously put his hand up. "My apologies. I did not mean to overstep my bounds. I would be more than happy to ride in your carriage."

Clarissa leaned closer to her brother, her voice lowered. "Fredrick's carriage is much more luxurious than ours. Perhaps we should take his?"

"No, Clarissa," Calvin snapped. "We will take ours."

"Very well, Brother," Clarissa responded in a soft voice, taking a step to the side.

Fredrick offered his arm to Emilia. "Allow me to escort you to the coach."

As Fredrick led her towards the main door, Emilia couldn't help but notice that Clarissa's gaze was downcast, and it was evident that Calvin's harsh words had affected her more than she had let on.

Fredrick must have noticed it, too, because he directed his comments towards Clarissa. "You are looking well."

"I am well," Clarissa said, but her words betrayed her true emotions.

Once they were situated in the coach, it jerked forward and Emilia found herself seated close to Fredrick. She couldn't help but notice the subtle scent of his shaving soap, with a delicate hint of orange, lingering in the air around him.

Calvin sat across from her and wore a pleasant smile. "It is a beautiful day for a carriage ride, is it not?"

"It is," Emilia agreed.

Calvin continued. "It isn't often that we have the pleasure of spending time with our father's prized godson, is it, Fredrick?"

Fredrick visibly tensed, but his next words sounded cordial enough. "It is true. I have been off fighting in the war for many years."

"Father always spoke highly of Fredrick, even to a fault," Calvin shared, his voice taking on a hint of bitterness. "No one could compete against him, despite my many attempts."

"Calvin…" Clarissa interjected.

Her brother spoke over her. "But we mustn't dwell on the past. It is much better to look towards the future."

The atmosphere inside the carriage grew tense as they entered Hyde Park through the south entrance. Emilia sighed inwardly, wondering if the situation could possibly get any worse.

Fredrick stood in the shadows, keeping a watchful eye on Lord Drycott's whitewashed, three-level townhouse. The entire building remained in darkness, without a flicker of light or any signs of movement, which was a promising sign.

He retrieved his pocket watch from his waistcoat. The time was nearing midnight, and Miss Delacourt was nowhere to be seen. For someone that had encouraged him to be on time, he found her delay somewhat surprising.

In the distance, he saw a hunched and slow-moving figure shuffling towards him. A beggar, no doubt. He turned his attention back towards the townhouse, but his thoughts soon drifted back to the events of their earlier carriage ride.

He hadn't realized that Calvin held such animosity for him, but the carriage ride only seemed to get worse as time went on. Despite the efforts of Emilia and Clarissa to keep the conversation lively, Calvin remained critical of him.

Fredrick had never taken a liking to Calvin, especially given he only seemed to care for himself. He couldn't help but find Calvin's sudden interest in Emilia to be rather disconcerting. What did he hope to gain by his association with her? A happy family seemed unlikely, so what were his true intentions?

"Do you have any coins, sir?" the beggar asked.

Fredrick reached into his pocket and removed a few coins. As he extended them towards the beggar, he suddenly noticed a familiar pair of wide, expressive eyes staring back at him from beneath a tattered cloak that covered her head.

"What are you wearing?" he asked, his eyes roaming over her dirtied face.

Miss Delacourt revealed herself, a hint of a smirk on her lips. "I thought it was appropriate, given the circumstances," she said. "Besides, no one gives a beggar any heed, no matter day or night."

Fredrick had to admit that she wasn't wrong. "You are late," he said.

"No, I am right on time," Miss Delacourt corrected. "The last light went off in the study about an hour ago."

"How long have you been waiting?"

Miss Delacourt shrugged one shoulder. "Long enough to determine everyone seems to be fast asleep."

"Then let us be quick about this," Fredrick stated. He crossed the street and reached the gate that led into Lord Drycott's gardens.

After opening the gate, he gestured that Miss Delacourt should go first. She entered, and he followed her inside, taking care to close the gate behind him.

They stayed close to the building as they made their way towards the rear of the townhouse. Fredrick was familiar with

A Suitable Fortune

the configurations of these townhouses and knew that the study had a window that faced the gardens.

Upon reaching the study, Miss Delacourt quietly opened the window. "It isn't locked," she whispered.

She climbed through the window, and Fredrick waited a moment before he followed suit, making his way into the study.

A desk sat near the windows with stacks of papers covering the surface. It was no better than the desk at Lord Drycott's factory.

Miss Delacourt stepped over to the desk and pulled out the drawers. "This is odd," she muttered.

"What is?" Fredrick asked.

"Nothing is secure," she replied with a frown on her lips. "The window was unlocked and so were the drawers."

Fredrick had an uneasy feeling about this, too, but they couldn't turn back now. They had an assignment that they had to complete. "Just quickly look through the files and see if you find anything of importance," he encouraged.

He pulled out a drawer and removed the papers from within. He started rifling through them, looking for something that would help their case. The moonlight streamed into the room, providing enough lighting to make out the words.

After a moment, Miss Delacourt held a sheet of paper up. "These are the buyers that are purchasing the smuggled goods."

"That is good, but did you discover anything that would point to the reason as to why the French spies came here?"

"Not yet," came her reply.

The door swung open, and Lord Drycott stepped into the room, a smug look on his rounded face. His black hair was slicked to the side, and his green jacket did little to hide his protruding belly. "Now who did I catch breaking into my office?" he sneered. "It is Lord Chatsworth, the war hero."

Fredrick lowered the papers to the desk. "Why is it that you don't look surprised to see me?"

"That is because I am not," Lord Drycott replied. "I know you broke into my office at my factory, along with your brother, and Mr. Bolingbroke. Do you really think I am so stupid as to not guard what is mine?"

"I don't know, considering you are smuggling goods out of France," Fredrick said. "That doesn't seem very bright to me."

Lord Drycott stepped further into the room. "It has made me a very rich man," he said.

"You will hang for your crimes," Fredrick asserted.

With a chuckle, Lord Drycott asked, "Who is going to arrest me? You?" He turned his attention towards Miss Delacourt. "I had not taken you for a man that would partner with a woman. She looks rather worse for the wear."

"I would not underestimate her," Fredrick advised.

Lord Drycott looked amused. "I would not underestimate *me*," he said with a flick of his wrist. One of Caleb's attackers from the alleyway stepped into the room and pointed a pistol at them.

Fredrick lifted his brow. "What is it that you want?"

"I want you dead, and your partner," Lord Drycott replied. "Then I will kill your brother and Mr. Bolingbroke. And anyone else who tries to defy me."

"Your plan is to just kill everyone? That doesn't seem like a good plan to me," Fredrick remarked.

Lord Drycott smirked. "Once I get the message across that anyone who dares to defy me will die, no one will come after me. I will be unstoppable."

Miss Delacourt spoke up. "You are wrong. You will never be left alone. Not only are you a smuggler, but you also willingly transported two French spies aboard one of your ships."

"I don't care who I transport as long as they pay," Lord Drycott declared. "And those two paid a pretty penny to be brought over from France."

"You committed treason," Miss Delacourt stated.

"Did I?" Lord Drycott mocked. "Oh, good heavens. I didn't mean to do such a thing. Please forgive me. I will send them back."

Miss Delacourt narrowed her eyes. "You think you are so clever—"

"But I am quite clever," Lord Drycott said, speaking over her. "I'm not sure who you are, but you must die, too. I normally avoid killing women, but I will make the exception with you."

"How gracious of you," Miss Delacourt responded. "But since I am going to die anyways, why don't you tell me what the French spies have planned?"

"How would I know?" Lord Drycott asked. "More importantly, why would I care?"

"You just let French spies come into England without knowing the intent as to why that was?" Miss Delacourt asked.

Lord Drycott pursed his lips together. "I am not a monster. I am merely a businessman."

"No, you treat your workers no better than slaves in horrendous conditions," Miss Delacourt stated. "I have seen it firsthand."

"No one has complained before," Lord Drycott said.

"I doubt that," Miss Delacourt responded.

Lord Drycott scoffed. "I truly don't care what you think, but you should stop talking now. You are trying my patience."

"Good, at least I am doing something right," Miss Delacourt said.

"Listen, you chit, you are nothing to me, and you will die a lonely, miserable death," Lord Drycott spat out.

Fredrick interjected, attempting to divert Lord Drycott's attention away from Miss Delacourt. "You can't be that naïve to think killing us will solve anything."

"It is late, Chatsworth, and no amount of talking will

change your fate." Lord Drycott snapped his fingers. "Kill them."

"I wouldn't do that just yet," Fredrick said.

Lord Drycott, his face etched with boredom, asked, "Why is that?"

"You never did ask if we came alone," Fredrick responded. "Did you?"

With an unconcerned glance over his shoulder, Lord Drycott inquired, "Who did you bring with you to die?"

"You have it all wrong. If you don't give up, it is you who will die," Fredrick asserted, his tone unwavering.

Lord Drycott seemed amused. "Me?" he huffed. "No one is going to kill me. Do you know how much money I have accrued in the past few years thanks to this war?"

"That means little to me," Fredrick said.

"It should be everything to you!" Lord Drycott shouted. "You stand there, judging me, but you don't know what I have had to do to ensure I become a very rich man. My father left me a bankrupt estate, and I had to take matters into my own hands."

"By opening factories that took advantage of their workers?" Fredrick questioned.

"That was only the beginning of my empire," Lord Drycott said, his arms outstretched. "You can't stop what I have put into motion."

"I can, and I will," Fredrick said.

Lord Drycott, growing increasingly impatient, reached behind him and retrieved a pistol. "I tire of this conversation. You will be the first to die," he said, pointing the weapon at Fredrick.

But before he could pull the trigger, Miss Delacourt swiftly positioned herself in front of Fredrick. "If you want to kill him, you have to go through me first."

"My pleasure," Lord Drycott said.

In a swift motion, Miss Delacourt produced a concealed

A Suitable Fortune

dagger and hurled it at Lord Drycott. The dagger found its mark, embedding itself in his right shoulder.

Lord Drycott looked at the dagger in surprise. "What did you do?" he asked, his voice laced with pain.

"That is a warning," Miss Delacourt responded. "If you don't put down your weapon, the next time my dagger will be aimed for your heart, and I assure you that I won't miss."

"Boss?" the burly man asked. "What do you want me to do?"

Narrowing his eyes, Lord Drycott growled, "She is bluffing. Kill them."

The sound of a cocking pistol could be heard coming from behind Lord Drycott. "I wouldn't do that if I were you," a familiar voice said.

Roswell, calm and collected, stepped into the room with a pistol aimed directly at the burly man. "If your finger twitches on that trigger, I will shoot you," he warned.

Fredrick seized the opportunity to draw his own pistol and stepped out from behind Miss Delacourt. "It is over," he said, addressing Lord Drycott. "You have lost."

With defiance in his tone, Lord Drycott asked, "Is it? We both know that I can claim privilege of the peerage, and this will all go away."

Kendrick stepped into the room. "That is assuming there is a trial," he said. "And in your case, I doubt there will be one."

"Who are you?" Lord Drycott asked.

"Someone that you will wish you never met," Kendrick replied. "We shall take it from here."

Two guards swiftly entered the room with their pistols drawn and proceeded to secure Lord Drycott and his henchman. With the immediate threat neutralized, Fredrick returned his pistol to the waistband of his trousers as Kendrick made his way towards them.

"We had guards stationed at this townhouse, watching

Lord Drycott and waiting for him to make his next move. I had come to speak to them when we saw Roswell positioned outside the townhouse, and he explained you were searching the study," the spymaster explained. "Did you discover anything of importance?"

Miss Delacourt spoke up. "We found a list of buyers for the smuggled goods."

"That is a start," Kendrick said. "Based on Lord Drycott's own words, he doesn't know the French spies' intentions for being here. Let's bring them in and ask them ourselves."

"Yes, sir," Miss Delacourt responded.

Kendrick tipped his head. "Report back when the spies have been apprehended," he ordered. "Now, if you will excuse me, I will need to deal with the servants that are milling around."

As Kendrick walked away, Fredrick turned towards Miss Delacourt and asked a question that had been weighing on his mind, "Why did you step in front of me?"

"I couldn't just let you get shot," she replied without hesitation.

Fredrick appreciated her bravery but insisted, "That was very noble of you, but don't ever do that again. I fight my own battles, and I have no desire to see another get hurt because of me."

Miss Delacourt, her chin slightly tilted, said, "A simple 'thank you' would suffice."

Fredrick felt some of the tension drain out of him now that the fight was over and he felt appreciation for what Miss Delacourt had done for him. "You are right. Thank you."

Roswell joined them, suggesting, "Shall we depart?"

"I think that is wise," Fredrick agreed. "Thank you for trailing behind us."

"It was a good thing I did, or else things could have ended very differently for you both," Roswell expressed.

Miss Delacourt smiled. "We had it handled, didn't we, my

lord?" she asked with mirth in her voice. "It is time I depart and return home."

"Would you care for us to escort you home—" Roswell started.

"No, thank you," Miss Delacourt said, speaking over him. "Good evening, gentlemen."

They watched as she climbed through the window and disappeared into the gardens.

With a shake of his head, Fredrick wasn't quite sure what to make of Miss Delacourt, but her act of bravery had touched him deeply. She had risked her own life to save his. Her actions were nothing short of courageous.

"Let's go home," Roswell encouraged.

Chapter Seventeen

Emilia could barely contain her excitement as she lay in bed. Today was to be her ball. She had never experienced a ball before, and the unknown filled her with a sense of wonder. But there was one thing she did know, and it caused her heart to race: the prospect of dancing the waltz with Fredrick. The memory of their previous waltz was never far from her mind, and she couldn't wait to be in his arms again.

She may hold Fredrick in high regard, but the feelings were unrequited. Not that she faulted him for that. He was an earl, and she was just a country bumpkin who happened to inherit a fortune. No, he deserved much more than her, no matter that she was already halfway in love with him.

Regardless, tonight would be magical; she was sure of that.

A knock came at the door before Lily entered the room. "Good morning," she greeted. "Your ballgown has just arrived from the dressmaker."

Emilia moved to sit up in bed. "That is wonderful news."

"I thought you would be pleased," Lily said. "But we must get you dressed. Mr. Livingston has come to call."

Her brows furrowed. "Calvin is here, at this early hour?"

Lily laughed. "It is not early. You just slept the morning away," she teased. "I have been up for many hours, preparing my plans for school today."

"How is the new teacher?"

"She is wonderful, but she isn't you," Lily said. "Although, the girls seem to be taken with her."

"That is good."

Lily grinned. "You can still visit the school and teach the girls a thing or two about the needle," she said. "Your needlework is exquisite."

Emilia placed her feet over the bed. "I don't wish to intrude."

"It is your school," Lily contended. "You can come and go as you please. Perhaps you can even bring Miss Clarissa on your next visit."

"You are right. I do believe I will come visit tomorrow and I will try to convince Clarissa to accompany me."

Lily approached the wardrobe and removed a pale green gown. "I still find it interesting that you and Clarissa are starting to grow rather close. You two are opposites, in practically every way."

"Yes, it is rather interesting," Emilia admitted. "But I am excited to have a sister. I have always wanted one."

"Having a sister is not like having a pet," Lily joked.

Emilia laughed at that comparison. "I know, but Clarissa is coming around, I can feel it."

"For your sake, I hope you are right." Lily held the gown up. "Now, let's get you dressed."

With Lily's assistance, Emilia got dressed and styled her hair into an elegant chignon. She departed from her bedchamber and headed for the drawing room, her curiosity piqued as to why Calvin was here.

She entered the drawing room and found Calvin pacing back and forth, his face clouded in agitation.

"Is something amiss?" Emilia asked, concerned.

Calvin stopped pacing and looked at her. "Emilia," he said. "Thank you for agreeing to meet with me at such an early hour."

She decided to lighten the mood by saying, "I have been informed by my lady's maid that it is not that early."

He took a step towards her. "I just feel awful about what transpired yesterday on our carriage ride and I was hoping for a chance to explain my behavior."

"There is really no need..." she attempted.

He spoke over her. "There is," he insisted. "My behavior was utterly unacceptable and I humbly beg your forgiveness."

Emilia gave him a weak smile. "You do not need my forgiveness, considering there is nothing to forgive."

Calvin released a heavy sigh. "You are being far too gracious, Emilia."

"Come, let us have a seat and discuss what has you so upset," Emilia suggested as she settled on the settee.

He took a seat across from her in an upholstered armchair. "I had promised you a pleasant carriage ride, but I ruined it by letting emotions get the best of me."

"You did seem rather bothered by Fredrick's presence," Emilia said.

"That is putting it lightly," Calvin admitted. "My father... or rather, our father would constantly compare me to Fredrick, and I always came up lacking."

Emilia's heart went out to Calvin. "It was unfair of Father to do such a thing."

Calvin nodded in agreement. "Yes, it was, but I wrongly directed my frustrations at Fredrick, and I let out all my pent-up emotions on him."

"It is understandable what you did, but as you said, it is not Fredrick's fault," Emilia said. "I hope you can move forward, letting go of the pains of the past."

"I hope I can," Calvin stated.

Dalby stepped into the room and announced, "Lord

Chatsworth would like a moment of your time. Shall I send him in?"

Emilia's face lit up with a smile upon hearing Fredrick's name. "Yes, please send him in."

After Dalby departed to do her bidding, Fredrick entered the room with a respectful bow. "Miss Sutherland," he greeted.

She tipped her head graciously. "Lord Chatsworth."

Fredrick's gaze shifted towards Calvin, his voice tightening. "Calvin," he acknowledged.

Rising, Calvin's eyes briefly met Emilia's before returning Fredrick's gaze. "I am glad that you are here. I wanted to apologize for my behavior yesterday."

"You do?" Fredrick asked.

"Yes, it was unfair of me to treat you so rudely, and I'm sorry," Calvin said, his voice coming out rushed.

Fredrick studied him for a moment before responding, "Thank you, Calvin. I appreciate your apology."

Calvin turned back towards her. "Well, I should be going," he said.

"So soon?" she asked. "You only just got here."

"I have things that I must see to before Clarissa and I attend the ball this evening," Calvin replied.

Emilia rose. "I am most pleased that you two have agreed to attend."

A warm smile crossed Calvin's face. "We wouldn't miss it. It will be a night to remember." His smile dimmed as he met Fredrick's gaze. "Good day, Fredrick."

After Calvin departed from the room, leaving them alone, Fredrick turned his gaze towards Emilia. "I don't think I have ever heard Calvin apologize to anyone before."

"People can change," Emilia defended.

Fredrick didn't look convinced. "Not that much," he remarked. "I am rather worried about his intentions towards you."

"His intentions?" Emilia repeated with a frown. "He is not my suitor; he is my brother."

"Half-brother," Fredrick corrected.

Emilia's voice carried a note of exasperation. "Regardless, he just wants a relationship with me."

Fredrick took a step closer to her, but still maintained a proper distance. "For your sake, I hope that is true."

"What else could Calvin gain from me?" Emilia asked.

"I don't know," Fredrick replied.

Emilia crossed her arms over her chest, determined to prove a point. "Not everyone has nefarious intentions, my lord," she said. "Some people are good and kind."

"I don't dispute that, but Calvin is not one of those people," Fredrick asserted.

"That is very unfair of you to say."

Fredrick closed the distance between them, stopping in front of her. "I have known Calvin my whole life and he is abhorrently selfish."

Emilia was unwilling to give up on her brother and thought it was best if she tried to reason with Fredrick. "Calvin just suffered a terrible loss…"

He spoke over her, his voice rising. "Stop looking for the good in everyone. Some people are inherently bad."

Fredrick was so close that she had to tilt her head to look up at him. She refused to back down, not when she believed she had right on her side. "Why don't you believe that people can change?" she asked.

"I know of your desire to have a family," Fredrick conceded, his voice softening, "but you are being blind to the truth."

"Yet you think you know the truth?"

Fredrick placed his hand on her sleeve. "I only want what is best for you. You must believe that to be true."

Their proximity left Emilia feeling vulnerable, yet, heaven help her, she did believe him. "I do," she admitted.

"Be wary of Calvin, please," Fredrick urged. "That is all I ask of you." His request was simple, yet it felt like a heartfelt plea.

Emilia held his gaze and saw the undeniable sincerity from within. She trusted him, in her heart and down to the very depths of her soul. And she knew she always would.

"Emilia…" he started.

"Yes?" she replied, her heart quickening at the intensity of his gaze.

Fredrick's eyes dropped to her lips and her breath caught. Dare she hope that he wanted to kiss her?

A maid stepped into the room, interrupting them, and announced, "I have tea, Miss." She said it much louder than was necessary.

Fredrick dropped his arm and took a step back. "I should go," he said, his voice hoarse.

Emilia wasn't quite ready to say goodbye, so she suggested, "Will you stay and join me for a cup of tea?"

"Tea would be lovely," Fredrick responded.

The maid placed the tea service onto the table and went to sit in the corner of the room.

Emilia made her way to the settee, reaching for the teapot. After she poured tea into two cups, she handed one to Fredrick.

"Thank you," he said as he accepted the cup and saucer.

"Would you care to sit?" she offered.

Fredrick let out a chuckle. "A chair would be nice," he said before taking a seat beside her.

They both sipped their tea in silence before Emilia remarked, "It is quite generous of your father to lead me in the first dance this evening."

"It is," Fredrick said. "I am not quite sure how Anette convinced him to do such a thing since he hardly attends social events anymore."

"Anette can be rather convincing," Emilia acknowledged.

"That she can be. Hence why I am here," Fredrick shared. "Anette wanted me to come over and personally ask if you needed anything for the ball this evening."

"How did she convince you to run such an errand?"

Fredrick smirked. "I'm not quite sure, but she is good," he said. "I daresay that Roswell has met his match in Anette."

"I just adore Anette. She has been nothing but kind to me since we first met."

"You are easy to be kind to," Fredrick complimented.

A blush crept into Emilia's cheeks and she tried to will it away. "You shouldn't say such nice things to me."

"You wish for me to lie to you?" Fredrick asked.

"No, I prefer honesty between us."

"As do I."

Emilia placed her teacup down onto the tray and asked, "How is it that you are not married?"

A flirtatious smile came to his lips. "Are you interested in the position?"

She reared back. "Good gracious, no. You have spoken of your aversion to it, but I am just curious as to how a man as handsome as you—"

"You think I am handsome?" he interjected.

Emilia felt her cheeks flush. "Well, I mean, surely you must know…" She pressed her lips together, wishing she could just disappear. She was mortified. Why had she even brought up such a thing?

Fredrick had sympathy for her because his next words were gentle. "I am just teasing you, Emilia. I won't get married, not because I am not able to, but because I can't."

"Of course you can," she said.

His tone grew somber. "No, you don't understand," he replied. "I can't. The things I have done, what I have seen. No, I am not worthy to be loved by another."

Emilia could hear the heartache in his voice, and she knew he believed the words he was saying. But he was wrong. She was determined to find a way to convince him otherwise.

Fredrick couldn't quite believe what he had just revealed to Emilia. What had he been thinking? He didn't want to have this conversation with her- he couldn't. She wouldn't understand his reasonings and he couldn't stand the thought that she might pity him. He didn't want anyone's pity, much less hers.

So why did he feel Emilia was the only one that could help him- truly help him? It was ridiculous to think anyone could help him. He was in a misery of his own making, and nothing would change that.

Emilia shifted on the settee to face him. "You are wrong, Fredrick," she said. "You are worthy of love."

He shook his head. "The things I've done, the things I've seen…" His words trailed off. "You couldn't possibly understand."

"You are right," she agreed. "But that doesn't mean I can't at least try, for your sake."

"No, you are too kind-hearted to ever fathom what I did," Fredrick said.

Emilia placed her hand on his sleeve. "You asked me to trust you, now I am asking for the same courtesy."

"It isn't that simple."

"Whyever not?" Emilia asked. "Tell me what troubles you."

Fredrick glanced down at her hand, knowing precisely how Emilia would react when he told her that he had killed a child. She would look at him with disgust and he didn't think he could endure that. He cared for Emilia, so much so that he needed to protect her from himself.

"I don't think I can," Fredrick admitted.

"Yes, you can," she encouraged.

Fredrick met her gaze and he could see compassion stirring within her. He knew her intentions were pure, but could he risk darkening her soul, just as his was?

In a soft voice, Emilia shared, "I want to help you, Fredrick. Tell me how to do so."

"I am past hope."

"I don't believe that to be true," Emilia said. "You are a good man."

Fredrick huffed. "You are wrong—"

She spoke over him. "I am not," she asserted. "I know precisely the man that you are. Kind. Honorable. Loyal. You helped me when no one else would."

"I owed your father a great debt. That is why I helped you."

"Perhaps, but you and I became friends along the way," Emilia said.

Friendship.

Is that what he wanted from Emilia?

Emilia continued. "I can see the pain deep within your eyes and I know your heart is troubled. Let me in, Fredrick." Her soft plea did inconvenient things to his heart.

Her words pierced through Fredrick's defenses, and he found himself admitting, "I killed a child."

Fredrick halfway expected Emilia to jump up and leave him after what he had just admitted. But, to his surprise, she remained where she was, watching him, listening.

"There must be more to the story," she said. "Will you share it with me?"

Knowing he needed her strength, he gently removed her hand from his sleeve and intertwined their fingers. "We were on a mission in a small village when we started taking fire from the locals," he shared. "They were no match for us, but when the dust settled, I was horrified to discover that I had killed a child." He hung his head. "I later learned that his name was Timmy and he was only three and ten years old. Why he had a weapon on him, I cannot say, but I shot him, dead. And his eyes still haunt me every time I close my eyes."

Emilia's voice was gentle as she said, "You did nothing wrong. Timmy would have killed you, given the chance."

"Does that make what I did right?" he asked, his voice rising.

"You were a soldier, and you were forced to make a difficult call," she said. "No one can fault you for that."

"I fault myself!" he exclaimed, jumping up from his seat. "I should have known better."

Emilia rose with him. "You are many things, but a fortune teller is not one of them. How would you have known the boy's age? All you saw was a weapon being aimed at you."

Fredrick's voice wavered as he admitted, "I wish it was me who died that day, not Timmy." His eyes filled with tears at his admission.

In the next moment, Emilia wrapped her arms around him in a comforting embrace. "Don't you dare say that," she admonished. "You changed my life, for the better. I need you in it."

"You would do just fine on your own."

"That is not true," she was quick to respond.

Fredrick returned her embrace, his chin resting on the top of her head. Despite what he had just shared, he felt something different stirring deep within him. It was something he hadn't felt in a long time- contentment. Having Emilia in his arms became an unexpected solace, offering a moment of peace amidst his haunted memories.

How could he not care for this woman? She had only shown him compassion as he bared his darkest secret, without a hint of judgment. He didn't know what his heart was trying to tell him, but he knew that something had shifted between them— something that prevented them from going back to the way they were before.

The discreet clearing of the maid's throat served as a reminder that they were not alone in the room. Reluctantly, he released Emilia, taking a step back. "I feel as if I must apologize…"

"Please don't. I do not regret my actions and nor should you," Emilia insisted. "But I do wish to say that you must be strong enough to realize that breaking isn't the same as being weak."

He pondered her for a moment before asking, "How are you so wise?"

She grinned. "I am not wise, but it is far easier to offer advice to another than to take my own."

"I haven't shared that story about Timmy since I returned from the Continent," Fredrick said. "Only my comrades know what happened that fateful day."

"I am glad that you shared it with me."

Fredrick returned her smile. "As am I."

They stared at one another, and Fredrick found himself entranced. He didn't think he could look away, even if he wanted to. Her eyes were telling him a story, one that he found he very much wanted to be a part of from here on out.

Anette's voice came from the doorway, breaking the spell that had come over Emilia and Fredrick. "Now what has you two so engrossed?"

Fredrick broke his gaze with Emilia and turned towards Anette. "We were just discussing something, weren't we, Emilia?"

"Yes, we were, and it was very important," Emilia responded, her words rushed.

Anette, looking rather curious, glanced between them as she ventured further into the room. "Interesting," she muttered. "When Fredrick failed to return, I was worried that he had gotten distracted."

Fredrick shifted uncomfortably in his stance, afraid of what Anette saw in him. "I was just about ready to depart."

"There is no need," Anette said with a wave of her hand. "I decided to just come see for myself if Emilia needed anything for the ball."

Emilia shook her head. "No, all preparations have been seen to, and my ballgown arrived this morning, as promised."

"Wonderful," Anette declared. "Shall we celebrate by going to Gunter's for an ice? My carriage is out front."

Emilia's eyes lit up. "I think that is a grand idea."

Anette shifted her gaze to Fredrick. "Would you care to join us?"

It was on the tip of his tongue to refuse but then he glanced at Emilia. He wasn't quite ready to say goodbye to her. "I would be happy to accompany you."

Emilia smiled in response, and Fredrick felt a curious flutter in his chest. What was happening to him? He had never been so wholly affected by a woman before.

"Shall we depart?" Anette asked, bringing him back to the present.

Fredrick realized that he had been caught staring at Emilia and he quickly turned his head. "Yes, that is a fine idea."

He offered his arm to Emilia, and he was pleased when she readily accepted it. They didn't speak as he led her towards the waiting carriage.

Once they were situated, the carriage merged into traffic and Fredrick retreated to his own thoughts as Anette and Emilia engaged in conversation. He didn't feel much like talking, considering he had made an utter fool of himself in front of Emilia. He had been far too vulnerable, too raw, and he couldn't help but wonder what Emilia thought of him. He stole a glance at her, attempting to discern any clues from her expression.

It was evident that she cared for him, but she only spoke

of friendship. Which was good. He wouldn't offer her anything more- he couldn't.

The carriage came to a stop outside of Gunter's and Fredrick exited first. Then he assisted the ladies out onto the pavement. As he led them into the shop, the sweet aroma of confections filled the air, eliciting a delighted gasp from Emilia.

He leaned closer to her and asked, "What shall you try?"

Emilia bit her lower lip. "What do you recommend?"

"The mango ice is my favorite," Anette shared. "But the lemon ice is quite popular amongst the patrons."

"I am more of the adventurous type," Fredrick admitted. "I will try whatever looks the most exotic."

A server approached them. "How can I help you, my lord?"

Fredrick turned towards the ladies and asked, "What shall it be?"

"The pineapple ice," Anette promptly replied.

Looking a bit hesitant, Emilia said, "Raspberry, please."

The server tipped his head in acknowledgement. "And for you, my lord?"

"I believe I shall have the burnt filbert," Fredrick responded.

It wasn't long before they each had their treats in hand and were making their way back towards the carriage. Once settled, Fredrick couldn't resist watching Emilia as she dipped her spoon into the glass and brought the frozen delicacy to her lips.

A bright smile came to her face. "This is delicious," she said, looking down at the ice.

Fredrick chuckled. "I won't disagree with you." He flicked his wrist at a worker. "I need a bag of your dry sweetmeats."

As the worker hurried to fulfill his request, Fredrick explained, "It is for my mother. It is the one indulgence that she has and I don't dare stop her from eating them."

"Nor should you," Anette said. "She is dying and deserves to eat whatever she wants."

Emilia placed her empty glass down next to her on the bench.

Fredrick arched an eyebrow. "You are finished, already?"

"Was I wrong to do so?" Emilia asked.

Anette chimed in. "You can eat your ice however you see fit. There is no right way to enjoy it. Is there, Fredrick?"

"Of course not. That was not my intention to imply such a thing," Fredrick replied. "Would you like me to get you another?"

Emilia put her hand up. "There is no need." She glanced around before lowering her voice. "Why does it feel like everyone is staring at me?"

"That is because they are," Anette said. "Do not give them much heed."

"Why are they staring?" Emilia asked.

Anette shrugged her shoulders. "Who knows, but they will go about their own business in a few moments."

The worker arrived back at the carriage with the bag in his hand. "Here you are, my lord," he said, extending the treats towards him.

Fredrick retrieved the bag before he handed the worker a coin.

Anette eyed the bag and asked, "Would you like me to ensure they are not poisonous?"

"Now you are sounding like Octavia," Fredrick joked. "But you are more than welcome to have one."

As he settled back to enjoy his ice, Fredrick recognized that he was truly enjoying this outing. It was far preferable to being stuck in the study, working on the accounts.

But he suspected the real reason why he was enjoying himself so much was because of Emilia.

Chapter Eighteen

As the sun dipped below the horizon, casting a warm glow across the study, Fredrick found himself seated at the desk, attempting to work on the accounts. However, his mind was on anything but. He couldn't stop dwelling on Emilia. She was quickly starting to occupy space in his heart, a heart that he had believed to be impenetrable.

Everything had changed between them when he shared what happened with Timmy on the battlefield. How was it that he trusted Emilia so much, even with his heart? She had managed to breach his defenses, making him feel like he wasn't alone in his grief anymore.

How was it that she believed in him when he didn't even believe in himself? She was a rarity amongst women. And he would be a fool to let her go. Yet the doubt started creeping in. Could he take a wife, knowing he would never truly be worthy of her?

Roswell stepped into the room. "We just received word from Miss Delacourt," he said. "She wants us to meet her at the boarding house where the French spies are."

"When?"

"Now," Roswell replied.

Fredrick stood up and walked around the desk. "Let's depart at once," he said.

As they made their way to the coach, silence hung between them. It wasn't until they were seated inside that Roswell broke it. "Now, will you tell me what has you so upset?"

"I am not upset," Fredrick lied.

Roswell shot him a knowing look. "Come now, surely you do not think I can be dismissed so easily."

"I don't wish to discuss it," Fredrick insisted.

With a smirk, Roswell remarked, "There is only one thing that would have you so upset and that is Emilia. Am I right?"

Fredrick adjusted his jacket's lapels. "You aren't wrong, but it changes nothing for me."

"Why not just marry her and put yourself out of your misery?"

"I never said I wanted to marry Emilia."

Roswell chuckled. "You didn't have to."

"You are infuriating," Fredrick muttered, "and not the least bit helpful."

Leaning back into his seat, Roswell said, "The attraction between you two is evident to everyone around you. Furthermore, Anette truly believes you would be perfect for one another."

"Emilia is a wonderful woman…"

"Why do I sense a 'but'?" Roswell interjected.

"…*but* she deserves better than me," Fredrick said.

Roswell lifted his brow. "You are an earl and will be the Marquess of Cuttyngham one day."

"That means very little to Emilia, which makes her that much more endearing to me," Fredrick said. "She just wants to feel accepted, loved, even."

"You can give her that," Roswell remarked.

"I could, but I am not quite the same since I returned home from the war," Fredrick shared. "I have nightmares to this day. And the terrible images that I still see, I do believe will haunt me forever. Can I in good conscience let Emilia into my misery, my pain?"

"Have you asked her this?" Roswell asked.

Fredrick shook his head. "I have not," he said. "I only just came to realize that I might love her."

"Might?" Roswell huffed. "You, Brother, can't stop staring at Emilia whenever she is around. There is no 'might' about it."

"I never wanted to marry," Fredrick sighed.

"It is all right to accept change," Roswell said. "It proves that you are still growing."

Fredrick shifted his gaze towards the window, a myriad of conflicted emotions whirling inside of him. As much as he wanted to dwell on Emilia, he didn't have the time or the luxury to do so. Two French spies were on the loose, and he couldn't afford to let his emotions cloud his judgment. Emilia would have to wait.

Roswell's voice broke through his musings. "Did you happen to read the newssheets this morning, specifically the article about Lord Drycott?"

"Yes, I did read that Lord Drycott was found dead last night. Presumably, his heart had failed him," Fredrick replied.

"We both know that isn't true."

"I know. But I can't say that I feel sorry for the man," Fredrick said. "He had blood on his hands."

"That he did," Roswell agreed.

The coach came to a stop down the street from the boarding house and Fredrick exited, not bothering to wait for the footman's assistance. His boots met the pavement with purpose, the gravity of the impending mission etched on his face.

Roswell gestured towards the boarding house. "That is the one," he said. "Now where the blazes is Miss Delacourt?"

No sooner had he uttered these words than they heard

Miss Delacourt's voice behind them. "It is about time you two showed up."

Fredrick turned around, and his brow shot up at the sight before him. Miss Delacourt was wearing trousers, a white shirt and black Hessian boots. Her brown hair was tucked under a brown cap, and she wore a handkerchief around her neck. If she thought her disguise was fooling anyone, she would be mistaken.

"What are you wearing?" he asked.

Miss Delacourt glanced down at her clothing. "I would say that it is fairly obvious."

"You are wearing trousers," Fredrick said, lowering his voice.

She took a step closer to him and matched his hushed tone. "I know, and so does everyone else. There is no need to whisper."

Roswell looked amused. "I see no issue with it," he stated. "Anette has worn trousers on occasion to ride her horse."

"You have a good wife," Miss Delacourt remarked.

Fredrick put his hands up. "My apologies. I shouldn't have said anything, considering we have more important matters to discuss."

"That we do," Miss Delacourt agreed. "I have since learned that the French spies are in room 3A."

"Have you seen them?" Roswell inquired.

She shook her head. "No, but the owner of the boarding house informed me that two people with French accents rented the room. They claimed to be brother and sister and they haven't left their room since this morning."

"Did you request additional agents?" Fredrick asked.

"I didn't think we needed them," Miss Delacourt replied. "There are three of us, and only two of them. Furthermore, we have the element of surprise."

Fredrick eyed her curiously. "I assume you brought a pistol to this fight."

"I did, but I am much more proficient with my daggers," Miss Delacourt said.

"Then let us end this," Fredrick asserted.

They headed towards the boarding house with a purposeful stride. The mission was simple, and straightforward. If everything went well, they should have the French spies in Newgate before it was time to get ready for the ball.

Miss Delacourt arrived first at the door of the boarding house and pushed it open. A thin, older man with pasty white skin met them in the entry hall.

"Mr. Treanor," Miss Delacourt greeted. "Has there been any movement in room 3A?"

"None at all, and I've been keeping a watchful eye over it, just as I promised," Mr. Treanor assured her.

Miss Delacourt's lips curled into a confident smile as she turned to Fredrick. "Will you pay the man? This clothing doesn't exactly make it easy to carry coins with me."

Fredrick produced a few coins and handed them to Mr. Treanor. "Your assistance is greatly appreciated."

Mr. Treanor pocketed the coins. "Any man that would pretend a woman was his sister is up to no good in my opinion." He reached into his pocket and pulled out a key. "This key will open 3A. Just try to keep down the noise. It is bad for business."

Miss Delacourt extended her hand for the key. "We shall try our best," she said.

With a brief nod, Mr. Treanor departed from the entry hall, leaving them alone. Miss Delacourt gave them both expectant looks. "Come along," she urged before she led them down the dimly lit corridor.

Fredrick retrieved his pistol and followed closely behind. When they reached room 3A, Miss Delacourt held up three fingers and initiated a silent countdown. Three. Two. One.

Inserting the key into the lock, she stepped back. Roswell swung the door open, and they entered the room, only to find it empty. The window was open, and the blue drapes billowed in the evening breeze.

Miss Delacourt looked stunned as she walked further into the room. "Where are they?"

"They clearly left at some point," Roswell replied. "The question now is, where did they go?"

Fredrick moved towards the hearth, crouching down. He noticed the burned edges of papers that had been discarded in the fire. "There is nothing recoverable here."

Roswell headed to the writing desk and started pulling out the drawers. "There is nothing in here," he said, slamming the last drawer closed.

"I don't understand," Miss Delacourt said, her voice hesitant. "I have been standing guard for hours. How could they have just slipped out right from under my nose?"

"It happens," Fredrick remarked.

"Not to me," Miss Delacourt insisted.

Fredrick didn't know much about Miss Delacourt, but he recognized enough to know that she was a competent agent. "We will get them," he reassured her. "You found them once; you will find them again."

Miss Delacourt's eyes held gratitude. "Thank you, my lord."

"There is nothing for us here," Roswell said. "We should return the key and depart before we attract any unwanted attention to ourselves."

They filed out of the room and went in search of Mr. Treanor. They found him in a room off the entry hall.

"Did you get the man and woman you were after?" Mr. Treanor asked.

"I'm afraid not," Miss Delacourt replied. "They were already gone when we got there."

Mr. Treanor blinked. "That is impossible. I have been watching that door all day."

"They slipped out the window," Miss Delacourt informed him.

"Those scoundrels. They skipped out on paying their bill," Mr. Treanor grumbled. "I even brought them the newssheets this morning, just as they requested."

A thought crossed Fredrick's mind. "I can't help but wonder if they saw the article about Lord Drycott. Perhaps that is what scared them off."

"Most likely," Roswell agreed.

Miss Delacourt returned the key to Mr. Treanor. "Thank you, sir. You did your best. That is all I could have asked of you."

Mr. Treanor's eyes crinkled around the edges. "You remind me so much of my granddaughter, Olivia. I have caught her in trousers a time or two."

Fredrick interjected, "Would you describe the people we are after?"

With a bob of his head, Mr. Treanor replied, "The man was tall, dark-haired and had a thin face. His nose was slightly crooked, as if he had broken it before. The woman was similar in appearance, but she was shorter than her companion. That is why it was feasible that they were brother and sister."

"That is most helpful," Miss Delacourt said. "Thank you." Once she finished saying her words, she departed from the boarding house.

Fredrick and Roswell hastened to catch up to her on the pavement, easily matching her stride. "Who wants to inform Kendrick of what happened?" Roswell asked.

"I will handle it," Miss Delacourt replied. "After all, it was my failure. Besides, don't you two have a ball to prepare for?"

"Are you not attending?" Fredrick asked.

Miss Delacourt came to a stop in front of a black coach and a footman exited his perch to open the door. "I will be there, but I doubt you will notice me. Not with Miss Sutherland being there and all."

Fredrick cleared his throat. How was it that everyone could see that he was falling for Emilia? Was he so obvious in his affections?

But Miss Delacourt was right. He had a ball that he had to attend, and he was rather looking forward to it. However, this conversation was not over, at least not yet. There were too many questions that remained.

"I think it is safe to assume that the French spies were scared off by Lord Drycott's death," Fredrick said. "What do you think their next play is?"

"I don't know," Miss Delacourt replied. "But I will ask Kendrick to post guards at Lord Drycott's townhouse in case they are foolish enough to go there."

Roswell crossed his arms over his chest. "And I will reach out to my informants and ask them to keep a look out for anyone that matches their descriptions. We will find them. It is only a matter of time."

Miss Delacourt nodded. "I shall inform Kendrick of this, and with any luck, he will let me continue working on the assignment."

Fredrick bowed. "Until later, Miss Delacourt."

As Fredrick made his way towards his waiting coach, he noticed a quickened pace in his step. He was to dance the waltz this evening with Emilia, and the mere thought of holding her in his arms, if only for a moment, filled him with a profound sense of joy. And in that moment, it struck him- he had undeniably and irrevocably fallen in love with Emilia.

Emilia stood in the parlor, her anticipation palpable, as she waited for Lord Cuttyngham's arrival to escort her into the ballroom for her first dance. Nervousness coursed through her, overshadowed only slightly by the excitement she felt within. The uncertainty of how she would be received by the *ton* quickened her heart.

"I can do this," she muttered for what felt like the thousandth time. Amidst the whirlwind of emotions she felt within, she held on to the knowledge that Fredrick was waiting for her in the ballroom. He would help her; she was sure of that. Her trust in him was not misplaced.

Fredrick may not care for her as she did for him, but she would take him as he was. She wanted to be in his life, now and forever.

Emilia turned towards the large mirror that hung on the wall and marveled at her ballgown. She had never worn such an ornate gown before. The cost of this single gown was more than she would ever earn as a teacher at her old boarding school.

The gown itself was a delicate shade of pale blue, adorned with a net overlay intricately embroidered with flowers and dotted with small jewels. It was truly magnificent. She felt beautiful- something that didn't happen very often in her life.

The door swung open and Anette stepped into the parlor with a broad smile on her lips. "Your ball is a *crush*," she declared.

Emilia found herself smiling in response. "That is wonderful."

Anette perused the length of her. "That ballgown is exquisite," she said. "I have never seen anything quite like it."

"I helped the dressmaker design it," Emilia admitted.

"Well, you should be proud of yourself, because I doubt Fredrick will be able to keep his eyes off of you," Anette said.

"Fredrick?" she asked.

Anette waved her hand in front of her. "My apologies. I meant the *ton* won't be able to keep their eyes off of you."

Emilia wasn't sure what to make of Anette's slip of her

tongue. It sounded deliberate, but she didn't dare press her friend. Not now. Her greatest fear was that Anette saw right through her and knew of her feelings for Fredrick. What a mortifying thought.

"I am slightly nervous," Emilia admitted.

"As well you should be," Anette replied. "A little fear doesn't hurt anyone, especially since everyone in that ballroom is waiting for you to fail."

"They are?"

Anette nodded. "But you aren't going to fail, are you?" she questioned. "You are going to keep your head held high, knowing you have earned your rightful place in high Society."

Emilia started fidgeting with her hands. "I have earned nothing," she admitted. "I just happened to inherit a fortune."

"A grand fortune, that is far more than suitable," Anette corrected.

"Regardless, is that enough to win the *ton's* approval?" Emilia asked.

A deep, resonant voice came from the doorway. "No, it is not," said a tall, white-haired man. It was evident that this was Lord Cuttyngham because he bore a striking resemblance to Fredrick.

Lord Cuttyngham walked further into the room. "There will always be some naysayers that claim you don't belong amongst high Society because you are an upstart. There will be others that say you don't belong because Sir Charles was only a baronet," he said. "But none of those opinions matter; only yours does. Don't give the naysayers any heed."

Emilia gracefully dropped into a curtsy. "Thank you, my lord."

The marquess came to a stop in front of her. "You are enchanting, my dear," he said with a warm smile. "I can see why you have bewitched my son."

Her eyes grew wide. "I have done no such thing," she said. "We are just friends."

"Ah, my mistake," the marquess responded lightly.

Anette interjected, breaking the moment. "Shall we adjourn to the ballroom?"

Lord Cuttyngham extended his arm to Emilia. "Shall we, my dear?" he asked.

She rested her hand on his sleeve and allowed him to lead her from the parlor. As they walked to the ballroom, she wanted to express her gratitude. "Thank you for agreeing to do this. I know it must come as a great hardship to you since you were forced to leave your wife's bedside."

"It is my privilege to help one of Fredrick's friends," Lord Cuttyngham said with amusement in his voice.

Emilia felt her heart quicken as they approached the ballroom.

In a gentle voice, Lord Cuttyngham encouraged, "Don't forget to breathe."

"I am trying to," Emilia confessed, "but I fear my heart will pound right out of my chest."

Lord Cuttyngham paused, turning to face her. "Just try to remember that this is your night. Do try to enjoy yourself."

"I will try."

A look of understanding came to his eyes. "Before his death, Sir Charles told me about you and your circumstances. He was so very proud of you that you had found your own way after the death of your mother, and I know he deeply regretted not being a part of your life."

"I wish he had been," Emilia murmured.

Lord Cuttyngham placed a hand on her sleeve. "You are enough, and I hope you know that," he said. "His absence in your life had nothing to do with you and everything to do with him."

Emilia offered him a weak smile. "Thank you."

"Have I offered you enough advice yet?" Lord Cuttyngham asked with a twinkle in his eyes. "After all, your guests are waiting for you."

She squared her shoulders and took a deep breath, mustering a façade of confidence. She could do this. "I am ready," she announced.

As Lord Cuttyngham walked towards the ballroom, two impeccably dressed footmen moved to open the door, revealing the crowd of people within.

After she stepped through the doors, her gaze sought Fredrick amidst the crowd. They locked eyes and a reassuring smile played on his lips. A sense of calm washed over her, ensuring her that everything would be all right.

The soft glow of chandeliers cast a warm light over the ballroom as Lord Cuttyngham guided her towards the chalked dance floor. He came to a stop and asked, "How are you faring?"

"Quite well," she replied, stealing a brief glance in Fredrick's direction.

Lord Cuttyngham nodded approvingly. "Then let us dance," he declared, extending his hands.

The enchanting melody of the orchestra filled the air, and Lord Cuttyngham led her into the dance. Her gaze remained fixed on the marquess as she attempted to ignore the blatant stares of the other guests.

"You are doing remarkably well," Lord Cuttyngham praised, his voice a soothing reassurance.

"That is only because you are such a fine dancer," Emilia said.

Lord Cuttyngham grinned in response as they continued their dance, and Emilia found herself relaxing in his arms.

Once the music had died down, Lord Cuttyngham brought the dance to a close, dropping his arms with practiced elegance.

Emilia dropped into a low curtsy.

Turning towards the assembled crowd, Lord Cuttyngham, with a voice that carried authority and warmth, announced,

"May I have the privilege of introducing the lovely Miss Emilia Sutherland."

The room responded with polite applause and Emilia felt a sense of accomplishment wash over her. She had managed to get through the dance without embarrassing herself or Lord Cuttyngham.

After the applause died down, the marquess directed his attention towards her. "Well done," he praised. "If you will excuse me, I am going to return to my wife's side."

"Thank you for what you did, my lord," Emilia said, hoping her words conveyed her deep gratitude for his sacrifice.

"You are most welcome," Lord Cuttyngham responded before departing from the dance floor.

Anette broke through the crowd and hurried over to her. "You were flawless," she declared. "I challenge anyone to say otherwise."

"It wasn't as awful as I thought it would be," Emilia admitted.

Lord Roswell joined them, standing next to his wife. "I must assume that my father departed to be with my mother."

Emilia bobbed her head. "He did," she confirmed. "You must thank him again for me. I know it couldn't have been an easy decision for him to leave his wife."

Lord Roswell's eyes reflected a touch of sadness. "My father hardly leaves her side now. I know it has taken a great toll on him, but he doesn't speak of it."

"Your mother is a good woman," Anette murmured.

"The best of mothers," Lord Roswell responded. "But we are here tonight to celebrate Emilia. It is her ball, after all."

Anette brought a smile to her lips. "You are right, of course," she said. "Come, I wish to introduce you to someone."

Fredrick's voice came from behind her. "Do I not get to congratulate Emilia on a job well done?" he asked.

Emilia turned towards Fredrick, her heart skipping a beat at his presence. "Hello," she greeted.

"Hello," he replied, his eyes holding approval as he perused the length of her. "You look lovely this evening."

She held out the sides of her skirts. "It is the dress," she said, a modest smile gracing her lips.

"Although the dress is indeed lovely, that is not the reason why everyone is staring at you this evening," Fredrick responded, a subtle intensity in his gaze.

Emilia felt a blush forming on her cheeks. "You are most kind, my lord."

Fredrick leaned closer, his tone teasing. "I see that you have finally learned how to take a compliment."

"I learned from the best," she replied as she held his gaze.

Anette stepped closer to them, drawing their attention. "Perhaps we should remove ourselves from the dance floor before the next set begins."

"That is a wonderful idea," Fredrick said, holding out his arm to Emilia. "Would you care for a glass of lemonade?"

"Yes, please," Emilia replied as she placed her hand on his sleeve.

As Fredrick led her off the dance floor, Emilia couldn't escape the scrutiny of the crowd. A blend of critical and curious glances followed her every step. Some of the young women tried to catch Fredrick's attention, batting their eyelashes and offering coy smiles, but his focus remained on Emilia.

"I wish everyone would stop staring at us," Emilia whispered.

Fredrick offered her a reassuring smile. "I have learned to just ignore it."

"How are you able to do so?"

Fredrick's smile widened. "I do not care as deeply as you do when it comes to what people think of me."

"That is because you are an heir to a marquessate," Emilia remarked.

They found a spot near the refreshment table, and Fredrick reached for a glass of lemonade, extending it to Emilia.

"Thank you," she acknowledged.

Fredrick picked up another glass for himself. "Are you at least enjoying yourself?"

"I am." Her gaze swept over the elaborately decorated ballroom. "It just seems so unbelievable that this is my life now."

"You will get used to it," Fredrick assured her.

"I hope not," Emilia admitted. "I want to savor every moment, to never let this extraordinary life become ordinary."

Fredrick took a sip of his drink before saying, "I'm afraid it is a life that I have taken for granted far too often."

"That is because you were born into it. You know no different, and I could never fault you for that," Emilia responded.

A movement in the crowd caught Emilia's attention and she saw Clarissa hastily making her way towards the doors leading to the veranda.

Fredrick followed her gaze. "What do you suppose has Clarissa so upset?"

"I don't rightly know, but I should go to her," Emilia said as she placed the glass on the table.

"Would you care for me to join you?" Fredrick asked.

"You are kind to offer, but I should go alone," Emilia replied.

Fredrick tipped his head. "Very well, but do not forget that we are to dance the waltz soon."

With a furrowed brow, Emilia asked, "I thought the waltz wasn't until the end of the ball?"

A playful glint came into Fredrick's eyes. "I asked Anette to change the order of dances this evening."

"For what purpose?"

"Because, my dear, I didn't wish to wait until the end of the ball to hold you in my arms," Fredrick replied.

Emilia stared up at him, surprised by the genuineness in his voice. Could it be that he harbored feelings for her? The notion sent her heart aflutter with anticipation.

But now was not the time to act like a love-craved debutante. Clarissa needed her attention. She took a step back. "I shall return shortly."

"See that you do," came Fredrick's reply, his gaze lingering on her.

Emilia spun on her heel and headed towards the doors through which she had seen Clarissa disappear. She couldn't help but smile at Fredrick's admission. What it meant, she did not know. But it was promising.

Chapter Nineteen

Fredrick watched Emilia's retreating figure as she made her way towards the veranda. He hadn't meant to be so bold in his words with her, but he couldn't help himself. He wanted her to know how he felt. But what that meant, he did not know.

His desire to take Emilia as his wife was growing. With her by his side, he felt like he would have a new lease on life. She lifted him up in a way that no other woman ever had. However, the haunting memories of his past still lingered, tormenting him. Could he bring Emilia into his life, knowing he might not truly be free of them?

His eyes swept over the hall, noticing young women vying for his attention. But he had no interest in any of them. His heart resided with Emilia.

Miss Delacourt's voice came from next to him. "I spoke to Kendrick," she revealed. "He is not pleased with my failure."

"*Our* failure," Fredrick corrected. "We were assigned to work together."

"You are gracious, but we both know that I let them slip right out from under my nose," Miss Delacourt said as she reached for a glass of lemonade.

"We will find them," Fredrick said.

Miss Delacourt took a sip of her drink. "Kendrick wants us in his office tomorrow, along with Caleb," she revealed.

"I will be there," Fredrick said.

"Good," Miss Delacourt responded. "I should return to my companion before she starts to question why I am taking so long to get a glass of lemonade."

Fredrick's curiosity sparked. "How is it that you can evade your companion during the day but not at a ball?" Fredrick asked.

"Very carefully, my lord. It is a skill that I have perfected over time." Miss Delacourt smirked. "If there is nothing else, I shall take my leave."

"Good evening, Miss Delacourt."

As she gracefully returned to her seat among the other wallflowers, Fredrick couldn't help but be intrigued that a young woman of Miss Delacourt's undeniable beauty could go unnoticed by the *ton*. She was a perplexing woman, yet an unquestionably competent agent.

Fredrick's gaze wandered towards the veranda, wondering what was keeping Emilia. He hoped she would return shortly for their dance.

Greydon and his wife made their way through the crowd and approached Fredrick. "Something is different about you," he commented as he came to a stop next to Fredrick.

"Nothing is different about me," Fredrick insisted.

Greydon studied him for a moment. "You seem happy," he commented. "Making me wonder *who* has had this effect on you."

Fredrick should have known that his friend would see right through him, but he didn't want to continue down this line of questioning. He bowed to Lady Rushcliffe. "My lady," he greeted.

"I do believe I asked you to call me Enid, on multiple occasions," she responded with a warm smile.

Fredrick returned her smile. "It is good to see you looking so well."

Greydon took a step closer to him. "Do not think I don't know what you are doing."

"What is that?" Fredrick asked.

"You are trying to avoid my comments, but it won't work," Greydon said, a knowing glint in his eyes.

Enid playfully swatted at her husband's sleeve. "Leave Fredrick alone. He has a right to his own secrets."

"It isn't a very well-kept secret," Greydon joked. "Anyone with eyes can see that Fredrick is enamored with the lovely Miss Sutherland."

"I think it is sweet. Although, I am not acquainted with Miss Sutherland," Enid said. "But Anette speaks very highly of her."

Fredrick nodded. "I do believe that Anette and Miss Sutherland have grown rather close as they planned the ball together."

Enid's eyes swept over the ballroom. "Yes, and what a splendid ball it turned out to be. I have no doubt people will be talking about it for weeks to come."

"Where is Miss Sutherland?" Greydon asked.

Fredrick gestured towards the back wall. "On the veranda with Clarissa."

"I found it to be an odd choice that she invited Clarissa and Calvin to the ball," Greydon remarked. "And it was even more surprising that they agreed to come. I can't imagine they have been received very well this evening."

"Miss Sutherland has a soft spot for them, and she wanted to ensure they were included in the festivities," Fredrick explained.

Enid nodded approvingly. "Miss Sutherland seems like a kind-hearted young woman."

"She is," Fredrick rushed to say. "I have never met anyone who has such a loving heart for everyone."

"Then you best not let her go," Enid advised with a twinkle in her eyes.

Fredrick decided it was best to be honest with his friends, but not too honest. "I care for Miss Sutherland, but I still do not know if offering for her is the best idea. My past has caught up to me, and I don't know if I can care for her as she deserves."

Greydon exchanged a telling look with Enid before saying, "Have you been honest about your past?"

"I have told her about the war, but I still have some secrets that I have not shared, particularly that I have been working as a spy," Fredrick admitted.

"My advice to you is to be honest about everything," Greydon said. "Don't hold anything back and let her decide if she can step into your life."

Enid nodded her agreement. "Greydon is right. You must be honest with Miss Sutherland if you want your marriage to work."

"What if she thinks it is all too much?" Fredrick asked.

"Then you will know your answer," Enid replied.

With a resigned sigh, Fredrick said, "That does not sound easy."

Greydon slipped his arm around Enid's waist. "Love never is, but it is worth it, my friend."

Fredrick saw no reason to correct Greydon. His heart belonged to Emilia, and he didn't care if everyone knew. But it was more important that Emilia knew. He had to tell her the truth, and he truly hoped that she would reciprocate his affection.

The next set was announced and it was to be the waltz. He wondered what was keeping Emilia. He didn't want to pass on the chance to hold her in his arms.

"Excuse me, but I must go see to Miss Sutherland," Fredrick said with a slight bow.

He didn't wait for their responses before he headed

towards the veranda. Once he stepped outside, he saw no sign of her. Or Clarissa. Where in the blazes could they be?

Had they taken a walk on one of the many paths that lined the expansive gardens? He let out a groan. It could take a while to search for them, and he didn't have time for that.

He didn't want to miss the waltz, but it appeared to be inevitable. As his eyes roamed over the gardens' grounds, an uneasy feeling came over him. It was a feeling that he had learned to trust, but he wasn't sure what it meant.

Fredrick started down one of the paths, hoping he would come across Emilia and Clarissa sooner rather than later.

The moon hung high in the sky, casting a pale glow over the gardens. Emilia sat on a bench in the rear of the gardens where it was more secluded. She wanted to give Clarissa some privacy as she swiped at the tears that were falling down her cheeks. The leaves rustled softly in the breeze and the occasional chirping of crickets filled the air.

"I'm sorry for my display of emotions," Clarissa said in between sobs.

"You have nothing to be sorry about," Emilia responded.

Clarissa looked over at her. "We both know that isn't true. I am ruining your ball."

Emilia placed a comforting hand on Clarissa's sleeve. "You are doing no such thing," she insisted. "I am happy to be here with you."

"You are very kind," Clarissa said, wiping away another tear.

Emilia gave her a knowing look. "You would do the same thing for me," she remarked. "Now, what has you so upset?"

Clarissa looked up at the night sky, as if searching for an answer among the stars. "I wasn't prepared for the harsh comments that were directed at me, but I suppose it was inevitable."

"Now it is my turn to apologize," Emilia said.

"Whatever for?" Clarissa asked, looking bemused.

"Perhaps it wasn't wise for me to invite you to the ball, given your recent change in fortune," Emilia admitted with a sigh.

Clarissa shifted on the bench to face her. "But I wanted to be here to support you."

"You did?" Emilia asked.

"I did," Clarissa confirmed. "That is what sisters are for, is it not?"

Emilia smiled broadly. "It is."

Calvin's voice emerged from the darkness behind them. "What do we have here?" he asked, his tone cold.

Turning towards Calvin, Emilia saw that he was holding a pistol, and it was pointed at her.

Emilia rose. "What are you doing?"

"Isn't it obvious?" Calvin asked. "I am here to kill you."

"But why?"

Calvin laughed dryly. "When you die, everything that you have will become ours, and we will finally be free of you." He paused. "What did you think would happen when you made us your beneficiaries?"

"I did so because we are family," Emilia said.

All humor left Calvin's face. "We are not family," he spat out. "It was just a fantasy on your part, making it so easy to manipulate you."

Emilia shifted her gaze towards Clarissa. "Surely you are not a part of this?"

Clarissa's expression was one of indifference. "I am not your sister, and I never will be," she replied as she went to stand by her brother. "I just said precisely what you wanted to hear."

"How could you do such a thing?" Emilia asked.

Clarissa tilted her chin haughtily. "How could I do such a thing?" she repeated back. "You came into our lives and ruined everything. You are nothing to us."

Emilia tried not to react to the harshness of their words, but it stung anyways. "But I gave you back your dowry."

"Yes, you did," Clarissa said. "But upon your death, we get everything back that was rightfully ours."

"It is not rightfully yours. Father gave it to me," Emilia declared.

A flush stained Clarissa's cheeks and her nostrils flared with rage. "He is not your father; he is mine!" she exclaimed. "I was forced to put up with him and he betrayed me in the end."

"He didn't betray you," Emilia attempted. "He did leave you some money."

"A paltry ten thousand pounds," Clarissa said. "But with you gone, I will be an heiress again and regain my place within high Society."

Calvin took a step closer to Emilia and cocked his pistol. "Enough talking," he ordered. "I need to return to the card room before anyone notices I am missing."

"You won't get away with this," Emilia attempted.

Calvin's lips twitched. "Who is going to stop me?"

Slow clapping echoed from the shadows of the trees. A familiar figure emerged.

Fredrick.

Emilia felt relief at the sight of him, but that was short-lived. What if Calvin shot Fredrick? Her heart pounded faster as a wave of fear surged through her at that thought.

Fredrick came to a stop next to Emilia. "That was excellent theatre, but it is over."

Calvin turned his pistol towards Fredrick. "What are you doing here?"

Appearing completely unruffled by the weapon that was

being pointed at him, Fredrick said, "I have come to retrieve Miss Sutherland for the waltz."

"She is not going anywhere, and neither are you," Calvin declared.

Fredrick looked at him curiously. "What is your plan exactly?" he asked. "Dare I point out that you have one bullet in that pistol?"

Calvin's face grew hard. "You think you are so clever, don't you?"

"More so than you," Fredrick replied. "Did you ever anticipate all the ways that this could go terribly wrong, considering people would hear the shot echo through the gardens and would come to investigate?"

"That is why I was going to sneak back into the card room during the commotion, and none would be the wiser," Calvin said.

Fredrick lifted his brow. "Your alibi was going to be a room full of drunken gentlemen?" he asked.

"Yes," Calvin replied.

"I see, and what of Clarissa?" Fredrick asked. "People saw her leaving with Emilia following close behind. Wouldn't they be suspicious of her?"

Calvin shifted his weight from one foot to the other. The ground beneath him was damp and gave way with a squelch as he moved. "I care little about what happens to her."

Clarissa's mouth dropped. "You would betray me- your sister?"

"Do not look so surprised," Calvin responded. "You would do the same to me, given the chance."

"I would not!" Clarissa's voice was shrill and defensive. Her hands balled into fists at her sides. "We are family, and we are supposed to stick together."

Calvin looked uninterested by Clarissa's remark. "Save me the theatrics," he said, speaking slowly, deliberately. "We both know that your heart is as cold as mine."

Fredrick looked at Emilia and winked. She felt her pulse quicken, and in that moment, she knew that everything would be all right. She didn't know how, but she trusted him.

The indecision was on Calvin's expression as he shifted the pistol between Fredrick and Emilia. "Both of you will still die tonight," he growled.

"How, exactly?" Fredrick asked. "You are no match for me, or Emilia, for that matter."

The pistol's swaying stopped on Fredrick. "I hate you," he seethed. "My father was constantly comparing me to you, and I despised him for that."

"That was hardly my fault," Fredrick said.

"Regardless, I will shoot you and then kill Emilia with my own bare hands," Calvin declared.

Fredrick put his hands up. "Brilliant," he said. "But have you killed anyone before? I only ask because it is much more difficult than people imagine."

Calvin sneered. "As if you would know."

"You seem to forget that I fought in a war," Fredrick stated. "I was forced to kill more people than I care to admit, and it takes a toll on you."

With a sadistic grin, Calvin aimed the pistol. His cold, dark eyes stared straight at Fredrick as he said, "I will rejoice when you are dead. Then I won't have to hear your grating voice anymore."

Emilia moved quickly between them, blocking Calvin's view of Fredrick. "Don't shoot him!" she begged desperately. "I will give you my entire fortune. Just leave us be."

"You don't mean that," Calvin said.

"I do," Emilia asserted. "I don't care about the money."

Fredrick placed a hand on Emilia's sleeve and gently turned her to face him. "What are you saying, Emilia?"

She stared up at him, her heart beating a little faster as she felt more vulnerable than she ever had before. "I want you in my life, more so than the money," she confessed.

His face softened, and his green eyes seemed to pierce her very soul. "You would be willing to give up your fortune for me?"

"I would," she said.

As she uttered her words, a tall, dark-haired young woman strolled down the path towards them. She stopped and gasped as her eyes landed on the pistol in Calvin's hand.

Calvin turned the pistol towards the young woman. "Get out of here," he ordered.

"Why are you pointing a pistol at Lord Chatsworth and Miss Sutherland?" the young woman asked.

"It is none of your business," Calvin growled.

Clarissa stepped closer to her brother and said, "We can't just let her leave. She is a witness to this."

The young woman shook her head. "I won't say anything. I promise. Just let me return to the ballroom."

Emilia couldn't help but feel sympathy for the distressed young woman before her. She seemed so unsure of herself, and she was caught in an unfortunate circumstance.

"Let her go," Emilia urged. "Your business is with me, not her."

Calvin shifted his attention towards Emilia, allowing the young woman to swiftly release a dagger that found its mark in his right arm. He dropped the pistol and reached for the dagger.

"You stupid chit!" Calvin exclaimed, his voice laced with pain.

Seizing the opportunity, Clarissa bent down, snatching up the pistol, and aimed it at Emilia. "This is all your fault! You ruined everything when you showed up!" she shouted. "You need to die."

Fredrick immediately moved to stand in front of her, but Emilia put her hand out to stop him. This was between her and Clarissa. "She isn't going to shoot me."

"Yes, I am," Clarissa said.

Emilia shook her head. "No, because I believe, deep down, that you are a good person."

Clarissa scoffed. "You don't know me. Everything you think you know is wrong."

The sound of booted footsteps came from behind Clarissa. "But I do," Roswell said. "It is over, Clarissa. You have lost."

Clarissa's eyes widened in desperation. "No! She can't win, not again," she shouted. "I won't go back to Cheapside."

"You may change your mind when you see the accommodations at Newgate," Roswell joked. "Lower the pistol or else Miss Delacourt might release another one of her daggers."

With a defeated expression, Clarissa reluctantly lowered the pistol to her side, allowing Roswell to move in and secure the weapon.

Roswell shifted his gaze towards Fredrick. "Will you inform Anette that I might be a little late returning to the ball? I am going to see them to Newgate."

"Newgate?" Clarissa asked. "You cannot be in earnest. I won't go."

Calvin's face was pale. "I need a doctor."

"They will send for one when you are in Newgate," Roswell said. "If you don't cooperate, we will be happy to parade you through the townhouse."

"You wouldn't dare," Clarissa snapped.

"Try me," Roswell responded.

Clarissa tossed her hands up in the air. "Fine. We will go, but we shall be out by morning when they discover who we are."

"I wouldn't count on that. You did threaten to kill two people, one being an earl," Roswell remarked. "Let us depart. I tire of waiting around."

After Roswell guided Calvin and Clarissa out through the back gate, Emilia turned towards Fredrick, who regarded her with a furious expression.

Chapter Twenty

A myriad of emotions coursed through Fredrick as he stood before Emilia. Anger. Frustration. Relief. He couldn't quite bring himself to believe how close he had been to losing her. If he hadn't chanced upon them, the outcome could have been dire.

What had she been thinking when she moved to stand in front of him, and then later when she practically challenged Clarissa to pull the trigger? He was the one that was supposed to protect her, not the other way around.

He watched as Emilia approached Miss Delacourt and smiled. "Thank you for your help in saving my life," she expressed.

Miss Delacourt returned her smile. "You are welcome," she said. "When Lord Chatsworth failed to appear with you to dance the waltz, Lord Roswell and I went in search of you."

"I am relieved that you did so."

With a knowing glance at Fredrick, Miss Delacourt remarked, "I am sure that you and Lord Chatsworth have much to discuss. Although, I shall remain close for propriety's sake."

Emilia turned back to face Fredrick, and she clasped her

hands in front of her. She looked hesitant, and that hadn't been his intention. He wanted to run up to her and wrap his arms around her. But so much needed to be said between them.

"What were you thinking?" he asked. "You could have gotten yourself killed."

"Clarissa wouldn't have shot me," she insisted.

"I disagree," he replied. "You were so desperate to have a family that you overlooked that Calvin and Clarissa were just using you."

Emilia lowered her gaze. "I was wrong to do so."

"Yes, you were," he said, taking a step towards her. "And I tried to warn you, multiple times, in fact."

"I know, and I am sorry." Her voice was soft.

Fredrick closed his eyes. What was he doing, he thought. He should be confessing his love for her, especially after she had been willing to give up everything for him. Surely that meant that she cared for him, loved him, even.

"Perhaps we should return to the ball," Emilia suggested.

No.

So much still needed to be said between them.

Fredrick closed the distance between them and Emilia tipped her head to meet his gaze. Her emotions were laid bare, and he could see the uncertainty that was in her eyes. In the moonlight, she appeared stunning, a vision of beauty that captivated him.

"It is I that should be apologizing to you," Fredrick said.

She furrowed her brows. "For what?" she asked. "You did nothing wrong."

"But I did," he confessed, his voice carrying a weight of vulnerability. He paused, allowing the words to linger in the air. "I should have been praising your bravery, not belittling your actions. I was just scared."

"You, scared?" she asked, her tone a delicate blend of surprise and disbelief. "Of what?"

He gently reached for her gloved hand. "Of losing you."

Emilia's expression softened, and she responded with quiet certainty, "I am right here."

Fredrick continued to hold her hand, his fingers intertwining with hers. "I wanted to be the one that protected you, not the other way around."

"Perhaps we can protect each other from here on out," she suggested.

"I like the sound of that," Fredrick said.

Emilia's eyes reflected a sincerity that resonated deeply with him. "I was in earnest, though. I would have given up my entire fortune in exchange for your life."

He couldn't help but react, his words emerging harsher than intended. "Why would you do something so foolish?"

With a slight wince, Emilia replied, "I was born with nothing so I wouldn't miss it too much. I just needed to make sure you lived to see another day."

"That was sheer madness on your part," he asserted.

"I did not see it as such."

Fredrick knew it was time that he told Emilia how much she meant to him, and he hoped he didn't botch it up. He blurted the first thing that came to his mind. "Marry me."

Emilia's eyes widened in surprise. "Pardon?"

"Marry me, please."

She pursed her lips, a hint of hesitation in her expression. "Is this because I offered to give up my fortune?" she asked. "Because if so, that is truly not necessary."

"No, it is not just because of that. Although, that did play a part in it." Fredrick sighed, sensing his own awkwardness. He was blathering, and he was not one to do so. He took a deep breath, determined to express himself more clearly.

Fredrick brought her hand up to his lips and spoke earnestly. "I have fallen in love with you, Emilia. I tried not to, but I failed, time and time again. You have my whole heart."

Emilia blinked. "You love me?"

"I do," he replied. "I never wanted to take a wife, but you convinced me otherwise. I have since discovered that I don't just want you in my life, but I *need* you in it. You took a broken man, and you have given me hope once more."

"What of my past?" Emilia asked. "We were raised so differently."

Fredrick grinned. "I care little of your past. I only care about your future, assuming that I am in it, of course."

Emilia bit her lower lip, still uncertain. "I would make a terrible countess."

"Possibly, but I do believe you are precisely what the *ton* needs."

"And what of your family?" she inquired.

Fredrick chuckled. "They have been conspiring against us behind our backs. I have no doubt we have their approval."

Emilia shook her head. "I don't believe this," she whispered. "This is all too... perfect."

"Before you say yes, there is one thing I must confess to you," Fredrick said in a more serious tone. "When I served under Wellington, I was one of his spies, and I have worked a few cases since I returned to England."

"You are a spy?" Emilia asked, a line between her brows appearing.

"I am."

A bright smile replaced Emilia's initial surprise. "I adore spies," she replied. "I do hope you will regale me with some of your adventures."

"Not all of them are adventures," Fredrick clarified.

Emilia's eyes lit up. "May I say yes now?"

"You may."

"Then, yes. A hundred thousand times, yes," she gushed.

He dropped her hand and pulled her into his arms. "I love you, Emilia."

"I love you, too," she replied.

Fredrick leaned back and looked at her, truly looked at her.

"I promise that you will never question my love as long as you live."

"I hope that is a very long time," Emilia responded.

As they stared at one another, Fredrick's eyes dropped to her lips and he asked, "May I kiss you, my love?"

"Yes, you may," she breathed.

He slowly leaned in until his lips met hers, initiating a soft and thorough kiss. In that moment, as Emilia returned his kiss, Fredrick felt complete. It was the type of kiss that he knew would be etched in his memories forever.

A discreet clearing of Miss Delacourt's throat reminded them that they were not alone.

Fredrick broke the kiss but remained close. "Should we go back inside and announce our engagement?"

"Now?"

"I think it is the perfect time, is it not?" he asked.

Emilia nodded. "I suppose it is."

"I will post the banns tomorrow, and we shall marry in three weeks' time, assuming you have no objections," Fredrick said.

"I have none."

Fredrick took a step back and reached for her hand. "Now that we are engaged, I intend to dance with you twice this evening."

"I have something to look forward to, then," Emilia responded.

As they strolled down the path, it dawned on Fredrick that it wasn't that he didn't want to get married. He was merely waiting for the right person to come along. That person, he now knew, was Emilia. She saw the real him, and yet she loved him anyways. How could he not love her?

With the morning sun streaming through the windows, Fredrick sat at his mother's bedside as she peacefully slept. He wanted to share the good news with her, but he didn't dare wake her. So instead he watched her sleep, feeling immense gratitude that she was still alive.

His mother's eyes fluttered open and a bemused look came to her expression. "Good morning," she greeted.

Fredrick smiled. "Good morning."

"Where is Alfred?" his mother asked.

"He is having breakfast, but I offered to sit with you while he was doing so," Fredrick explained.

His mother sat up in bed. "You remind me of someone I used to know."

A glimmer of hope came into his heart. Perhaps today, she would remember him. "I do?"

"Yes, my father," she replied. "Do you know him?"

"I did," Fredrick replied, though a tinge of disappointment lingered. He reminded himself that his mother was doing her best, and he needed to be patient and understanding.

His mother furrowed her brow. "Did something happen to him?"

Not wanting to upset his mother, Fredrick shook his head. "Not that I am aware of."

"That is good," his mother sighed. "I have a son that is fighting in the war. Do you know him as well?"

"I do."

"He is so brave, but I fear for him," his mother said, her voice tinged with concern. "My brother went to war and never returned."

Fredrick leaned forward in his seat, ready to share the comforting truth with her. "Your brother did return, and he lived a long life."

"What wonderful news," his mother responded.

"Speaking of wonderful news," Fredrick started, a smile brightening his face, "I am engaged to be married."

His mother's eyes sparkled with interest. "How wonderful! Who is the lucky lady?"

"Miss Emilia Sutherland," he replied with pride. "She is the daughter of Sir Charles Sutherland."

"Do I know Sir Charles?" she inquired.

Fredrick nodded encouragingly. "You do," he replied. "He was a friend of Father's."

"Well, I hope you have a lifetime of happiness," his mother said. "Marriage has enriched my life so deeply."

"I aspire to be as happily married as you are with Alfred."

The door opened, revealing Roswell and their father.

A soft smile came to his mother's face as she greeted her husband. "Alfred," she said. "Did you hear that this young man is engaged?"

"I did hear that," his father responded. "Emilia will make a fine bride for him."

"Do you think our children will ever get married?" she asked.

With a reassuring look, his father took a seat on the edge of the bed. "I do," he said. "And they will be just as happy as we are."

"I hope so," she responded.

Roswell approached Fredrick with a sense of urgency, leaning in to whisper, "We need to depart to see Kendrick."

Fredrick rose from his seat and bowed. "It was a pleasure to speak to you," he said, addressing his mother. He knew he was being overly formal with her, but she didn't remember him.

"What was your name again?" she asked.

"Fredrick."

No sign of recognition emerged in her eyes as she tilted her head. "Thank you for sitting with me and good luck with your wedding."

Fredrick acknowledged her words with a nod, his heart carrying a multitude of emotions as he followed Roswell out of the room, leaving behind the bittersweet reality of his mother's condition.

As they walked down the corridor, Roswell remarked, "Mother seemed to take the news well about Emilia."

"She did, but I am just a stranger to her," Fredrick said.

"As am I," Roswell responded. "She didn't even acknowledge me when I stepped into the room with Father."

"At least she is still alive."

"For now, but for how long?" Roswell asked, his tone reflecting the weight of their mother's fragile state.

Fredrick didn't want to dwell on the inevitable. The thought of his mother's eventual passing weighed heavily on him, and he didn't look forward to that fateful day when their lives would drastically change. The only thing that gave him solace was that Emilia would be by his side and she would be a great comfort to him.

As they stepped out of the townhouse, Mr. Rymer approached Fredrick on the pavement. "Lord Chatsworth," he greeted. "I was the late Sir Charles' solicitor and he asked me to deliver this letter once you announced your engagement to Miss Sutherland."

Fredrick accepted the letter from Mr. Rymer and asked, "What does it say?"

Mr. Rymer shrugged. "I do not know, but Sir Charles was explicit in his instructions. He wrote it shortly before he passed."

"But how did he know I was going to get engaged to Miss Sutherland?" Fredrick pressed.

"Again, I cannot answer that, but I suspect all the answers that you are seeking are in that letter," Mr. Rymer said with a tip of his hat. "Good day, my lord."

Roswell came to stand next to him on the pavement and inquired, "What was that about?"

"I'm not quite sure," Fredrick admitted before he entered the awaiting coach. As it merged into traffic, he unfolded the letter and read it, scarcely believing the words on the page.

"What does it say?" Roswell asked.

Lowering the paper to his lap, Fredrick replied in disbelief, "This is the precise outcome that Sir Charles had hoped would happen when he made Emilia his heir. He anticipated that I would help her ease into high Society and that we would fall in love."

"Sir Charles planned the whole thing?"

"Apparently so," Fredrick remarked. "He wanted me to know that he wholeheartedly gives his blessing and hopes we have a lifetime of happiness."

Roswell's eyes held approval. "That was well-played on Sir Charles' part," he acknowledged. "I am glad that Emilia helped you face the demons from your past."

"They are still there, but my burdens seem lighter somehow, as if she is helping to carry the load now," Fredrick confessed.

"Anette did the same thing for me," Roswell reflected. "When do you intend to post the banns?"

"Right after we meet with Kendrick."

Roswell chuckled. "What is the rush?" he joked.

Slipping the letter into his jacket pocket, Fredrick replied, "I would marry Emilia by special license, but I do not wish to bring any scandal to our union."

"Her ball appeared by all accounts to be a tremendous success. That bodes well for her standing in high Society."

"That it does," Fredrick agreed.

It wasn't long before the coach came to a stop in front of the agency's headquarters. Stepping onto the weathered pavement, they made their way into the dilapidated building.

A familiar guard met them by the back wall. "I wish you luck," he said as he opened the door for them. "Kendrick is in a foul mood."

Fredrick made his way towards Kendrick's office and noticed that Caleb and Miss Delacourt had already gathered there. With a polite nod, he acknowledged Miss Delacourt.

In return, she offered a courteous response, "Lord Chatsworth."

Kendrick spoke up, his voice gruff. "Close the door," he ordered. "We have much to discuss."

Following Kendrick's instructions, Roswell closed the door and came to stand by Fredrick.

Kendrick leaned back in his chair, his expression stern. "We have two French spies that are unaccounted for and we are no closer to finding them than we were before."

Miss Delacourt opened her mouth to interject, but Kendrick put his hand up, stilling her words. "I don't need excuses. I need answers," he asserted. "Which is why I am going to assign Caleb and Miss Delacourt to work together to apprehend these spies."

With a barely discernible frown, Miss Delacourt responded, "I work better on my own. I just need more time."

"Time is not a luxury that we have, Agent," Kendrick remarked sternly. "You will work with Caleb or I will remove you from this assignment."

Miss Delacourt pressed her lips together, the displeasure etched on her face. "As you wish."

Kendrick turned his attention towards Caleb. "Are you in agreement?"

With a quick glance at Miss Delacourt, Caleb replied, "I am."

"Wonderful," Kendrick muttered. "Now that Chatsworth is useless to us since he got engaged, we need to focus on what we do know, which isn't much."

Fredrick interjected, "I can still assist on the assignment."

Kendrick shot him a dubious look. "You focus your time and energy on courting Miss Sutherland. Caleb and Miss Delacourt can work this assignment."

"What about me, sir?" Roswell asked. "Caleb and I have been partners since we started working at the agency."

"That you have been, but I do believe Caleb and Miss Delacourt working together will be for the best," Kendrick responded. "I have another assignment for you."

"Very well," Roswell said.

Miss Delacourt fidgeted with the reticule around her right wrist. "I should go. I need to return before my absence is noticed."

Caleb stepped forward. "Allow me to escort you to your coach."

"That won't be necessary," Miss Delacourt said.

"I insist," Caleb responded.

Miss Delacourt looked as if she were going to refuse but propriety won out. "Very well," she conceded, a forced smile on her lips.

As Caleb went to offer his arm, Miss Delacourt brushed past him and stepped out of Kendrick's office. Caleb cast a brief, exasperated glance heavenward before following her.

Roswell shifted his gaze to Kendrick. "Miss Delacourt and Caleb working together is an interesting choice."

"It is, but desperate times call for desperate measures," Kendrick said. "Miss Delacourt is a competent agent, but she needs to learn some restraint."

Kendrick reached for a stack of papers on the edge of his desk. "I thought you should know that I called in a favor and Mr. Livingston and his sister will be aboard the next ship to Australia."

Fredrick, surprised by the swift action, inquired, "They are being transported so quickly? What of a trial?"

"A trial would no doubt besmirch Miss Sutherland's name, so I convinced a judge to sign off on it," Kendrick explained.

Gratitude welled up inside of Fredrick as he expressed, "Thank you, sir."

For a fleeting moment, Kendrick's usually stoic face softened, revealing a rare glimpse of emotion. "Consider it a wedding present." He paused and concluded, "That will be all, Agents."

After they had departed from the spymaster's office, they returned to their waiting coach. Now that they had met with Kendrick, Fredrick felt a renewed sense of purpose- he was ready to go and post the banns.

Roswell must have sensed his urgency. "Shall we go post the banns?"

"I think that is a brilliant idea," Fredrick said.

As the coach traveled to the chapel, Fredrick stared out the window, his excitement building. He couldn't wait until Emilia became his wife. Never had he been so happy before.

Fredrick didn't need much in his life. Wanted very little. But the only thing he truly needed was Emilia.

Roswell's voice broke through the silence. "You are smiling, again."

"I am," Fredrick admitted, his smile growing. "I don't think I can dwell on Emilia without smiling." And that was the truth.

Fredrick loved her, of course, but better than that, he would choose her, day after day. In Emilia, he had found his match.

Epilogue

One year later

Emilia stood by her baby's bedside and let out a sigh of contentment. Her entire life had led her up to this point and she had never been so happy. She had everything she ever desired.

As Rosie slept, Emilia couldn't help but watch her, knowing everything about her was perfect. Her toes. Her fingers. Her smile. There was not one thing about her that she would ever change or want to change. She just hoped that Rosie could feel the depth of love she had for her.

The door opened and Fredrick entered the room with light steps so as not to disturb their sleeping daughter.

Fredrick slipped his arms around Emilia's waist from behind and leaned into her. "Your guests are waiting for you downstairs."

"Let them wait," Emilia said. "Can you believe that we created something so precious?"

"It still boggles my mind."

Emilia turned in his arms, wrapping her arms around his

neck. "Have I properly thanked you yet for what you have given me?"

Amusement danced in Fredrick's eyes as he teased, "No, and you could stand to do it more."

"I love you," Emilia declared.

Fredrick's demeanor turned solemn. "The greatest thing I have ever done in my life is ask you to marry me," he confessed. "You have brought me more joy than I can hardly contain."

"I feel the same," Emilia responded.

"I hope that we can fill this nursery with children and watch as our joy increases with each new addition."

Emilia smiled. "Perhaps we should wait until Rosie is a little older to give her a brother or sister."

Fredrick leaned in, pressing his lips against hers. "I do hope I make you happy, my love."

"You do," Emilia said. "Because of you, I am not a nobody anymore. I am a wife and a mother. I have the family that I have always dreamed of."

"And we have only just started," Fredrick said.

"Perhaps we could name the next one after your mother, assuming it is a girl," Emilia suggested.

Fredrick's eyes became moist. "I would like that very much. It would be a fitting tribute to my mother." He paused. "I miss her."

"I know you do, but she is out of pain now."

"That is the only comfort that I have with her passing."

Emilia brought her hand up to cup his right cheek. "I did not mean to distress you by speaking of your mother. Forgive me."

"There is nothing to forgive," Fredrick insisted. "I am just grateful that my father handled her death far better than we all anticipated."

"He seems lonely, though."

Fredrick nodded. "That was inevitable. The love that my

parents shared was one that just doesn't go away when one of them passes. I do believe it is forever."

"I love that thought."

"It is the love that *we* share," Fredrick said, his tone carrying a deep resonance. "You took me at my worst and made me a much better man."

"You were already a good man, but I just had to convince you of that," Emilia remarked. "I just wish you saw yourself how I saw you."

"How is that?"

Emilia met his gaze, her eyes filled with sincerity. "My everything."

Rosie let out a soft cry in her sleep, breaking the spell that had come over them.

Fredrick dropped his arms and took a step back. "We should leave so we don't wake Rosie with our incessant declarations of love," he said, a playful lightness in his words.

Quietly exiting the nursery, Emilia acknowledged the nursemaid stationed just outside the door with a subtle nod.

As they walked hand in hand down the corridor, Fredrick asked, "Would you care to go riding tomorrow?"

Emilia made a face. "I would prefer a carriage ride."

Fredrick chuckled. "I have never met someone that had such an aversion to riding a horse."

"I do not mind riding a horse, but I do not like side saddles," Emilia admitted. "I prefer the freedom of riding astride at our country estate."

"That is rather scandalous of you, my dear," Fredrick joked.

"I did warn you that I would make a terrible countess."

Fredrick grinned. "You did, but you are selling yourself short," he said. "The *ton* adores you, and your latest ball was a rousing success."

"I only planned the ball so I could dance the waltz with you," Emilia remarked.

"I will dance with you whenever, wherever," Fredrick said.

Emilia glanced over at him. "You promise?"

"I will gladly take every opportunity to hold you in my arms." He came to a stop at the top of the stairs. "Let us dance."

"Now?" Emilia asked in disbelief. "Here?"

Fredrick pulled her close to him and placed a hand on her waist. "I think this is the perfect place to dance."

"What about our guests?"

He leaned closer and whispered, "Let them wait." Their shared laughter echoed through the hall as they surrendered to the impromptu dance, relishing the joy of being wrapped up in each other's embrace.

The End

Next in Series...

Two unlikely partners must risk their secrets- and hearts- to unravel a web of treachery and save England.

Next in Series...

Miss Simone Delacourt, a seemingly unnoticed wallflower in the eyes of the *ton*, hides a secret life as a spy, enjoying the freedom her anonymity affords. When she's reluctantly paired with Mr. Caleb Bolingbroke, a man she can barely tolerate, her carefully crafted life is thrown into turmoil.

Mr. Caleb Bolingbroke isn't pleased that he is assigned with the obstinate Miss Delacourt, but he is pleased when he is able to convince her to give their partnership a chance. Pursuing elusive French spies is their shared mission, and the stakes are high. Despite Miss Delacourt's initial mistrust, Caleb is determined to win her over.

As they delve into the pursuit of the French spies, Caleb and Simone discover the need to depend on each other. The case unravels a web of secrets and lies, challenging their perceptions. In this intricate game of treachery, they must risk everything, including their hearts, to save England from an impending threat.

About the Author

Laura Beers is an award-winning author. She attended Brigham Young University, earning a Bachelor of Science degree in Construction Management. She can't sing, doesn't dance and loves naps.

Laura lives in Utah with her husband, three kids, and her dysfunctional dog. When not writing regency romance, she loves waterskiing, hiking, and drinking Dr Pepper.

You can connect with Laura on Facebook, Instagram, or on her site at www.authorlaurabeers.com.

Made in United States
Orlando, FL
17 May 2024